Scorned

Scorned

The Anderson Brothers Series
Book 3

MARIE LONG

To Robert
A great friend and amazing teacher.

Acknowledgments

I owe all of my creative talents to my Lord and Savior, Jesus Christ, for without Him, nothing is possible.

To Mom, Dad, and my big brothers who have continued supporting me in my creative efforts. Thank you, and I love you.

To all of my online and offline friends (male and female) who let me pick your brains during my process of writing Dominick, Kevin, and Michael's stories. Thank you very much for your help and advice.

Thank you again to the superheroes and heroines at Red Adept for continuing to work wonders on my manuscripts.

Many thanks goes to my critique partners of the Dragon's Sandbox who have helped me perfect my writing voice.

Thank you to the wonderful ladies of First Coast Romance Writers for the motivation and support you've given me during my journey in Romance writing.

Many thanks to the reviewers and bloggers who have volunteered their time to read and review this book.

Last, but certainly not least, *thank you*, dear reader, for allowing me the opportunity to share the world of the Anderson Brothers with you.

Scorned

Chapter 1

I bounce on the balls of my feet, my adrenaline pumping. A refreshing breeze sweeps across my face, bringing some relief from the dry September air. I inhale the stench of sweat and burned rubber, and I can smell the coppery tinge of old metal. The noise of the crowd echoes from beyond the long corridor of rusted shipping containers. My heart races.

Dante—my trainer, mentor, and most trusted friend—pats me on the shoulder. "Ready for this?"

I nod as I undo the silver cross I wear around my neck, kiss it, and tuck the chain in a pocket of my jeans. I flip up the hood of my black sweatshirt and proceed through the makeshift passageway, which is lit only by the moon.

"Don't fuck up," he says.

Of course I won't. Because I want to do more West Coast fights. If I prove myself here in Los Angeles tonight, then Dante will get off my ass about me not being ready.

Hell, I'm almost twenty-six. Been fighting full-time since I was eighteen. You would think my 23–2 streak this year would convince Dante, but no—he keeps me fucking hand-cuffed to the smaller venues on the East Coast. I can't be mad at him. He saved my life. I owe it to him to work hard no matter where he has me fight.

But this past week, Dante has gone out of his comfort zone and landed me a headline fight. And here I am, some-where in LA in the middle of an abandoned fucking rail yard on a Sunday night.

I'm not expecting to steamroll my opponent. Not this time. I looked him up a couple nights ago. Craig Stiller, aka Atomic—twenty-eight years old, six-nine, and three-twenty. His rap sheet included attempted murder—which got him locked away for nine years—drug possession—the hard shit—and aggravated assault. I'm sure he's out to prove a point just like the rest of them. I need to be on my game to-night—more than ever.

At the end of my walk, I stare out at a crowd packed into an open-ended, abandoned warehouse, which is dimly lit by several strategically posted citronella torches. In the midst of the crowd stands a raised platform constructed of metal grat-ing. Distorted music starts blaring from a pair of small speakers at the base of the platform. It's screaming death metal. I have no idea what the artist is singing—if you'd call it that—but the music riles the crowd to a violent level. People roar death threats, head bang as they flash hand signs, and jump around, acting crazy. I take a deep breath. Glancing over my shoulder, I notice that Dante is no longer behind me. He's found his way into the crowd, out of my line of sight. Thank God. It'll rattle my nerves if I see him watching me with that "don't fuck up" look on his face.

Craig emerges from the crowd, a muscled, tattooed—way more ink than me—freak of nature with short, spiky hair. He raises his arms in the air and makes his way to the platform, waving for the crowd to scream and cheer louder. And they do. This crowd is out for blood. Craig walks around the ring, flexing his bare chest and arms as he eyes random people, perhaps looking for me. His face is hard and mean, as if he's ready to chew a hole in the metal grating.

I smile under the hood. *He's trying way too hard.* I've fought plenty of people like him. They put on the tough-guy front and end up getting their bells rung with one solid punch. But I can't assume that's the case with Craig. Underestimating my opponents was what caused this year's two losses.

The death metal fades out—thank God—and my theme song, "C.R.E.A.M.," starts to play. People crane their necks and look around with curious looks on their faces, probably expecting to see a tall, muscly guy. There are few cheers as I quietly snake my way through them and onto the platform. I mostly hear murmurs.

I shrug off my hoodie and toss it out of the ring. I'm only six-one and weigh one fifty-five. Muscular? Pfft. Yeah, right. I'm definitely some kind of genetic failure because I can't seem to gain much muscle despite all the intense workouts I do. Or maybe God just hates me. Either way, it fucking sucks.

Craig stops his flexing, looks me over, and then smiles, the flickering torchlight winking off platinum from one of his bottom teeth. I stare back at him, emotionless, hoping my not reacting to his display fucks with his head. That usually works with my opponents, but I think he's onto me.

My theme song fades out, and a guy in a flashy red-and-gold jacket and wearing sunglasses comes between us. He waves a handful of betting slips over his head and addresses the crowd in a thick Asian accent. "All bets are in! All bets are in!" He points to me. "Knox from da Bronx!" There's barely a murmur in the crowd. Then he points to Craig. "LA's own 'Atomic' Craig Stiller!"

The cheering shakes the floor. I might have a bigger fight on my hands if I end up beating this guy. I stare out at the spectators, assessing how much of a challenge this is going to be. Lots of guys in the crowd look as if they might be con-tenders, too. But for a moment, my eyes settle on a girl standing in the front, her arms crossed, chewing gum, not engaging in the wild craziness around her. She's silent, and she's looking straight at me as she blows a pink bubble.

The announcer runs out of the ring and yells, "Fight, mothafuckas!"

My attention immediately snaps to Craig. I position my-self in a fighting stance. Craig's hands are up, and he stands almost like a boxer, keeping light on his toes. He throws a jab at my face with such speed it's almost a blur. I weave to the side and land one of my signature roundhouse kicks to his solar plexus. My foot stings. *Damn, he's solid.*

But even so, he groans and bends forward from the blow. I may be small, but my feet are like sledgehammers. At least, that's what Dante always says whenever we spar.

As I advance, he moves as if he wants to try and take me to the ground. He swings wildly with a right hook. His fist makes contact with my ribs. I groan, but in that split second, his face is wide open. In one motion, I move in and uppercut him in the chin. His head snaps back. He staggers backward. Blood trickles from his mouth, and he immediately grabs it with his hand.

Sweet. He has a glass jaw. I come at him with a fury of punches to his face and kicks to his ribs. The boos rise from the crowd.

Growling, Craig rushes me like a bull, breaking my combinations. I sidestep away from his line of destruction. I don't anticipate his arm extending and clotheslining me.

With a grunt, I'm slammed to the ground. The back of my head hits metal. Something shiny glints across my line of sight then disappears. Craig pins me down and whips his fist across my face. I'm seeing stars, the looming image of him becoming a blur.

The boos are replaced by cheers, whistles, and other shit in Craig's favor. They quickly start to sound distant. I don't even hear Dante. Hell, I don't *want* to hear Dante. I need to get my shit together fast. If I end up losing, Dante will never let me fight out west again.

For a few moments, my vision goes clear, and I see that girl again. She's not too hard to spot because of her purple hair, which is styled like a Mohawk with the sides cut short and the top untouched and tied back. She's kneeling down, focused on something on the floor. She must be bored out her mind. I guess her boyfriend dragged her here.

Craig moves into my line of sight, and all my attention is back on his blurry image. The image moves. Anticipating he's drawing back for another punch, I pull my legs up, move one of them around the side of his neck, and force his head to whip to the side. Bending my knee, I have half of his neck pressed against my calf and thigh. I squeeze, applying a little pressure to the artery. His face starts to turn red and purple. While he coughs and gasps, I shift my body out of the lock but keep him in my control. I swing my other leg under his torso in a half scissor then finally yank one of his arms up and across the top of my thigh. It's a perfect setup for an arm break. Pressing against the joint, I hear him cry out in pain.

Tap, damn it. This guy's stubborn. It's going to take me actually breaking his arm or snapping his neck for him to tap out.

No, I won't snap his neck. Instant death. And that's one thing I can't do—one thing I *won't* do: kill. My vision clears again, and I watch the rowdy crowd yell like the savages they are. Except for Goth Girl. She's back to standing and looking at me.

With Craig still tangled like a pretzel, I squeeze my legs harder against his torso and that artery in his neck, intending on putting him to sleep instead. His head turns a deeper purple than that mysterious girl's hair. His body flinches in my hold and finally goes limp.

The crowd boos, and some scream obscenities as I unwrap myself from my opponent and stand. I bounce on my toes and watch him, ready, in case he's just playing opossum. After a few moments, I know he's not.

The announcer comes rushing back in the ring and holds up my arm in victory. "Winner! Knox from da Bronx!"

Three young guys swarm Craig, trying to wake him up. As I turn to leave the ring, Dante's standing there, holding my discarded hoodie. He pats me on the shoulder and casually leads me through the thick, angry mob as if nothing's wrong. But *everything* is wrong. The look of death is in all their eyes as I walk past them. They lost a shit-ton of money tonight. And I think I just earned one of the biggest payoffs of my career.

We snake through the maze of rusted shipping containers as we head back to where Dante parked the car. The adrenaline wearing off, I can feel the stinging pain in my jaw and ribs. I bet my right eye is swollen as fuck.

"You did good," Dante says, grabbing his keys out his pocket.

"How much did we win?"

"Two Gs." He unlocks the door. "Get in."

Relieved but exhausted, I slump down in the passenger seat with a sigh. The softness of the seat feels great in comparison to that metal grating. The absence of the noisy crowd makes my ears ring. I wipe away sweat and dirt from my face and chest then grab my glasses, which are sitting on the dashboard. I slip my hand down my pocket and pause.

I blink. *Where's my necklace?* "Dante, we need to go back."

Dante raises an eyebrow at me. "For what?"

"I lost something important. I need to go back and—"

"Kid, did you *not* see that pack of angry wolves back there? They're ready to chew your head off."

"I don't give a fuck, man! I need to find it!"

Grumbling, he starts the car but doesn't put it in gear.

I smile slightly at him. "Thanks, man. I'll be right—"

"Shit, they're already here." Dante nods toward the passenger-side window.

"Huh?" I follow his gaze toward the silhouette of a female figure rapping on the glass. Dark purple streaks glint from her hair. *Holy shit—it's that girl again.*

"I'm getting us the fuck outta here," Dante says, throwing the car in gear.

"Wait." I don't know why, but something about her tells me that she's not part of the angry mob. I flip on the overhead reading light and roll down the window.

She leans on the edge of the rolled-down window, tapping her black-painted fingernails against her biceps. She studies me with light-brown eyes accented with thick lashes and shadowed with black powder. *Shit. What if she's a cop? Naw. If she were a cop, Dante would know.*

"Yeah? Whatdya need?" Dante says in an annoyed tone.

She looks from Dante to me. I check out the tattoos that run down her neck and arms and across her exposed cleavage. My God, she's got a nice set of tits. Lip, nose, and eyebrow piercings cover her pasty-white face. Two metal gauges cover her earlobes. She dresses completely in black—and here I thought all that gothic shit was just a phase in high school.

She wears black lipstick on that nice set of lips. Around her neck is a black choker with a thorny rose entwining a skull. I bet she's a very pretty girl beneath that angsty facade. "Knox." Her voice is rough, but there's a hint of sweetness in her tone. She sounds like a girl I would definitely never underestimate.

I scrunch my brow. "Uh, yeah, that's me."

She nods, slips two fingers down her shirt, her large tits giving a happy bounce, and presents my silver necklace. "You dropped this."

I widen my eyes. I don't know which is more amazing: her tits or the fact that she found my necklace. In the end, my reasonable side prevails over my lust, and I take the necklace. "Thanks. I thought I lost this."

She smiles and then turns to leave. "Be more careful next time, eh?"

CHAPTER 2

I OPEN MY EYES TO THE MUTED MORNING SUNLIGHT between the blinds of my South Central motel room. My body is throbbing like a motherfucker. My eyes cut to the alarm clock sitting on the night table, its red illuminated numbers reading 11:30. The green notification light on my cell, sitting next to the clock, blinks repeatedly. Groaning, I grab the phone. The screen awakens to show the two missed calls: one from Dante, and one from Uncle Adam. Staring at Uncle Adam's name, I frown as memories—bad memories— of a past life flood my mind.

God. What does he want now?

Ever since I totally screwed over the family big time by missing Mama's fiftieth birthday last year, my chats with her and Uncle Adam have been few to none. And my brothers, Kevin and Dominick . . . they've pretty much banished me from the family. I don't even try talking to those two any-more. I don't blame them for hating me.

I fucked up bad. Again. I can't expect to redeem myself after so many years of running, fighting, doubting . . . *hoping.*

I punch Dante's name with my thumb and call him back. I switch to speakerphone and lie back in bed.

"Hey, kid. About time you returned my call," Dante's gruff voice says.

"Sorry, man," I say groggily. "What's up?"

"You're just getting up? You mean you haven't even gone out training yet?"

I clench my jaw. Dante's cool and all, but sometimes he acts like an annoying parent. I can't be mad at him, though. He's had a rough life. He divorced his wife and lost both of his kids to gang shootings. I'm pretty much the only "son" he's got, and I don't mind. Anyone's a better father than the one I had.

"Naw, I haven't gone out yet," I reply. "Last night was rough. Give me some time to heal, will you?"

"Right. I'm going to book a couple of plane tickets so we can be back in New York by tomorrow."

My eyes widen, and I bolt up in bed. "What the hell, man? You mean all I get is one fight out here?"

Dante is silent, and I seethe. "This is fucking LA!" I con-tinue. "It's taken me this long to convince you I'm ready, and now all I get is one fucking fight? Seriously, man."

"I figured you'd be tired of this place already. Fine. I'll see what else I can find. But if we're gonna stay out here, you better get your ass up and train. I have a friend named Brett who owns a gym not far from the motel. Called Black Knights Arena and Athletics. Check it out. He's probably got some guys you can spar with."

I hiss through my teeth. "Yeah, whatever, man." Rolling over, I reach for my phone, ready to shut it off. "That it?"

"Yeah," he says, a little less enthusiastically. "I'll call you later."

I hang up and run my hand over my hair, sighing. *What the hell's his problem?* He's been acting like this ever since I first asked him about fighting out west last year. As if he doesn't *want* me to get better. Well, fuck him. I'll show him more than he thinks he knows about me.

As I move to get out of bed, I spot the necklace lying beside the phone. Reaching for the silver cross, I think about the mysterious girl who found it. Who the hell was she to track me down like that just to give it back? I mean, honest people don't exactly attend those kinds of events. She wasn't even paying attention to the fight. It makes me wonder what she *was* doing there in the first place. I run my thumb over the pendant then bring it to my lips. I catch a whiff of strawberries. It must be *her* scent. *God*—and this was between her amazing tits . . .

Shit. I blink out of my fantasy. *I can't be thinking that. My mother gave me this necklace.* I put it back down and head to the bathroom.

I crank up the volume of my MP3 player and stick it in my back pocket. The bass and steady beat of "Survival of the Fittest" flow through the earbuds and put me in the zone. I secure the straps of my backpack, adjust my glasses, and begin the seven-block run toward Brett's gym. Mouthing the hip-hop lyrics keeps me conscious of breathing properly while I run. I snake through the busy streets of the grungy neighborhood, my feet hitting the cracked pavement of the sidewalk at a steady pace. Shady onlookers glance my way as I run past, and then they nervously turn their gazes elsewhere. By the time I arrive at the gym, my white tank top is soaked with sweat, and my legs and lungs are burning.

The small industrial building looks old, with boards covering bashed-in windows. Graffiti is scrawled everywhere on the crumbly brick wall, including the gym's crookedly hanging plastic sign. The front door is boarded up, and there's a sign on it that says, "USE OTHER ENTRANCE" with an arrow pointing toward the side of the building. I hear muted rock music, voices, and the rhythmic thud of bags being punched from that direction, so I follow the sounds.

Standing under the rolled-up overhead door, I take off my backpack and peer inside the musty gym. There are mostly guys in it but also a few women—young and old— pumping iron, hitting hanging bags, and stretching. Toward the back is a large, caged octagon constructed of chain-link fencing and lined with a padded wall. I glimpse the tops of two heads moving around.

A man who looks about Dante's age sits behind a desk in an enclosed office, chatting on the phone. I assume that's

Brett, so I lean against the wall and wait. Everyone's training hard; they don't even acknowledge me. That's awesome. They're focused and serious. Some look like pro contenders by their builds and the way their bodies move. The energy in this place makes me hungry to train as well. I observe one of the female trainees punching at two hand targets. She bobs and weaves after a series of jabs and then repeats the exercise.

"You here to train or what?"

I blink then snap my attention to a man who's appeared in front of me: the guy I'd pegged as Brett. He barely comes up to my neck. A few streaks of grey show in his dirty-blond hair. Shallow wrinkles line a hard, weathered face half-hidden by a stubbly beard. He looks up at me with expectant blue eyes.

"Uh," I stammer.

Brett crosses his arms. "Look, kid. This ain't a peep show. Either you're here to train, or you're a spectator. No loiterin' in my gym."

"Dante sent me. Dante Coleman."

Brett raises an eyebrow. "DC? You train under him?"

"Something like that."

He smiles. "Well, hot damn. You're definitely welcome to train here. I just need you to fill out a waiver first." He beckons me to follow him to the office, where he hands me a form and a pen. "I didn't know he was in town," he continues while I skim through the standard liability form—won't sue them if I die, yada yada yada—and then fill it out. "How's he doing these days?"

"He's all right," I say. "We're just in town for the week."

"Cool. Hopefully, I'll see him before he leaves."

I sign and initial the form and hand it back to him. "How much is it to use the gym?"

"You came at a good time. It's free open gym till five on Mondays and Wednesdays. After that, ten bucks." He pauses to look over the form then nods and thumbs over his shoulder with a smile. "You're good to go. Get outta here, and have fun."

I smile back and leave. My first stop is the weight machines—the leg press specifically. I toss off my tank top, lay my glasses on it, and set the press weight to four hundred and thirty pounds. As I work on my reps, I catch glances from the other trainers. Some nod to me. It's cool. I already feel like I belong here.

In four hours, I've touched every machine at least once and blasted through my usual routine of five hundred push-ups and ab workouts. My final stop is the bench press, and I pile the bar with two hundred and twenty pounds. I retrieve a towel from my backpack and drape it across the bench, lie back, and as I reach for the bar, a woman looms over me. I blink and stare up at her face a moment before my eyes drop to the visible peaks of her nipples poking against her sports bra. I grip the iron bar tight as I try to control the sudden surge of heat in my shorts.

"Hey, need a spotter?" she asks, reaching for the bar.

I swallow. I really don't want one, but with my dirty thoughts racing, I don't trust the stability of my arms. I stare back up at her sweaty, mocha face and will my eyes to remain there. "Yeah, sure. Thanks."

"I'm Chanelle, by the way."

"Knox."

We don't chat anymore after that, and I push through my three sets of ten reps, keeping my eyes focused elsewhere. Last night crosses my mind again, and I remember that mysterious girl. I don't know why I'm thinking about it—about *her*—so damn much. I guess because no one's looked out for me like that before. Well, no one except Dante.

When I finish my last set, I reset the bar and sit up, swiping the towel from beneath me and wiping sweat from my face with it. My arms are burning—just how I like it. Chanelle ogles me.

"I've seen it, and I still don't believe it," she says, shaking her head.

I draw a blank. "What?"

"The fact that you just did thirty reps of two twenty. You don't look like you weigh any more than a buck fifty."

I get up from the bench, irked that she had to go and state the obvious. "Yeah, I get that a lot."

"Seriously, what's your secret? Are you juicing or something? Pills?"

I blink. "Fuck no. I don't do that shit." I grab my tank top and slip my glasses back on. "Thanks for spotting, by the way."

"No problem." She looks me up and down. "Hey, you fight?"

"A little here and there. Why?"

She nods toward the cage, where four people are gathered near the pad-free door, watching the sparring session beyond. "You should get in on that."

I follow her gaze, feeling a little lackluster. I probably *should* do a little munching before I leave. Checking the clock on the wall, I see it's almost four-thirty, so I have plenty of time to spare before the "happy hour" of open gym comes to a close.

I turn back to Chanelle. "You know, I think I just might."

She grins, showing me a set of too-white teeth. We walk to the cage and peer at two new contenders inside, grounding and pounding away.

"So what's your foundation, if you don't mind my asking?" Chanelle asks during the small dips in spectator noise.

"Tae Kwon Do," I reply, not taking my eyes off the match inside. One of the guys has the other pinned to the ground in an arm triangle choke submission.

"No, seriously, what's your foundation?" she asks again.

I finally look at her and scowl. Amusement is all over her face. "Tae Kwon Do," I repeat.

"For real? I mean, no offense, but isn't that the kiddie stuff?"

I narrow my eyes. This girl just got uglier. "No, it's not," I say through gritted teeth.

One guy in front of us looks over his shoulder. "Dude, Tae Kwon Do? Seriously?"

I unclench my fists and clench them again. "Yeah? What's it to you?"

"My seven-year-old niece does that shit in some after-school program." He snorts. "What a joke."

Very few things trigger my anger, but disrespecting what I love is one of them. Without thinking, I lunge at the guy and shove him against the wall of the cage. "I'll show you a motherfucking joke, bitch!"

The guy's eyes go wide, and the commotion scatters the other three spectators. Even the fight in the cage has halted.

"Hey!" Brett calls, coming between us. I have no idea where he came from so fast. The little guy's stealthier than a ninja. He separates us and turns to me. "You need to settle some shit? Take it in there." He points to the cage. His eyes are raging, pupils contracting, as if lasers will shoot out of them and burn a hole through my face. *Holy shit. And I thought Dante was scary when he got mad . . .*

The other guy nods, his nose wrinkling from the sneer he gives me. "Yeah, that's right, Tae Kwon Bitch. I'm gonna fuck you up good."

"That's enough, Preston," Brett warns. He turns to the cage and whistles, signaling for the guys in there to leave. When they do, Brett looks back at me expectantly.

Frowning, I empty my pockets, take off my glasses, and set my stuff aside before walking through the chain-link door of the cage.

Chapter 3

Brett closes and locks the cage door behind Preston, who moves around eagerly on the balls of his feet, eyeing me like a predator. *Why the hell am I about to fight right now? I don't feel like fighting. I'm tired—exhausted. Worked out extra hard today.* But I can't back out. Not now. Not when I let that punk disrespect me like some bitch.

Brett doesn't even bother initiating the fight. The slammed door was enough. A group of spectators crowd near the door, egging us both on. Preston holds a stance that I immediately recognize as some sort of kickboxing style, like Muay Thai. His fingers curled like tiger claws, he advances slowly.

I keep moving, bouncing. This isn't a real fight. It's just some punk who wants to prove a point. Why am I in here again? I want to leave, get some grub. All that working out worked up a serious appetite.

A fist comes toward my face, and I lean back. My attention snapping to Preston, I weave around his forward-leaning body and counter with a ridge-hand strike to the side of his neck. He crumples, stumbling forward, but recovers quickly. I keep moving, no longer hearing the crowd. If I remain a moving target, maybe he'll get frustrated enough for me to finish him off. But instead, he stands there, planted in his defensive stance, his knee poised. Both of us seem to be too chickenshit to strike next.

"That all you got?" he taunts.

Great.

"Told you that shit was all a joke." He turns to the rest of the crowd. "Tae Kwon Bitch is a pussy! He can't handle none of this!" That gets the crowd cheering louder and shaking the cage in anticipation.

I remain focused, unmoving. I know what his game is, and I'm not falling for it. He advances with a quick lunging punch. I sidestep and block the attack. His offense is strong and faster than I anticipated, and he breaks my guard. He follows through with a punch toward my face. I fall backward, hitting the padded wall of cage. Preston advances, cornering me there, and knees me in the gut.

I double over. I underestimated my opponent again, and now I'm screwed. My mind is all sorts of rattled right now. My heart's not in this fight. I don't want to be in here. But I have something to prove and my honor to uphold.

"Finish what you start," Master Rho always used to say. God, the old man's probably rolling over in his grave right now.

Preston elbows me across the face, and I smell and taste iron—blood. *My* blood. *Fight, damn it.* I will my body to move, but it resists my command, and I'm forced to cover my head and torso with my arms. Left, right, left, Preston punches the sides of my ribcage over and over. My body goes numb, and I collapse to the canvas floor. The sound of the crowd outside gets farther and farther away. Preston presses his weight on me, and I suddenly feel pain from my shoulder all the way down to my forearm. The bastard got me good, and there's nothing I can do about it.

Gritting my teeth, I slap the canvas repeatedly as hard as I can. The weight on me lifts, and the pain lessens. The cheering gets louder. I'm lifted up, and I hear Brett's rough voice in my ear. "Get cleaned up."

My feet guide me out of the cage, but I have no idea where I'm going. Then, someone takes my hand. It feels soft like a female's touch. My eyes shift sideways. It's Chanelle.

"Hey, take it easy," she says then leads me toward the back of the gym.

Why the hell is this girl helping me? We reach the bathroom door, and I yank my hand from hers. "I'm fine."

Her eyes dull for a moment, then she purses her lips. "You sure? You got some nasty bruises there."

"I said I'm fine!" I snap, opening the door.

She flinches, and her expression hardens. "Well, fuck you then, asshole." She turns abruptly and leaves.

I look daggers at her back as she joins another girl, who's punching a speed bag. *Fuck these people.*

Flipping on the bathroom light, I stare into the smudged mirror above the sink. Cuts and bruises pepper my face. The adrenaline rush is gone, and pain suddenly surges through me. It's only now I realize just how badly Preston fucked me up. Both areas of my ribs are swollen and bruised purple and blue. A line of dried blood runs from my nose to the top of my upper lip. My jaw cracks a little when I try to move it. I turn on the sink, hold my hands under the cold running water, and bring them up to my face, washing away the sweat, blood, and grime.

But this water will never wash away the shame and dishonor.

Despite getting mentally and physically fucked up at the gym today, I'm starving, so I hit up the closest burger joint. Sitting alone in a booth, I indulge in my one and only unhealthy meal of the day. Dante's ringtone goes off in my pocket, and I hesitate. I wonder if he talked to Brett today. Sighing, I stare at his name on the screen then finally answer. "Yo."

"Where are you?" Dante's tone is icy.

"I'm at Out the Box over on Florence Ave. Why?"

There's a brief pause. "We need to talk."

Shit. I bet he *did* talk to Brett. I exhale. "Whatever, man."

"I'll be over there in ten." He ends the call.

I scowl at his name staring back at me on the screen. I decide to make better use of my time surfing the Web. I sign in to a private website for my underground fight circuit and the results of Sunday's fight. As usual, the odds were against me, 97:2. No one ever has faith in the little guy's ability—especially a little guy whose foundation is apparently a kiddie sport. I've proven them all wrong time after time, and yet, I seem to get nowhere.

Well, fuck those people. I know who I am. So why does it always piss me off whenever someone talks shit about my art?

Scowling deeper, I swipe my finger down the screen and check out the rest of the website. I reach the bottom of the page and notice a small icon on the right. It's so tiny it's easy to miss. There's something familiar about that icon, though. I've seen it before.

I zoom the screen in as far as it'll go. Adjusting my glasses, I lean my face closer. The icon is an image of a thorny rose entwining a skull. Memories of last night's fight come to the forefront, and I picture that purple-haired girl wearing a necklace with that same symbol. It's *her* symbol. *I wonder if I can click on it?* I guide my finger over the icon and tap the screen once. The image highlights, as if it's clickable, and then the phone suddenly shuts off.

I blink. *What the hell?* I power the phone back on. When it's fully booted up, I notice a text notification at the top of the screen. I arch an eyebrow and check the message, which comes from an unknown number:

Naughty boy.

Whoa. This is getting all kinds of freaky—in a bad way. I muster the courage to text back:

Who is this?

I wait a few moments. To my surprise, I get a reply:

No one important.

It figures I don't get much info from this conversation. But still, this person is talking to me, so maybe if I keep texting, I'll find out something. I type back:

so how'd u get my #?

The reply comes quickly:

ppl obtain #s all the time.

Maybe this person is a cop or FBI. I hope not. Maybe I should stop while I'm ahead. Just as I'm about to shut off the phone, another text appears:

urs just happened to conveniently pop up on my screen.

I swallow. They must have me mistaken for someone else.

i never called u…

I kno u didn't. but u were still naughty.

What the hell does that even *mean?*

ur not making sense. Either tell me who u r or leave me alone.

I can't really do that, but maybe we can meet somewhere.

That definitely sounds like cop talk.

hell no.

I wait for a reply, but surprisingly, there is none. Someone slides into the booth seat across from me, and I look up to Dante's raging red face. I almost drop my phone. "Geez, man! You scared the shit out of me!"

"Good. And what the hell are you doing eating this shit?" He motions to the burger wrapper and fry box on my tray. "You're not gonna last five minutes in a fight with processed garbage in your stomach."

I roll my eyes. "Jesus H. Christ. Is that why you came here—to berate me for my fucking diet?"

"No." He shifts in the seat, his gaze drifting to the table, and then he sighs. "Look. I think we should go back to New York for now. Take a break from the scene for a while.

I grit my teeth. *Not this again.* "No, man. I want another fight. Why is that so fucking hard?"

He looks around the restaurant. The place is not too crowded, with mostly families and teenagers occupying smaller tables. Still, I can tell what he really wants to talk about is not meant for public ears.

"Even the greatest fighters need to unwind every now and then," Dante says.

I know he wants to say more, but this place prevents him from doing so, and I don't want to give him the satisfaction of moving the conversation elsewhere. "I unwind every time I go to the gym. I don't need a vacation, Dante. I need to fight."

He rubs his temples and shakes his head. "Yeah, I heard what happened over at Brett's gym."

I purse my lips. I'm expecting that look of rage to return to his face, but it doesn't. In fact, he looks hurt, disappointed. It eats me up inside whenever he looks like that, but I don't want him to think it bothers me, so I sit back in my seat and fold my arms.

Dante clears his throat. "All I'm gonna say about that—and I've said it for years—is you can't fight the world, so stop trying."

I shake my head. "I'm not fighting the world. Just the assholes who try me."

He sighs and slides out of the booth. "Right. Well, whenever you're ready to talk, I'll be back at the motel."

Not uncrossing my arms, I watch him leave. I remain there mulling over my thoughts for I don't know how long. Despite what Dante says, I *have* to fight the world. I've been doing it since I've been out on my own. No one ever gave a damn about me.

But I deserve this misery. I deserve it all.

Chapter 4

I'M BACK AT THE MOTEL BY SEVEN IN THE EVENING, AND MY aching, sore body doesn't feel any better. Neither has my mind recovered from getting weirded out by the mysterious texter. And now, Dante wants to give me shit. Fortunately, he's staying in a room at the opposite end of the hall.

I take a long, hot shower, and by seven thirty, I'm relaxing in bed in a pair of sweatpants, channel surfing. Nothing seems worthwhile to watch, and I'm getting hungry again. I was on a strict diet, eating six small meals a day. But when I came to California last week, that plan went out the window. Dante is still pissed at my little "rebellion," of course. But I promised him I'd get back on my regimen when we returned to New York. I'll definitely regret the lapse. I mean, I'm still eating healthy for the most part, but I can't deny I do enjoy the spontaneous splurging.

I flip through channels, not looking for anything in particular. I rarely watch TV, and when I do, it's usually an action movie or a silly cartoon. Yeah, I may be twenty-five, but don't fuck with me and my cartoons.

I stop at a sports channel, where the commentators are talking with professional basketball players. "April's draft has seen some promising talent," a male commentator says as the TV pans through pictures of various basketball players. "It will be a year of rising stars this season as these rookies will be defining a new era of professional basketball. And now, reporting from New York City is Lydia Williams."

The camera shifts to a female commentator. "Thanks, Mark. I'm here at an undisclosed training center with one of the league's most promising rookies this season, eighteenth overall draft pick, Kevin Anderson."

My thumb falls away from the buttons on the remote. *Kevin. Anderson. No, the name's generic. It's probably not—*

"Kevin hails from the University of Washington with quite a long list of athletic achievements. You may remember him two years ago during the championship game against UCLA. Check out these highlights."

I blink and sit up in bed. The TV is showing old footage of Kevin playing college hoops while the commentator begins rapping out all of his achievements. I think about my little brother, back in the day, when he loved playing basketball. While I practiced Tae Kwon Do forms alone in the backyard, Kevin played pickup games with the neighborhood kids. I haven't talked to Kevin since last year, and I haven't seen him since I was fifteen.

And now, here he is on national TV. My little brother is a college all-star! He's playing pro!

"Ho—ly fucking shit," I mutter.

Why hasn't Uncle Adam called me about this? He's usually the town crier of the family these days. Maybe he thought I wouldn't care. He told me that Kevin got himself a sports agent sometime last year, but I didn't hear anything after that.

As I continue watching Kevin's old footage, I realize just how out of touch I've become with my own family. The people I grew up with are moving forward in their lives, and here I am, staying stagnant. Looking at Kevin makes me realize how much of a fucking failure I've become.

The footage ends, and the camera pans back to the commentator and then zooms out to reveal Kevin standing next to her. Kevin's a giant compared to the woman, who has to hold the hand mic high for him. He must be pushing six-five, maybe six-seven. And damn, he's ripped. It pisses me the hell off that he looks like that, and I bet he's not even doing half the workouts I do in the gym. I swear, God is having a field day, screwing with me like that.

> Kevin is living his dream. He seems happy. That's all I'd ever wanted for my brothers. Kevin's grown up into a fine young man with a great future.

He turns to the interviewer, and the lights catch the string of tattoos on the left side of his neck and down his arm. There seem to be more beneath his T-shirt, but the visible ones are all I need to see before my eyes start to burn. Memories take over, bad memories of what I thought of as home—a place that ended up being a nightmare. The feeling of regret takes over. I can't even hear what Kevin is saying to the commentator.

All I can think about is *that night* ten years ago: coming home from grocery shopping with Mama and discovering what my father had done to Kevin and my baby brother, Dominick. I keep recalling the look of hurt and anger in my brothers' eyes and how I hadn't been there to save them from that shit.

I swallow a lump in my throat. "I'm sorry, K," I whisper to Kevin's image on the TV. "God, I'm so sorry." Unable to watch the taped interview anymore, I shut off the TV. I clench my fists and rip a pillow from the bed and punch it hard. "I'm fucking sorry, man!" I yell, my view of the pillow wavering from the welled-up tears that muddle my vision. I punch the pillow again and again, its softness yielding to my fist. I finally toss the pillow aside, wipe the stray tears from my face, and grab my cell from the night table. I need to clear my mind, so I play a game of spades, check my email, and visit the website again for fights, but Dante still hasn't scheduled any for me. I scroll farther down the page to see if that weird icon is still there. It's in the same spot as before. *I wonder if my phone will freak out again if I touch it.* Curiosity gets the better of me, and I test my luck.

I press my finger over the icon once, but nothing happens. The phone doesn't shut off or anything. Maybe it was just a fluke last time. Whatever.

As I'm setting the phone back on the night table, it buzzes, and the screen lights up, revealing an incoming text from that unknown person again.

U know what curiosity did to the cat

I frown. This is starting to get freakishly annoying. I text back:

who r u and what do u want?

i should be asking YOU that

I dont know what ur talking about…

Let's meet somewhere. or would u rather me stop by ur motel room? ;)

I blink. *How the hell did—?* I don't reply. This is definitely a cop. Maybe I should let Dante know. He's been keeping me under the radar with all the underground fighting I've been doing. And being an ex-cop himself, he knows the ins and outs of things that go on behind the scenes. I change out of my sweatpants and into some jeans, slip on a T-shirt, then grab my wallet, phone, and room key, and I leave.

I pound on Dante's door, and he answers it right away. He's on the phone, but when he sees me, he steps aside to let me in.

"Hey," he mutters into the phone. "Gotta go. Let me call you later . . . all right. Peace."

I sit on the edge of one of the twin beds, lean my elbows on my knees, push my glasses up atop my head, and bury my face in my hands.

"What the hell's wrong with you?" Dante asks.

I sigh deeply and look up at him. "I think we got cops on us, man."

He blinks. "What?"

I show him my phone and explain about the website incident and the unknown texts. While I'm explaining, he's carefully analyzing the screen.

"No, this ain't a cop," he says when I finish.

"It's not? Then how do you explain how they know I'm at a motel?"

He shakes his head. "It's not a cop. Hacker, maybe, but not a cop. But if it *is* a hacker, then you might be in some deep shit. Could be a blackmailer or stalker who might have obtained your personal information."

"What should I do, man? I feel like someone's watching me. It's freaking me out."

"When we get home, I'll talk to some friends who can investigate this a bit more. But for now, there's not much I can do."

I somehow knew he was going to say that. "Damn it, Dante."

He squeezes my shoulder. "Listen. It's time we went home. This has nothing to do with your ability to fight. But I'll be frank. I'm tired of living in the world of the underground, tired of hiding. I've been doing this shit for ten years. I need a new life. And so do you."

I shrug off his hand. "Really, Dante? You're gonna just abandon me now? What the fuck?"

"No, you know I'm not gonna abandon you. But I can't keep doing this. I'm sure whatever you've got to prove to the world has been proven already."

No, it'll never be proven. I'll never find peace because I failed my family.

"Let's go home." He looks at me with hopeful eyes.

I narrow mine at him. "No. I can't. I won't. *You* go to New York. I'm not running like a scared bitch anymore."

"This is the thanks I get for saving your little punk ass?" he growls.

I ball my fists and pop up from the bed. "Fuck you."

He prods me in the chest with his finger. "Listen . . . *Michael.*"

I freeze. Anger boils in me as that fucking name reverberates in my mind—the name I've been cursed with since birth. The name I wanted so desperately to forget. "Don't call me that."

"I can call you whatever the hell I want if it'll make you listen to me."

I clench my jaw and don't reply.

"You're better than this. You don't need a damn cage to prove who you are. It's in your heart. Take those skills you got and teach someone else. Help them." He pauses, and his eyes become glassy. "I lost my two little children to stupid shit. I'm sure as hell not gonna lose you, too."

I deflate. *Why the hell did he have to go and bring that up?* "Is that why you're so insistent in me not fighting anymore?"

"No." He sighs and paces in front of me. "I thought I could get back at the world for what those punks took from me by training you to be my weapon." His face darkens. "But as time went by, I realized that I was being selfish, and I gave up the underground shit. You seemed to be enjoying it, so I let you have your fun. But now when I look back, I realize it wasn't enjoyment you were getting out of those fights."

"This calms me, man. It's therapy," I say. "Don't you see that?"

"It's a dangerous sickness. A drug. And you know how I feel about drugs."

"Look, I have family shit I have to deal with."

"I thought you resolved your family issues when you went to see your mom for her birthday last year?"

I swallow. I never did tell him the details of that day. I never told him how I didn't make it past Chicago because the flight to Seattle got cancelled due to bad weather. Or how I screwed up so bad that day that Kevin banished me from the family. "Stay out of our lives. You're a fucking disease," he'd said.

I'm a disease. That's putting it mildly. But it might as well be true. The family's broken because of me. *I* did it.

"Fighting is what's keeping me alive, man," I finally say.

He heaves a deep sigh. "Come back to New York. I want to start a gym like Brett's got going here. You can work with me as a trainer. It'll be good, honest work. You're not a kid anymore. It's time to stop playing around with these punks. Besides . . . " He looks away.

I raise an eyebrow. "What?"

He looks back at me carefully. "I got word that there's been probing going on about some syndicate running the gambling ring. One of my buddies suggested I lay low for a while."

"One of your cop friends told you this?" I say.

"He's not a cop anymore. But yeah."

"So that's the *real* reason you want me to quit."

"It's *one* of the reasons."

I shake my head, reset my glasses, and head for the door. "Fuck this shit."

"Where are you going?" Dante calls after me.

"Food. I'm starving."

"Find something healthy this time, damn it."

I roll my eyes as I open the door. "Yes, Mother."

"Hey, so you coming back to New York with me or what? I'm gonna try getting the plane tickets tonight."

I stop in the doorway and sigh. My mind's too rattled to decide right now. "I'll get back to you on that," I say and then walk out.

It's after nine o'clock, and I'm scouring the streets for a good restaurant. Even at this time of night, the streets are busy. It's reminiscent of New York in some ways. As I walk, I realize I'm nearing Brett's gym. The side door is still rolled up, the lights are on inside, and people are moving around in there. As tempting as it is to stop by, I decide against it and cross the street to a small strip of stores. Unfortunately, there's no restaurant. I head down another block and catch a whiff of grilled steak, garlic, roasted fish, potatoes—food, actual real food and not fast food. I've been looking for a hole-in-the-wall, mom-and-pop place to eat like the ones back home, and this could be it.

A commotion ahead breaks into my thoughts. A well-dressed couple is standing near a car parked by the curb outside a nightclub. The man's swaying like he's had too much to drink, and the woman is in his face, prodding his chest as she goes off on him. I slow to a casual saunter and listen as I draw nearer. I don't know what they're saying, but the sharpness of their tones indicates it's not good. Then out of nowhere, the man shoves the woman backward. She stumbles but recovers and slaps him across the face.

"I'm taking a cab. Go fuck yourself." She spins on her high heels and clips off down the sidewalk.

The man rubs his face then chases after the woman. "Bitch! Get back here!" He grabs her arm and pulls her into an alley.

Passersby notice the scuffle and cross the street to avoid it. Some people get on their cell phones, but I've no idea if any of them are calling the cops. Even if they are making phone calls, the police will be too late to save that woman. A few people move toward the alley, aiming their phones at the scene as they start recording it.

Fucking sick people. I really shouldn't make this my business, but—

"No! Stop!" The woman's screams echo from the alley.

I run toward the sound. The muted amber glow from a nearby streetlight reveals the guy pinning the woman against the wall. She struggles and flails her arms about with wild punches and kicks at the guy's groin. He dodges the blows and holds her firm, one hand at her throat, the other groping around under her short skirt. The two of them don't seem to notice me.

"Don't you *dare* embarrass me like that again, you hear me?" he mutters through clenched teeth.

She spits in his face. I hear fabric tearing, and the guy removes his hand from under her skirt, revealing a small piece of ripped clothing.

I look around again to see if anyone is bothering to do something, but some continue walking by as if these two people are ghosts while others continue to stand around and film the scene on their phones. I hate feeling I need to do something, but the woman's suffering reminds me of how my mother was mistreated by my father. I can't let that shit happen to someone else.

I shove past the group of onlookers and approach the guy. He looks in my direction when I'm but a few feet away. The woman's eyelids flutter. The guy's holding her throat tight. She's losing consciousness fast.

"Hey, get the hell outta here, man," he says. "This don't concern you."

I shake my head. "Let her go."

"Mind your own fucking business, man!" he growls louder.

The woman's eyelids open and close slowly. I lunge at the guy, grab him by the collar of his fancy silk shirt, and slam him against the opposite wall. He lets out a grunt, and the back of his head smacks against the brick.

"Show a little more respect for the opposite sex, asshole." I slug him across the face. That one punch ends up knocking him out. He collapses.

I go to the woman, who's slumped on the ground, and try to rouse her by gently patting her cheek. "Hey, you okay? Can you hear me?"

She lets out a small cough and then moans.

"C'mon." I help her to her feet. "I'll get you a cab. You need to go to the hospital or something?"

"No," she mutters. "Home . . . please . . . "

I carry her out of the alley and lower my head as I brush past the group of video-taking idiots. The last thing I want is my damn face shown all over the Internet, but it's probably too late now.

"Holy shit, man, that was epic!" one person says. I notice him out of the corner of my eye, aiming his camera phone in my direction.

I hear police sirens in the distance. "You sure you're okay?" I ask the woman.

Her eyes open a little wider, and her face relaxes. She nods.

I hail a cab and help her into the backseat. The sound of the sirens is getting closer. The video-taking spectators finally put away their phones and disperse from the scene. I hustle across the street. When I reach the other side, I hide among the line of parked cars along the curb. Two police cars pull up in front of the alley, and some of the passersby stop and look. I really should leave now.

My phone suddenly buzzes in my back pocket. I take it out and check it. That unknown texter has contacted me again.

Need a ride? ;)

I blink and look around at the parked cars. Is that person here now? I don't bother replying and hustle up the street.

"Slow down, Knox," a familiar female voice says.

I stop in my tracks. *That voice.* I turn toward its source—a small red sports car parked beside me. The passenger window is rolled down, and the purple-haired girl from the other night grins at me, her metal piercings glinting in the light.

"Hey," she says. She's not wearing that black lipstick or any of that gothic shit this time. She's actually dressed quite plainly in jeans and a white T-shirt, which stretches over the swell of her big tits. I was right. She *is* pretty underneath that angsty facade. But what is she doing *here?*

"You looked like you were lost," she says again when I don't respond.

"Uh . . . " I stare at her, completely enamored and a little freaked out that she's here now. The staticky sound of the police radios in the distance brings me back to reality. "I need to get out of here."

"Yeah, I can see that. Hop in."

I look at her warily, still not thoroughly convinced that she's not a cop, too, but she is my best bet for leaving fast and unnoticed. Without another thought, I get in the passenger side, and we speed off down the street.

Chapter 5

I WATCH THE STREETLIGHTS GO BY AND WILL MYSELF TO NOT look over at the girl beside me because I know if I do, I won't be able to take my eyes off her. My mind races as I try to piece things together. *Is she the mysterious texter?* I check my phone for any recent texts, but there are none.

"So where're you headed?" the girl asks, breaking the silence.

"I was on my way to find some food." I take in the exposed tattoos covering her arm, and then admire her hips, which the grungy, ripped jeans hug nicely.

"I could dig some food right about now, too," she says, and my lingering gaze returns to her face. "I saw what you did back there, by the way. That was pretty badass of you. And noble."

"Eh . . . " I shrug. "I have a problem with guys mistreating women."

"Ditto. But sometimes, women mistreat men." She frowns when she says this, keeping her eyes focused on the road.

"Yeah, true." I sigh. "Soon, all of the Internet will see that shit when those phone videos get posted."

Her frown lifts slightly. "Camera shy are you? Well, don't worry. I can fix that."

I wrinkle my brow. *What does she mean by that?* "So who are you? It's crazy that we're meeting again like this."

"My name's Alexis, but you can call me Lexi."

Lexi. "Cute. I'm Knox."

"Yeah, I know." She glances at me and smiles coyly.

"Oh, right. From the fight." I nod absently. "Hey, sorry if I'm sounding weird or something, but I've been getting these strange texts, and it's freaked me out."

She raises her eyebrows. "Yeah? What do they say?"

"Things like . . . I've been naughty, and some other shit. It's really weird."

"Well . . . you *have* been a little naughty."

"So, that *was* you! What the hell?"

She waves her hand dismissively. "First, food. You like Italian?"

At the mention of food, my stomach growls, and I put the topic of texting aside for now. "I *love* Italian."

"Great. I know just the place."

I have no idea what part of town we're in or how far I am from the motel. But I don't care at this point. The flashing red-white-and-green sign of the Italian restaurant we pull up to has my fullest attention. We order our food to go, and we're back on the road again. Lexi drives as if she knows exactly where she's going. Why am I a little disturbed by that?

"Uh, where are we headed?"

"There's this spot up in Baldwin Hills I used to visit when I was in high school. Trust me, you'll like it."

"You sure you're not a cop?"

She chuckles. "If I was, I wouldn't have been your getaway back there." Her face softens. "I promise you I'm not a cop."

"You working for anyone?"

"Yes. Me, myself, and I."

I shift in my seat. It's disturbing to think that she's driving me to Hell knows where. But somehow, I trust this girl, even though I barely know her. Besides, the car already smells like minestrone and lasagna from the bag of food in the backseat, so I'm willing to go just about anywhere in order to satisfy my hunger.

Five minutes later, we veer off the highway and onto a dirt road that leads through a car-sized hole in a mangled chain-link fence. The road heads up a steep incline, and as we go higher, I start to see the city lights in the distance. They spread out below us like twinkling stars. She pulls up near a large steel structure and puts the car in park. The headlights shine on a metal railing guarding the cliff beyond. She rolls down the windows, letting in a wave of mild, dusty air, and shuts off the headlights and engine. I lean out the passenger-side window and see that we're beside the base of a cell tower. Way up above us, a tiny red light blinks at the tower's summit.

I pull my head back in and stare out the windshield at the mass of moving and blinking lights and buildings beyond the cliff—a breathtakingly beautiful sight of LA's night scene. It reminds me of New York only with fewer tall buildings.

"What do you think of the view?" Lexi asks.

"It's . . . kinda hard to explain in words."

"Yeah, I think so, too. That's why I always liked coming here." She reaches into the backseat for the carryout bag.

I poke a straw in my cup and take a long sip of iced tea while she divvies out the covered, aluminum-plated takeout containers. Questions begin swimming in my mind, but they're muddled by my hunger.

"I know what you're thinking," she says, edging the plastic lid off her lasagna. "And the answer is no, I'm not stalking you."

I pause and look sideways at her, my minestrone-filled spoon hovering at my lips. *That wasn't really what I was thinking, but . . .* "If you're not stalking me, then how did you know where I was tonight?"

"I tracked your phone via GPS. It's not that hard, really."

"How did you even get a hold of my phone like that?"

"You found my little beacon on the website. It sent me your information. When I found out who it was, I couldn't help but have a little fun with you."

"You call that fun?" I scowl. Then I remember what Dante said about a hacker possibly getting my information. "Wait, so you're a hacker . . . "

She casually eats her lasagna. "That's such a dirty word."

"It is what it is." I narrow my eyes at her as I swallow my soup. "What kind of information do you have on me?"

"Just stuff from your phone, since that's what you used to trigger my tracker."

That's more than enough information for my taste. "Get rid of it."

"Don't worry. I'm not gonna do anything with it. However, I need to keep track of who's been visiting the site."

"Why?"

She runs her plastic fork along the cheese and sauce, creating four little lines. "You ask too many questions, y'know? You sure *you're* not a cop?" She raises her eyebrows.

I snort. "I'm most definitely *not* a cop."

"An undercover cop would deny he's a cop while he's working." She finishes her lasagna and tosses the empty container in the bag.

"I swear, I'm not a fucking cop! I'm trying to *avoid* the cops more than anything."

She smiles, seeming convinced. "And why are *you* so scared of the cops? You an escaped convict or something?"

Sure feels like it. I wolf down every last drop of minestrone and uncover my main course: chicken marsala. "Naw, nothing like that. But being engaged in illegal fighting and all that for so long, I always have to be careful of who I associate myself with, if you know what I mean."

"Right." She leans her elbow over the driver-side window and nurses her soda. "So, let's lighten the mood, eh? You're from New York?"

I'm about to ask her how she knows, and then I realize she probably got it from my phone number. "Yeah. I'll probably be going back soon, though. What about you?"

"Originally from Santa Monica, but I live in Seattle now."

"What are you doing down here?"

"One of my friends graduated from UDub this past spring, and she moved to Inglewood, so I'm visiting her for a couple of weeks. And it was just my luck that there were some fights going on around here." She smirks.

As I process this, I finish my food and toss the empty container in the bag with the rest. I recline a little in my seat, the back of my head leaning against the headrest, and I stare out at the city lights. Bringing my fist to my lips, I let out a low burp.

"You good?" she asks, looking at me with slight amusement.

"Hell yeah, that hit the spot," I murmur.

She runs her finger along the steering wheel. "So, when are you going back to New York?"

I half shrug. "I dunno. My trainer wants me to go back with him tomorrow, but I kind of wanna stay out here and fight some more." I look over at her. "Why?"

"Just curious."

It's my turn to smirk. "You know what curiosity did to the cat."

She guffaws. "Lame."

Her laughter invigorates me, makes me forget about the goth girl from the other night. Maybe this is who she *really* is. I lazily glance at her body. The way she lounges in her seat with a confident vibe is all sorts of hot.

She reaches into the console and pulls out her phone. The screen lights up with the time—12:49 a.m.

"I guess I should take you back to the motel," she says, grabbing her keys, which are still in the ignition.

But I don't want to go. Not now, not yet. I like this secluded spot away from the world. It's just me and this girl, looking down at the chaos below, which is camouflaged by sparkling lights. "Wait," I say, putting my hand over hers and stopping her. Her hand is soft, smooth, and warm.

She tenses and looks at our hands and then over at me. I remove my hand. "Sorry. I mean . . . I think I wanna stay out here a little longer. I'm not ready to go back yet . . . well, unless you are, that is."

She shakes her head. "No, I just figured that . . . " She lets the unfinished sentence hang in the mild air.

The silence becomes a little tense. I probably *should* leave. But here I am with this girl who's more than piqued my interest. Beautiful? Hell yes. Smart? Amazingly so, and badass, too. It'll suck if I go back to New York and never see her again.

But she said she lives in Seattle. Some of my family members live around there. But Kevin told me to stay away. *I'm a disease.*

I push the thought aside as Lexi moistens her lips with her tongue. My gaze drifts to her lips, and I wonder if she tastes as good as she smells—like strawberries.

She smiles. "What?"

"Uh, nothing," I mutter, staring at the lip ring in fascination. "Think we can get to know each other a little more, Lexi?"

Her gaze falls lower, perhaps to *my* lips.

"Maybe." She shrugs. "Frankly, my girlfriends have been dogging me about me being single. They keep trying to hook me up with every guy they come across. It's amusing really."

My heart flutters a little. *Single? Sweet.* "No one's piqued your interest?"

"Not really." She returns her attention to the steering wheel and resumes running her finger along it.

Does that include me?

"How about you? Any girls on your to-do list?" she asks nonchalantly.

"No." My answer is quick—maybe a little too quick. I'm not exactly proud of my random one-night stands with bar girls.

She acknowledges my answer with a skeptical look. Maybe she knows. Girls seem to have a sixth sense about that kind of thing. She stares at the key in the ignition.

"We can go if you want," I say.

She hesitates then starts the car but doesn't touch the gearshift.

"I think maybe we *could* get to know each other a little more," she finally says. She turns to me, tilting her head slightly. "You look like someone I know."

"Oh?"

She nods. "He's cool. Really nice. You kinda remind me of him."

I feel a small lump forming in my throat, and my skin prickles. "Should I be asking who this guy is?"

"Don't worry." She smiles. "He goes out with one of my best friends. And he moved to New York a few months ago. Way out of my reach. He's hot, and he plays basketball."

No, it can't be. "What's his name?"

"Kevin."

I exhale. "Anderson?"

She looks taken aback. "Yeah. How did you—" Her eyes widen. "Wait, are you two related or something?"

I nod slowly. "Brothers."

She sits back in her seat and stares blankly at the dashboard. "Holy shit."

The way she reacts like that makes me wonder what Kevin told her about me. She must know everything. She'll not want to have anything to do with me now.

"I . . . honestly had no idea," she says, looking at me. "I mean, I've always seen Kevin and Dominick together. Never knew they had another brother."

"Yeah," I say, my voice getting a little quieter.

She smiles brightly and puts the car in reverse. "That's cool, I've met another Anderson brother. How many of you are there?"

"Just three."

"Okay. Well, you guys are cool. At least two of my girlfriends lucked out in that department." She backs out and heads down the dirt path toward the main road.

I'm not sure whether to be flattered or offended. And what does this mean for Lexi and me? "So you see Dominick and Kevin a lot?"

"Mmm . . . Dominick, yeah. He's still at UDub. Kevin, not so much since he moved to New York. But once the season starts, I'll be catching him on TV when I can. And I definitely have to catch Kevitron's House on Thursday."

"Kevitron's House?"

She scrunches her brow. "Yeah, Kevin's radio show. Don't tell me you've never heard of it."

I shake my head.

"It's only one of the hottest radio stations on the Internet. He spins live on Thursdays and Saturdays unless he has a game. I'll text you the link to the site later."

"Cool. Thanks." I'd forgotten how much Kevin loved deejaying. Man, I've been really disconnected. No wonder he's so angry at me.

We drive back to the motel with her mostly talking about her girlfriends' relationships with my brothers. It's weird, hearing about Kevin and Dominick like that, but it sounds as if they're happy. I wish I could move on the way they have.

Before I know it, we pull into a parking space in front of my motel door. She puts the car in park and waits for me to get out. "It was fun tonight. Thanks for hanging out . . . and buying dinner," she says.

I run my finger on the door latch but hesitate to open it. I just want this moment to last a little while longer. "No problem. And yeah, it was fun. Thanks for the ride."

Silence consumes the car's interior, aside from the low hum of the motor. I look at her. She looks at me. *I want to kiss her. Will she let me?* I look down to her hand, resting on the console, and slowly move my hand over hers. "When can I see you again?" I ask softly, with a gentle rub of my fingers.

Her eyelids flutter downward to our hands. "I dunno." She slips her hand out from under mine. "We'll figure out something."

I take her gesture to mean she's saying no to a kiss, so I start to open the door. "Okay. See you later then."

As I lean to get out the car, she grabs my arm. "Hey."

"Hmm?" I turn my head, and her face is so close to mine. Our lips touch. The cold metal of the lip ring sends a brief shiver through me. I lift my glasses up until they rest on top of my head. Then I answer earnestly, kissing her back. I taste a hint of strawberries from her lip gloss. She tastes ten times better than the sweet strawberry scent that fills my nose. My groin strains as I imagine kissing her like this all night. I reach over and caress her cheek. But then I feel her pull away. The moment is over before it began. My mouth partially open, I stare at her with need. I have an urge to wrap her in my arms and indulge in her sweet taste all over again. She looks back at me with an expression that tells the same story—but only briefly, and then she recovers and clears her throat.

"I gotta go," she says.

I nod absentmindedly, reset my glasses, and get out of the car. "Yeah."

"Later, Knox." She smiles and waves then backs out of the lot.

I wave back, my body still numb from the emotional high. "Bye, Lexi," I mutter though I know she can't hear me. While I stand there, she leaves the parking lot and speeds off down the street until she's out of sight.

Chapter 6

I END UP GETTING MY OWN LAST-MINUTE PLANE TICKET FOR New York and manage to catch the same flight as Dante though I have no idea where he is seated in this sardine-packed cabin. By three o'clock in the afternoon, I'm back in New York and on the metro bus on my way home to the South Bronx, having parted ways with Dante after we landed.

Since leaving California, I've been checking my phone in case Lexi texted me, but she hasn't. I even tried replying to one of the earlier texts, but she didn't respond. I haven't been on the website again, and I wonder if that's the only way to reach her? I can't call her because my phone lists her as "unknown," and her number is hidden. I don't know why she wouldn't give me her number when I asked. I guess it makes sense for her to keep quiet about that kind of info in her line of work. Or maybe she just can't trust me, yet.

Traffic is more ridiculous than usual, and I learn that there's a baseball game tonight. It takes me forever to get home. The bus finally stops a block away from my building on 148th Street, and I step off with my duffel bag in tow. Compared to California, the air is a little cool for a late September afternoon. I inhale the familiar aroma of Jamaican spiced beef patties and eggrolls drifting from the businesses farther down the street. Distant car horns welcome me as I near my building, bypassing a middle-aged lady pushing a heavy-duty cart full of laundry. A couple of old guys are sitting around on the stoop, talking and drinking from bottles covered by brown bags. One of the men is Mr. Whittaker, the obnoxious tenant who lives next door to me. Carrying my bag over my shoulder, I walk past them without so much as glancing their way and holding my breath so as not to breathe in their stink of cheap wine.

"I was wondering why it was so quiet around here for the past week," Mr. Whittaker says. "I actually got some damn sleep for a change."

I pause to slide a look in his direction. Both men are looking back at me, Mr. Whittaker smiling smugly. "The hell you talking about?" I say.

"You know *exactly* what I'm talking about, Mr. Playboy." He smirks, gives me a mock salute with his raised drink, and then takes a swig.

I roll my eyes. "Whatever, old man. You're drunk."

He laughs, openmouthed, revealing yellow, rotted teeth.

Cringing, I head inside.

"Don't go bringing any more of your damned skanks home, either! We've got enough rats in this building as it is!" The graffiti-covered entrance door slams shut behind me.

Fuck him. I climb the stairs to the third floor and pull my keys from my pocket. The strong odor of cooked fish that wafts from one of the neighbor's apartments makes me wrinkle my nose as I jiggle the key in the corroded lock. The muffled sounds of TVs and deep bass thumping reverberate from the floors above and below. Down at the other end of the corridor, one of the neighbors, Carlotta—a gorgeous Latina with curly, off-the-shoulder hair—exits her apartment and knocks on the door directly across the hall. I once tried to get with her, but she wouldn't give me the time of day. Now she's going out with some chump who's scared as shit of me.

She pounds hard on the door with her fist, each impact echoing throughout the hall. "*¡Oye, Rodrigo! ¡Te dije que le dijeras a tus chicos come mierda que dejen de llamar a mi teléfono!*"

I have no idea what she's saying, but *damn*, that accent sounds sexy. She looks my way, narrows her big brown eyes, scowls, and continues knocking.

I leave her to her drama and open my door. The decades-old one-bedroom apartment greets me with the smell of dust and mildew. I take in the peeling walls, popcorn ceiling dotted with occasional brown water spots, and rusted radiator under the window in the main room. Since I'm rarely home, I keep the place sparsely furnished, using the main open space to practice forms and use my bench press, which is tucked in one corner.

The place is stuffy, so I open the windows. Without bothering to unpack, I head to the bathroom to shower. While I relax, I consider Dante's offer to let me help him start up his own gym with me as a trainer. But I don't know if I'm ready to help others like that. I think about my own family and am reminded of why I'm not cut out to help anyone. *I ran away when they needed me the most.*

I leave the bathroom and rummage in the fridge. There are some weeks-old mystery leftovers in plastic containers that I'm too scared to open. It looks like I'll have to do a food run. For now, I decide to satisfy my hunger pangs with a can of beef stew. My phone buzzes on the counter, and I spot Uncle Adam's number, lit up on the screen.

Damn, I was supposed to call him back the other night. I take a deep breath and answer the phone. "Hey, man."

"Junior? I've been trying to reach you for the past week," he says.

I swallow a lump in my throat. "Yeah, well . . . I've been busy . . . "

"So it seems."

I run my finger along the white-tiled countertop. "What's up?"

"I haven't talked to you in a while, son. You have a birthday coming up in less than a week, and I'm sure your mother would love to talk to you."

It always sounds so weird whenever he calls me "son" and talks to me as if he were my real father. After what happened all those years ago, I wish he was.

"It's just another day, man," I say.

"Another day to stay away from the family?"

I ball my hand into a fist. I begin to smell the stew, and I return to the stove to take the pot off the fire. "What's the point? It's too late for that shit. I fucked up. When are you gonna understand that things will never be the same again?"

"No, things won't be the same, but that doesn't mean we can't start clean. What your mother wants more than anything is to see you again."

As I'm about to stir the stew, I pause and toss the wooden spoon into the pot. It clanks, and droplets of hot broth splash on my wrist. The stinging pain feels like a bunch of tiny ants biting my hand. "Shit!" I hiss. I head to the faucet.

"Everything okay, son?" Uncle Adam asks.

"Yeah, fine, man," I say, running my hand under the cold water until the pain subsides. "Look, I can't see Mama." *I'm a disease.*

"You're part of this family. We all love you."

"Fuck that. Me coming back will just remind Mama of *that day* again."

"That's not true. She always asks about you, wondering what you're doing."

My body goes rigid. "You haven't told her anything, have you?"

"Of course not. But how long am I—are *you*—going to keep hiding this from her?"

As long as I need to. I pour the hot stew into a bowl. "Hey, why didn't you tell me about Kevin going pro?" I ask, changing the subject.

"I did. Back in April, when it happened. At least, I *tried* calling you several times, but you didn't pick up. I even left you a voicemail."

I grit my teeth. *Damn it. I'm such a failure.* When he called, I must've been fighting and then forgot to check my messages.

"You never got my message?" Uncle Adam asks.

"Naw, I guess I missed it," I say, fishing for a spoon from the utensil drawer.

"Your mother cried when the league commissioner announced his name. She was so happy. We are all very happy for him."

I try to envision Mama shedding tears of joy, but it's hard. I've seen way too many of the other kind of tears coming from her.

"Now that Kevin's in New York, you should go see him," Uncle Adam says.

Like that's going to happen. "Kevin doesn't want to see me right now—or maybe ever. Anyway, he probably wouldn't even recognize me."

"I know it's been a while, son, but now's a good opportunity to make up for lost time."

I plop down in a chair at the tiny dinette. "Look, I gotta go. I'm about to eat."

"Fine. Think about it at least."

We hang up, and I nurse my stew while the mix of police sirens, car horns, and the whooshing of trains keeps me on edge.

After that depressing talk with Uncle Adam, I just want to sleep the rest of the day away. Unfortunately, my body won't let me, so I head out to do my much-needed grocery run. It's seven o'clock in the evening, and as I'm walking home with my arms cradling grocery bags, I pass by CLR, my usual hangout bar. Laughter and music pour out the propped-open door, and I make out the voices of my friends from the gym. I slow down and peer inside. Weston, Reno, and Carlos sit on padded stools at the bar, shooting the shit over a couple of drinks. A girl with her back turned to me leans on the counter beside Weston.

Reno straightens in his seat and looks toward the entrance. His face lights up, and he waves. "Knox! You're back!"

Stepping inside, I smile slightly, unable to wave back due to the bags. "Hey, man."

The rest of my friends stop talking and look up.

"Hey, when did you get back?" Reno asks.

"Earlier this afternoon," I reply. The girl beside Weston turns around and grins, and I see it's Bonita. She's cute, with cinnamon-brown skin and a convincing curly weave that cascades down her back, but she's trouble. I've had a few good booty calls with her, but I could never get serious despite her obvious interest in me. I guess it's the instability I sense in her. She drinks like a fish when she's bothered about something or turns into a sex-crazed fiend when she's looking for company.

Bonita abandons Weston and approaches me, an eager look on her face. I know what she probably wants, but I'm not in the mood right now.

"Welcome back, Knox," she says softly, tracing my exposed bicep with her finger. "Missed you."

I roll my eyes. *You only missed my dick.* "How are you? Staying out of trouble, I hope."

She smirks, and her hand falls away from my arm. "As much as you are." She looks at the bags. "Need some help with those?"

"Naw, I got it." I turn toward the door. "See you guys at the gym tomorrow," I say to my friends, who wave and call back.

I feel Bonita's hand at the small of my back, and my body tenses. "I need to talk to you," she mutters.

I flare my nostrils. "Is it your dad again?"

She nods slowly, and I sigh. Her family situation is all sorts of fucked up. Her mom died of breast cancer last year, her pregnant sister was shot and killed by a psychopath boyfriend, and her father is a drug addict. No wonder Bonita's resorted to bar whoring.

"Fine, come over later," I say.

The TV's tuned to the cartoon channel, providing background noise while I pump out a thousand diamond push-ups. I finish in forty-five minutes. My body's drenched in sweat, and my muscles are burning.

I flex in the bathroom mirror and check out the results. My sore pecs and biceps feel three times bigger than before, but they sure don't look it. I'm cut and toned in several places but nowhere near the way I want to be. I definitely don't look as if I bust my ass in the gym every day, working out like a fiend. Yet all Kevin has to do is dribble a basketball, and he looks like a beast. Fuck him and his better genes.

My phone buzzes in the bedroom, indicating a text message. I hurry out of the bathroom and check it. It's from an unknown number.

Hope u got home safe. I'm heading back to seattle this weekend.

I smile.

lexi?

Shh! ;)

sorry. I wanna talk 2 u again. i enjoyed last night.

Last night was fun.

I exhale a breath I've been inadvertently holding in. I wonder if "fun" includes the kiss? I haven't stopped thinking about that kiss since I left California.

I wish I can see u again.

come out here when ur not fighting. gtg now.

I'm almost tempted to get a plane ticket now. But she must be busy if she has to leave so quickly. She's probably doing more Internet snooping. I text her back even though I know she probably won't reply.

Bye, lexi...

Shit, I wasn't supposed to mention her name. I wish I could delete that text. To my relief, it returns as a message-sending failure. "Recipient not found," the pop-up box says. Wow, she can shut herself off from communication on a whim. I have limited tech skills, but compared to her, I look as if I've never touched a computer in my life.

I scroll through the older texts while I fantasize about her—that stunningly beautiful body, and the ice-cold lip ring that sent pleasure pangs through me when we kissed. She has a mysteriousness that continues to feed my burning curiosity.

But suddenly, my mind tumbles back to reality when my eyes are drawn to an old, unread text sent by Kevin in November of last year. That was a few months after he ostracized me from the family, and I've done my best since then to stay far, far away the way he wanted me to. I never opened that text, and I wonder if I should now. Is it really worth seeing what other despicable things he said and feel even guiltier about my screw-ups?

My heart pounds as I guide my finger over the message to open it. I read carefully.

Never thought I'd ever have to use the stuff u showed me when we were little, but I did, and it saved my life last night. Thanks.

I blink several times. I read it over and over again, trying to make sense of it. Was Kevin attacked? I chew on my knuckle. *Kevin's life was endangered. My God.* I think about our time as kids when I taught Kevin basic self-defense. He was a quick learner. I mentally curse myself for just seeing this message now. I wonder whether Kevin is still mad at me. *Am I still a disease?*

Before I can think about it any more, there's a knock at the door. I tuck the phone in my pocket and leave my room. I peer through the front door's peephole. Bonita is standing there, holding a bottle of whiskey and wearing a tight black dress that's looking to split at the seams from her well-endowed figure. Sighing, I open the door. "Hey."

She smiles crookedly and lets herself in. "Hey, yourself," she says in a seductive tone.

I wrinkle my nose. Her breath stinks of alcohol. I take the whiskey bottle from her as she saunters by, and I get a whiff of that cheap sandalwood perfume I always like. She's desperate, scared, and confused. She'll drink and fuck her way to oblivion in order to feel better unless I stop her. Maybe my resistance is why she's always drawn to me. But I can't be with a girl like her.

She makes her way to the couch and plops down. I set the whiskey on the kitchen counter, turn off the TV, and join her. Bonita is such a gorgeous girl.

She scoots closer to me and rests her head on my shoulder. I wrap my arm around her and hold her close, more out of pity than compassion. "How much bail money do you need for him now?"

She sighs. "I don't want to talk about that right now. Can't I just be here with you holding me?"

"But you said you needed to talk to me about your dad."

"I do, just . . . not now."

I drop my arm from around her. "All right, well . . . whenever you're ready to talk, let me know. I need to take a shower. Stay as long as you want." I wriggle her head from my shoulder and stand. She looks up at me and pokes out that juicy bottom lip of hers. I've kissed those lips before plenty of times. But I think about Lexi's lips and feeling that metal lip ring when I kissed her.

I leave Bonita on the couch while I head to the bathroom to shower. When I finish, I exit with a towel wrapped around my waist. Bonita is still on the couch. Her head tips back as she guzzles some whiskey straight from the bottle. Sighing, I approach her and swipe the bottle from her hands. Some drops of whiskey spill down her cleavage, but she seems too drunk to care. The lightness of the bottle indicates I'm too late to save her from herself.

"Damn it, couldn't you have just waited till I was done in the bathroom?" I say, exasperated.

She hugs my toweled waist and rests the side of her head on my groin. She's drunk off her ass, and I don't think she can hear me. I want to pry her off me, but damn, she feels good down there. "Hey, why don't you get some rest? It's late."

She moans and nestles her head against my dick, which stiffens under the towel against her cheek. It takes every ounce of willpower to finally pry her off. I bring her to her feet, steady her, and walk her to my bedroom. I clear my discarded clothes from my bed and lay her down. I pull on a pair of sweat pants, grab an extra pillow from the bed, and go to the living room. I fix up the couch, and as soon as my head hits the pillow, I fall asleep.

In the middle of the night, I'm awakened from a wonderful dream of Lexi by a familiar weight on top of me. Bonita's seductive growl rolls in my ear. Her alcohol-tasting lips touch mine. I feel the softness of her breasts against my bare chest. Her naked body presses against me, and I kiss her deeply, my hands caressing her back and exploring all the way down to her ass. My mind is jumbled from the dream, and I can only think of Lexi in this moment—the way she feels, the way she tastes.

Bonita moans against my lips as I squeeze her luscious ass.

"Fuck me right now, Knox," she whispers in my ear. "Please."

But at that moment, the bulge in my pants shrinks, and reality gets clearer in my mind. I push her off me and get up from the couch. I flip on the living-room light. Bonita sits up and puts her arm over her eyes.

She's completely naked on the couch with every bit of her wonderfully toned, curvy body in full view. I try not to look at her bedroom-messy hair or her perfectly defined thighs and calves. I imagine it's Lexi sitting there like that, and my stiffness returns. I tear my gaze away from Bonita and go to the bedroom to retrieve the comforter. I wrap it around her, until her goods are fully covered, then I sit back down next to her.

She sits there like a bundled Eskimo, staring blankly at the floor.

"You ready to talk now?" I ask, breaking the silence.

Her eyelids flutter, and she nods slowly. "He was just in the wrong place at the wrong time. His friends sold some stuff to undercover cops. Dad wasn't dealing, but they still charged him with possession . . . "

"How much?" I ask, not caring about the rest of her story.

"Ten grand." She looks at me hopefully.

I exhale. I've helped her with her dad's bail before, probably more than I should, but this is the highest he's had to post. And there's no fucking way I'll be able help her now without going completely broke myself. I shake my head. "I can't do it this time. Sorry."

Her eyes turn glassy. "Please, Knox. He's all I got. I just . . . I . . . "

I purse my lips. "Stop using that as an excuse. You had all this time to be with your dad before he got in trouble again. But you took advantage of it by playing around. I can't keep doing this. I've got a life, too."

Tears stream down her cheeks, and she holds herself tighter. "You don't care. No one fucking cares."

I swallow and wrap my arms around her and pull her close in an embrace. I hold her with a little more compassion this time. "I care, Bonita. I really do. But I can't afford to help your dad and expect to survive. I can chip in two or three hundred, but that's all I can do."

She shakes her head and pulls out of my embrace. "It's not enough. The premium's a thousand bucks. I'm going to lose my father. I'm going to lose everything. You don't know how much this fucking hurts."

The words sting, and I stare at her sadly. "I know exactly how much it hurts. But you're better than this, Bonita. You're a strong, beautiful woman. Stop relying on guys to support you all the time, and stand on your own. Maybe it'll inspire your father to get his head on straight."

She wipes away her tears and glares at me. "You think it's that easy? Huh? You think you know something, bastard? You don't know shit about me or my father, so shut the fuck up!" She stands and storms back to my room.

I bury my face in my hands and run my hands over my hair. I hear footsteps approaching, and Bonita returns, fully dressed, and heads for the front door.

I hop up from the couch and go to her. "Where are you going?"

"Home," she says, sharply. "This is bullshit. I thought you cared about me. I thought you were different. I can't believe I actually had feelings for you. You're just like everyone else—a sorry piece of shit."

I hold the door closed so she can't leave yet. "Listen. You and I would never work out. It just . . . wouldn't. There's too much baggage between us."

"Baggage? You?" She laughs. "Since when did you have any fucking baggage? All you do is fight. You don't care about me or my feelings. You never did."

As if she can drive that dagger any deeper. "You've known me a long time, Bonita, but you never wanted to really *know* me."

She narrows her eyes. "Fuck you, Knox."

I say nothing more and release the door. She leaves in a semi-drunken huff and heads for the stairs.

Chapter 7

I'M UP EARLY, GOING THROUGH MY TAE KWON DO FORMS IN the living room while the sounds of the city soothe me. Something's been on my mind, a weird gut feeling, and I still can't figure out what it is. Usually, working out and doing martial arts puts me at ease, but this time, it doesn't seem to do shit. After I finish my forms, I head to the kitchen and whip up some eggs and toast for breakfast. Dante texts me, saying he wants me to be at the gym by eleven thirty to do some mitt work and sparring. I text him back with the okay, though my mind is still not all there. I keep thinking about Bonita and the way she acted a couple of days ago. I didn't see her at the bar last night, and I even called her a few times, but she didn't pick up. Maybe she's avoiding me.

The more I think about her, the more I realize that she and I aren't that much different. We both have baggage, and I understand what she's going through. But somehow, I don't think she really understands my issues. Maybe she thinks she has it rougher than I do. Maybe she's right.

I don't know what I would do if I were in her shoes. No family, no life, no hope . . . she's a good girl underneath all that baggage, but she hides it from the world with her antics. It's her way of lashing out after all that's happened in her life. I understand. But at this point, I'm not sure if I can even help her anymore.

I dial her number, hoping she'll pick up, but it just goes straight to voicemail. Her mailbox is full, so I can't even leave a message, so I text her instead. *Maybe she blocked my number.* After all, it's not the first time I've been blocked out of someone's life.

I take the subway to the Upper West Side of Manhattan and jog the rest of the way to XL Westside Athletics Gym. The place is full of people training, sparring, and working out on the weight machines. Dante's off in a corner, punching and kicking a hanging bag, his hands and feet moving with lightning speed. One would never think in a million years he was forty-seven—he moves like a seventeen-year-old.

Carlos nods as I pass by. He's on the weight machine, working on his upper body. Weston is doing reps on the bench press while Reno spots. I meet up with Dante and set my backpack down. He takes a break, pats his face with a towel, and drapes it over one shoulder. "You ready, kid?"

"Yeah, sure," I say, not feeling all that excited.

He tilts his head to the side, his brow furrowing. "What's wrong?"

"Nothing man," I say, shaking my head. "Let's train." I fish through my backpack for my sixteen-ounce sparring gloves and put them on. Dante holds up the two target mitts, and I stand ready for the first drill. He raps out a series of combinations to do, and I execute them on the mitts with ease.

"I did a little digging," he says in a low voice once I'm working the pattern at a steady rhythm.

"Oh?" I say, not breaking my concentration. My jabs, crosses, and uppercuts hit each target with perfect accuracy.

"It's a hacker, all right, and whoever it is, he's good. Totally fucked with the data transfer when we were investigating that website."

Still not faltering, I think about Lexi. I wish I'd known about her sooner. It freaks me out that she has my information, but part of me trusts that she's not one of those malicious hackers—one of those people who would expose who I am and everything I've done just because she can. No, I don't think Lexi would do that. *Would she?*

She could've kept my mom's necklace—pawned it, even—but she didn't. She could've run off to the cops with all my information, but she didn't. There're so many things she can do to me right now that would ruin my life forever, but she hasn't yet. Call me a fool, but I think this girl can earn a little of my trust for that.

Dante stops the first drill and gives me another set of combinations to perform, this time incorporating my feet.

"Hey, man, don't worry about tracking down that hacker anymore," I say, once I get the pattern. I slam one of the pads with a roundhouse kick.

"What do you mean?"

"I mean, don't waste your time on it. It's not important. I don't want more cops involved. It'll just delay my next fight."

He lowers the mitts, and I pull back my cross punch, which would have hit him squarely in the chin.

"Don't tell me you *still* want to fight?" Dante says. "I thought we were done with that?"

I punch my fists together and bounce on my feet. "I never said shit. Now hold those damn things back up."

He just stands there, glaring.

I stop bouncing and let my hands dangle at my sides. "Jesus Christ, man. Why the hell am I even busting my ass training for a fight that's never gonna happen?"

"You tell me, Michael."

I clench my jaw.

"You think you only need to train when you have a fight? I want you to see that there's more to this than the cage." He gestures at the other people working out. "Look. They can be your future students. Some of these kids in here have had it rough. They need guidance. They need a young guy like you who knows the ropes."

I glance beyond my friends to some of the other athletes, who look no older than sixteen or seventeen. They're training hard with looks of determination and anger on their faces. They have baggage, too, I can tell.

"They won't wanna learn from me, Dante," I say flatly. "My foundation's Tae Kwon Do. People think it's all a joke."

"Then it's your job to show them it ain't."

"What do you think I've been doing for the past ten years?"

"Many things, but obviously not that."

I scowl. It's something Master Rho would've told me, too. What *have* I been doing with my life? I just want to fight and release the anger and bad shit from this fucking body. Maybe I *do* need a break from this.

I take off my gloves and shove them back in the backpack.

"We're not done here yet," Dante says.

"I am for now, man. You're right. I need to take a break. Can I do that?"

His look of disappointment lifts, and he nods. "You can. Come back a new man. I'll be here."

I grab my backpack and sling it over my shoulder. "Thanks."

"Just don't take *too* long of a break." He cracks a smile.

I smile back and wave him off. I walk past my friends, who are all sitting on a bench guzzling from their water bottles and talking.

Carlos shrugs at me. "Hey, leaving already?"

"Yeah, you know. I got some things to take care of," I say casually.

He nods and takes another sip of water, his eyes turning toward one of the TVs mounted on the wall by the treadmills. He suddenly drops his water bottle and pops up from the bench. "Holy—"

Weston and Reno stop talking and look his way curiously.

"What's up, man?" Reno asks.

When Carlos doesn't respond, he and Weston look toward the TV, too. Their faces go pale.

I furrow my brow at them. "What's up with you guys?" I follow their gazes toward the TV, where a newscast is being shown. A picture of Bonita is displayed on the screen with a headline underneath: "Woman's body found under Westchester Ave. Bridge last night."

Chapter 8

I can't breathe. I can't even feel the ground beneath my feet as I step off at the Bronx River Avenue bus stop. The concrete jungle is all a blur as I run the few blocks from the bus stop to an overgrown lot surrounded by an old, rusted chain-link fence with barbwire on the top. Part of the fence has been torn away, creating a space big enough for an adult to fit through. I wade through underbrush and garbage and emerge from a line of shade trees at the muddy bank of the steady-moving Bronx River. In the distance, under the bridge, yellow police tape swings in the breeze near four police officers. Keeping myself sheltered by the foliage, I draw closer, watching and listening. Bonita's body is gone, and one cop is on his radio while the other three are talking among themselves.

"Geez. Such a pretty girl. It's always the pretty ones," one of them says.

"I know, it's crazy, man," another says.

I swallow. "Found dead at the scene from what appears to have been an extreme overdose," the newscast had said. I wish I could see her again just one last time. But I have no idea where they've taken her body, and it's probably best I lay low and not get interrogated over this.

I should've known. I should've seen the signs. Why the fuck didn't I see the signs? *It's my fault!* It's as if all of today's news suddenly comes down on me at once. *She's dead and not coming back—because of me.*

I chew on my knuckle and shut my eyes. She loved me. Why the hell couldn't I have just given her what she wanted and made her happy? She had a rough life, and I should've taken better care of her. I should've helped her dad the way she wanted me to. Me being broke is nothing compared to her being dead. *Any*thing's better than this girl taking her life.

I recall the last thing she said to me. *Fuck you, Knox.* My eyes sting. It's the story of my life.

It should have been me instead. I ran from the people who needed me the most because I was a coward. I don't deserve a second chance at life. But Bonita . . . she had no family. *No one but me.* She trusted me. *Loved* me. And I pushed her away. I fucked up. *Again.*

I stare at the scene until my vision wavers and blurs. Then hot, stinging tears roll down my cheeks. *It should have been me.* I need to get out of here. I need to run far, far away.

Wiping away my tears, I quietly retrace my steps back up the bank and through the abandoned lot, squeezing back through the hole in the fence and jogging several blocks to the Elder Avenue station. I climb the stairs to the upper level and get lost in the sea of waiting people. It's not long before the train arrives, and I'm swept up by the flow of commuters. I find an empty seat and, once I'm sitting, run my hands over my hair, my body jostling as the train starts moving again.

I don't know where I'm going. I just want to go. Somewhere. *Anywhere.*

With no particular destination in mind, I ride the train for a while, get off, walk a little, ride another train, rinse and repeat. I don't pay attention to my surroundings because I don't care. It's four o'clock in the afternoon when I finally decide to stop for good. My feet are hurting, and I suddenly realize that I've been walking for two hours. I take a good look around and see that I'm standing in an unfamiliar place. The town I'm in looks pretty peaceful. I'm definitely not in the city. A small sign on the street corner catches my eye:

KEEP EASTCHESTER CLEAN! DON'T LITTER!

Eastchester? I pull up a map on my phone. *Holy fucking shit.* I'm over an hour north of the city.

My phone vibrates in my hands, and I flinch. A notification pops up with a hyperlink, followed by text.

Kevitron's show is tonight @ 11!!! ^_^

Just seeing Lexi's text makes me smile. Her remembering to send me the info must mean she's thinking of me.

cool, ill b sure to tune in.

Thoughts of Lexi pushes the bad shit out of my head, and I feel focused even if it's only for a moment. I can finally feel my breath and the concrete beneath my feet. The real world exists around me again. I set a reminder on my phone for Kevin's show.

I wait a few moments for her to text again, but she doesn't. I hope she hasn't cut off communication already, so I text:

how are u doing?

My heart beats with anticipation.

good. Packing for tomorrow's trip

My grin broadens.

My trainer let me take a break from fighting 4 a while. Im thinking about going 2 seattle

k.

I bite my bottom lip and hesitate before typing the next text:

Think i can come see u sometime while I'm there?

Maybe.

I exhale slowly. It wasn't a no, at least. She texts again:

gtg now.

No use in me replying with a goodbye; I'm sure she's already cut off the communication. And as soon as she's gone, the bad thoughts invade my mind again. But this time, instead of Bonita, I see myself lying in a mass of pills. I shiver.

It's not the first time I've had suicidal thoughts. The only thing that stops me is the reminder that my father did it. And I'm not going to become him, even if I am cursed with his name. Many times I considered legally changing my name, but it wouldn't erase the guilt or memories. My family would call me Michael, regardless.

I stop walking and look around. Autumn-colored trees are everywhere, a stark contrast to the concrete jungle I'm used to. I glimpse part of the Bronx River that runs beyond the trees. Surprisingly, there are no people around this tiny section of town. The few abandoned buildings that dot the area and a massive covered chain-link fence that runs for half a block are the only indications of civilization. How long and far have I walked? I have no idea where I am. I should probably catch a bus or something and get the hell out of here.

Through one of the green slats of the fence I see a massive parking lot next to what looks like an industrial park so overgrown that it's probably been abandoned for years. Yet several cars are parked near one of the old, large, nondescript buildings.

Police sirens echo down the street, and my heart drops to my gut. I don't want to see another cop right now. The sirens get closer, and I hustle in the opposite direction. The fence's gate is partially open, so I slip inside and wait while the police car drives by, its sirens screeching. Deciding to lie low for a while, I shove my hands in my pockets and observe the building. The sound of a car behind me catches my unawares, and I turn. The flashing orange-and-yellow lights on the vehicle's roof indicate that it's a security guard. *Damn.*

The window rolls down, and a bearded man looks me up and down. "Hey, you all right?"

I swallow a lump in my throat. "Um . . . yeah, uh . . . "

"This ain't the place to be taking a break, y'know. Your teammates are running around over there." He points toward the other side of the parking lot.

Teammates? "Right. S-Sorry." I start heading deeper into the parking light in a brisk jog. *Holy shit, that was close.* Who did he think I was? And where the hell am I?

Some of the parked cars look expensive. Like, over six-figures' worth. The windows are tinted so dark I can't see inside. I keep walking, trying not to stare too much at the shiny rims or amazing paint jobs on some of those vehicles.

I better leave before—

I stop in my tracks as I notice the front doors to the building open. I hear several voices inside. A man in a suit and tie walks out. I duck behind a tricked-out SUV and watch the man get into an expensive car with an emblem on the hood and drive off.

I wait a few moments before emerging from my hiding place and continuing my jog.

"Hey, what're you doing, man? Coach said to do five laps."

I nearly jump out of my skin at the winded male voice behind me. I turn and look up at two guys dressed in basketball shorts and T-shirts. They easily dwarf me by almost a foot, and they are built like machines. This is all kinds of awkward.

I try to swallow away the dryness in my throat before attempting to speak. "Uh, um . . . " My voice cracks. If only I could run away right now, but my feet feel like lead.

One of the guys, who wears a blue, sweaty T-shirt, studies me a moment then wrinkles his brow. "Oh, sorry, man, I thought you were someone else."

I tip my head, trying to be as nonchalant as possible. "S'all right."

"You must be the guy on the scrimmage team we've been waiting on," says the other guy, who is wearing an orange T-shirt.

I look him over as I wrestle with my thoughts. "Uh, yeah. That's right. Sorry I'm late."

Orange Shirt smirks and elbows his friend. The two of them exchange glances. "Well, what are you waiting for? Go see the coach." He thumbs over his shoulder toward the building's front door.

The two guys leave and begin jogging together around the parking lot. I face the entrance and swallow again. *They, too, have me confused with someone else.* I spot the security guard's car creeping around the parking lot and realize I'm trapped. I probably won't be so lucky next time if I confront him. Sighing, I drag my heavy feet toward the doors and, with a shaky hand, open them.

The inside of this place is nothing like I expected. It's clean—immaculate. Posh. That smell of new leather and rubber welcomes me as I enter what looks like a grand lobby. The marble-tiled floor is polished, and there's not a speck of dirt to be seen. Glass cases along the walls display basketball and hockey championship trophies and plaques. An elevator sits between two trophy cases, and a posted sign indicates that the players' lounge, video-editing room, and classroom are located upstairs. Plush blue carpet runs beyond the lobby and splits off down three grand hallways. At the head of each carpet are the logos representing New York's professional hockey and men's and women's basketball teams. Voices drift out from down the basketball hallway. *This can't be what I think it is . . . is it?*

A couple of sweaty guys walk my way, talking to each other and laughing. I turn back to the entrance and am reaching for the double doors when they suddenly fling open and Orange Shirt and Blue Shirt nearly trample me.

The guys in the hallway stop and look at me.

"Sorry, man, didn't see you," Blue Shirt says.

With nowhere to run, I take a deep breath. "No prob. I was, uh . . . just looking for the coach."

They give me odd looks, then Blue Shirt slowly raises his finger toward the basketball hallway. I nod in thanks and brush past the two other guys, who watch me.

The hallway seems to go on forever, with framed jerseys and photos of past all-stars and legendary basketball players lining the walls. My feet sink into the carpet, which also smells new. I notice the echoing sounds of feet scuffling on wood floor. Signs are posted, pointing to the gym. I walk past doorways, glimpsing inside the open ones. One room that makes me slow my walk is the weight room. The place is huge—almost as big as XL Westside. And it's full of every type of exercise equipment imaginable. Some guys are on the machines, and they all look like beasts. I've been working out pretty hard every day, but if exercise can make a guy look like that, then damn, I'm not doing nearly enough.

The door to the women's bathroom farther down the hall opens, and a heavyset woman wearing jeans and a blue shirt exits. She looks my way, squints, then smiles politely and continues walking in the direction of the gym. Her phone suddenly chirps, and she fishes through her trendy-looking woven purse. She slows her walk as she checks her phone then gasps. Her thumbs move like crazy as she starts texting.

I follow her, keeping a short distance away. The woman is gorgeous, with flowing, curly hair and chocolate-toned skin. I wonder what she's doing here among all these guys?

I walk beside her and look at her face. She's got a beautiful smile, her dark brown eyes so full of life. She stops texting and looks over at me, her smile broadening.

I can't help but smile back. "Hey there."

"Hi!" she says cheerily. Her smile falters a little, and her brow furrows slightly. "Do I know you?"

I quickly look away. "Uh . . . no, I don't think so."

Voices filter out from the weight room, and a group of sweaty guys with towels draped over their shoulders emerge and walk in my direction. The girl beside me smiles at one of the guys and goes to him for a kiss. The rest of them whistle and make teasing noises while they continue on toward the gym. I want to follow those other guys, but I'm frozen in place because the guy in front of me is the last person I wanted or had hoped to see. He looks even bigger than when I saw him on TV the other night. He's decked out in his practice uniform with the number four printed on the front of his shirt. That's his favorite number. It's weird that I can remember something like that from so long ago.

"Oh my God, Kevin! I have to tell you something!" the girl says when they break from the kiss.

I start walking past the couple, keeping my head lowered. Kevin doesn't seem to notice me, or perhaps he doesn't realize who I am. He hasn't seen me in over ten years, after all. I need to go. Now. *Come on, feet. Move faster!*

"Is it an emergency?" Kevin asks, hooking his arm around her waist.

"Well . . . no, but—"

"Kevin! Where are you?" a man's voice booms from the direction of the gym.

Kevin looks at the woman apologetically.

"Tell me later, babe, else Coach is gonna have my ass for being late for the scrimmage."

She pouts. "Oh, all right."

He gives her another kiss. "I'll make it up to you. Tonight. Promise."

She smirks wickedly at that.

I'm a few feet ahead of the couple when I notice in my peripheral vision that Kevin is starting to walk in my direction. I quicken my steps and head to the gym.

A group of guys dressed in shorts and practice jerseys are on the floor, dribbling, shooting, and working on other basketball drills. I'm dressed pretty much like them, so it's no wonder I was mistaken for one of them. But I suck at basketball, and there's no fucking way I'll be able to keep up this charade for too much longer. As I'm searching for an exit, a whistle blows, and I jump. A balding man wearing black windbreaker pants and a white T-shirt brushes past me. He stops, looks over his shoulder, and narrows his eyes. "Who the hell are you?"

I swallow and look around frantically for the exit. "Uh . . ." My searching stops for a moment when I spot Kevin's girlfriend making her way to an empty chair on the sideline, where other spectators are sitting.

"He's on the scrimmage team, Coach," Blue Shirt says from behind me, and my attention immediately returns to the situation at hand. "Isn't he the guy you said was gonna be running late?"

"Yeah. Nathan made it in twenty minutes ago." The coach thumbs over his shoulder at a pale-skinned, lanky guy stretching on the sideline.

"Oh, damn. Then who's this guy?" Blue Shirt asks, his gaze bouncing from the coach to me.

"That's what *I'd* like to know." The coach's expression hardens.

"Sorry, I, uh . . . I guess I made a wrong turn somewhere," I stammer. "I'll get out of here."

"Damn right you will," the coach snaps. "Come around here again, and I'll call the cops on you for trespassing."

"Yes, sir, I understand. It won't happen again."

Kevin comes up from behind me and stands beside the coach. Kevin easily dwarfs the older man. "Everything all right, Coach?" Kevin asks.

"Everything's fine, Kevin," the man replies, not taking his eyes off me. "Just some fan sneaking his way in here." He points to the nearest exit at the other end of the gym. "Get the hell out. *Now*."

I cast a quick glance at Kevin, who glares back at me, furrows his brow, and then does a double take. But before I can wonder whether or not he's recognized me, I lower my head and rush past him to the exit's double doors. I don't look back.

Chapter 9

It's after eight at night when I finally return to my apartment, still shaken from the day's events. From Bonita's suicide to seeing Kevin, today has left me emotionally exhausted. Fuck, I need to leave New York even if it's just for a little while. Dante wanted me to take a break, and now's as good a time as any.

I move around in the kitchen, cutting veggies, sautéing steak slices, and steaming rice for dinner. I don't consider myself a great cook like Mama or even Dominick. I'm just someone who can make a meal when he has to. And right now, I need to keep my hands moving because they'll only start shaking again if I remain idle. While the food's cooking, I call up Dante.

"What's up, kid?" he answers.

"Hey, man. Just letting you know I'm going to Seattle for a couple weeks. I'm packing tonight."

"Gonna see your mom again?"

I clench my jaw. "Yeah, I guess."

"You need this, Knox. Trust me—it'll do you a bit of good to get outta here. Clear your head."

"Yeah . . ."

"Hey, by the way, I wanted to let you know that I got some more leads on the website probing. My friend Kurt traced the source of the hacker to a spot just outside Inglewood, California."

I blink. *Lexi.*

"Some of Kurt's guys snooped around once they got that tip. Didn't find anything though. Kurt said the trail went cold." He pauses a moment. "I suggest we quit while we're ahead, kid. I'll train you for pro, if that's what you really want. It'll be honest work, at least."

I've always wanted to fight pro, but I'm too flustered to make a big decision like that right now. "I don't know, man."

"Your choice. But you going pro means you—*we*—won't have to keep hiding like this. This underground network's nationwide. It won't be much longer before they're snuffed out by the Feds. And I don't know about you, but I'm not ready to rot in prison. You need to think seriously about this, kid. I love you like a son, but I can't do this anymore. I'm gonna find a place and start up that gym with or without you."

My throat tightens when he says that. He knows I can't do this without him, because he's in with certain people who'll make sure I don't get arrested for illegal fighting. I guess that's a perk for being an ex-cop. "Fine. Whatever, man. Do what you gotta do."

I hear him sigh. "Stay in touch, Knox."

"Will do. Later, man."

I end the call and toss the phone on the couch.

After dinner, a long shower, and a much-needed shave, I spend the rest of the evening packing and surfing my laptop for cheap plane tickets. A couple minutes before eleven o'clock, my phone alarm buzzes, reminding me that Kevin's show is coming on soon. I type the link into the browser, and a snazzy-looking website pulls up with a banner at the top saying "Kevitron's House." Photos of Kevin wearing sunglasses, headphones, and baseball caps fill the page as if he's a celebrity. I do a double take when I see how many people are currently tuning in—almost three thousand. *Wow, talk about a following.*

The speakers blare with house music, followed by Kevin's voice. "What's up, guys? Welcome to the party. This is DJ Kevitron comin' at you live from the NYC. Got any requests? You know the deal . . . "

His smooth introduction makes me crack a smile. *Damn, he sounds good.* More and more listeners tune in. I wonder if he'll break five thousand.

"Now, I'm gonna start things off a little differently to-night. My beautiful partner in crime told me something awesome today, and I'm gonna announce it to all of my fans out there. My baby brother, Dominick, just got engaged to his college sweetheart, Denise. So, all you Seattleites who know Dom, congratulate him, and maybe embarrass him a little for me, too." Kevin chuckles.

My jaw drops. *Dominick's getting married?* This is unreal.

"I'm gonna do a little something special for him," Kevin continues. "I know you're listening, bro, so this one goes out to you. Congratulations, man."

A familiar song I haven't heard in years starts playing—"Keep Their Heads Ringin'." It was Dominick's favorite song when we were growing up. But Kevin adds his own personal mix to the song, making it more upbeat and catchy enough that it has me bobbing my head. Wow, Kevin is a master at this.

But the more I listen, the guiltier I feel for being such a coward all these years. The more I listen, the more I realize how much I miss my brothers. I lie in bed and stare at the ceiling as the music consumes my mind, taking me back fourteen years—back to memories I wish I could forget.

Kevin, Dominick, and I were in the backyard playing football, because none of Dominick's friends could come out and play with him that day. Dominick was only eight and still a bit scrawny but was starting to bulk up a little from playing on the junior football team in elementary school.

Not realizing my own strength, I accidentally tackled Dominick a little too hard. He cut his knee on the sharp edge of a twig in the grass and cried like I don't know what. Kevin and I rushed him into the house so Mama could look at his bleeding wound, but she'd gone out to the post office. Pops was there, though, watching a football game on TV, a beer in his hand. At the sound of Dominick's wailing, Pops slammed his beer on the coffee table, rose from the couch, and glared at the three of us. "What the hell's all that noise?" he growled.

I spoke up for my brothers. "H-He's bleeding."

Pops seethed, yanked Dominick from our grasp, and held the poor boy up by the arm. Dominick didn't stop crying. I took a step forward, thinking I could save my brother, but one menacing look from Pops, and I froze on the spot.

"You gonna raise up to me, boy?" Pops barked, lifting his eyebrows at my near defiance.

I shook my head quickly, too scared to speak. I retracted my foot. Kevin kept his head lowered, his body visibly trembling.

Pops returned his attention to Dominick. "What did I tell you about all that damn crying! Crying's for pansies. Be a fucking man, and clean that shit up your damn self!" He released Dominick, and the little boy crumpled to the floor. He sniffled and whimpered. Pops pointed down the hall. "Now you three go to your rooms and stay there. Don't you fucking bother me again while I'm watching the damn game, you little punks, understand?"

Kevin left without another word. He disappeared into the bathroom a moment then came out and dropped off some items in Dominick's room before going to his own. I walked a little slowly, waiting for Dominick, who struggled back to his feet. There was a small spot of blood on the floor. I hoped Pops hadn't seen it, but when he raised his hand to Dominick, I knew he had.

"You got blood all over this fucking carpet!" Pops shout-ed and smacked him hard on the ass.

The crying started all over again. I came between the two of them and shut my eyes, anticipating getting smacked by my father. "I'll clean it up! I'll clean it up!" I blurted as I pushed Dominick behind me and hoped he'd get up and go to his room. To my relief, Dominick's crying grew fainter, and I heard his bedroom door close.

Pops gritted his teeth at me and pulled off his belt. "If I see one fucking speck on that carpet, I'm gonna whip your ass." He pointed the folded belt at me warningly. "And you better be done before your mother gets home, or I'll whip your ass for that, too!"

I nodded quickly and rushed to the kitchen for the soap, a bottle of hydrogen peroxide, and a dishcloth.

I blink back to the present. So much time has passed since then. How much can I really salvage if I see my brothers again?

My phone chirps with a text, and I reach over to check the lit-up screen. Lexi's text stares back at me, and I smile, the bad thoughts momentarily erased from my mind.

R u listening? :D

yep. Kevin's amazing.

Yeah, since he's been doing the internet shows, the seattle clubs haven't been the same without him.

I imagine my home city and wonder when Lexi will be there.

r u in Seattle yet?

Nope. Tomorrow.

im heading that way tomorrow, too… i hope i can see u.

Typing those words makes me hope even harder.

yeah, that would b cool.

how can I contact you?

Don't worry. i'll find u ;)

A bitter taste forms in my mouth.

no, don't do that, plz. i need some privacy.

K. Let's meet somewhere then.

She sends me an address. I type it in a new browser window on my computer, and it pulls up a bar. I text her back:

Chauncey's?

Yep. Best hangout spot in town. u game?

yeah, sure. How bout 9pm tomorrow?

Perfect. Gtg now. Enjoy the show!

u too.

"Bye, Lexi," I whisper, staring at the phone screen until it dims.

A new song is playing now, one I've never heard of that has another catchy beat. The site has surpassed four thousand listeners, and the number continues to rise. It's cool to

see Kevin living his dream and so many people supporting
him.

I search my phone for an old text Kevin sent me last year
with Mama's home address. Tomorrow, I'm going back, but
I doubt I'll be welcomed with open arms.

I take an early flight the next day and close my eyes as soon
as I'm in my seat. By the time I open them again, it's eleven
o'clock in the morning. I step off the jet bridge and into the
busy Seattle-Tacoma airport. Toting my large duffel bag over
my shoulder, I make my way toward Ground Transportation, where a sea of yellow and bright-green taxicabs is waiting. I make a beeline for one and hop in the backseat. A
curly-haired woman wearing a backwards baseball cap read-
ies the meter on the dashboard.

I read her Mama's address from my phone, and the driver
types it in on her GPS. The ride is silent, much to my relief.
I'm not really in a socializing mood right now. I stare out the
window at the passing trees, which display the colorful or-
anges, reds, and browns of autumn. But my mind is filled
with gloomy greys and blacks. My stomach clenches as I
think about what I'm going to say or do when I see Mama.
She'll probably cry, and that's the last thing I want.

My ears pop as we drive down a hill. I wince. My ears haven't stopped popping since I arrived. It's been a little over
ten years since I've been here, and everything about Washington seems foreign. We go up another hill, and I glimpse a

line of hazy bluish-purple mountains in the distance—not exactly something you see every day in New York City. Why does a beautiful place like this have to hold such ugly memories?

We pull up to a little blue house. I pay the driver, grab my bag, and slowly get out. The sky is overcast, and the air is cool and crisp, fresher than the grit I'm used to back home. No cars are parked in the driveway, and the garage door is shut, so I have no idea if anyone's home. But I'm taking a chance in hopes of facing my fears and finding some sort of resolution to this nagging emotional pain.

I drag my heavy feet up the pebbled walkway, taking in the scents of fall flowers and glimpsing the sparse yellowed leaves of the azalea bushes that line the path. I remember helping Mama plant these bushes when I was little. They were so small then, but Mama loved her azaleas. They looked beautiful when they bloomed in the spring. I climb the stairs of the stoop, the second step creaking under my weight just as I remember. I'd always heard the sound from the living room, letting me know we had a visitor.

Orange and yellow leaves litter the floor and the white railing of the front porch, some crunching under my foot as I step onto the weathered brown welcome mat with pictures of flowers on it. I run my hand along the blue doorframe, which looks as if it's been recently painted with a fresh coat, and I finally build up enough courage to ring the doorbell.

But no one answers. I wait a few moments and ring it again, then knock, but all is quiet. *Maybe no one's home.* It's my fault for not calling beforehand to make sure someone would be home. I don't know what I was thinking, being such a chickenshit.

Or maybe Mama is *home, but she's too upset to open the door. Upset at me for abandoning her.* Despite what Uncle Adam said, I know Mama. She's very emotional. I blame my father for that.

I check my phone, wishing I had Lexi's number. But she's still in ninja mode, and I'll have to wait till tonight to see her. I locate Uncle Adam's number and stare at it. Leaning against the porch railing, I hit the Dial button.

"How're you doing, son?" Uncle Adam greets.

"Good, man." I swallow a lump in my throat. "I'm . . . I'm in Renton now."

There's brief silence. "Are you at your mother's?"

"Yeah."

"That's great, son. How's she doing?"

"I dunno, she's not home."

"Ah . . . she must still be at the farmers' market. She usually goes there every Friday."

"Know when she'll be back?" I ask.

"Not sure. Hey, how long are you going to be in Renton?"

"Just a couple weeks or so." I run my finger along the wrought iron banister.

"Okay, I'll try and get up that way maybe sometime next week or on the weekend."

"All right."

"I meant to call you last night to tell you the good news," Uncle Adam says.

"About Dominick getting married? Yeah, I know."

"Oh, good. Sorry, it was late here when I found out, and I figured it was really late in New York to be calling you."

"Yeah I'm happy for him." I rest my elbows on the railing.

"I need to go now, but I'll be sure to make it over there before you leave. I love you, son."

I swallow again, his words making the back of my throat clench. "Love you, too."

I end the call and slump down on the porch steps, setting my duffel bag beside me. Guess I'll have to sit here and wait for Mama to come back. I don't know why I'm doing this. My body's so tense. Everything about this place reminds me of why I ran away in the first place.

CHAPTER 10

I DON'T KNOW HOW LONG I'VE BEEN SITTING ON THE STEPS before I finally pick up my duffel bag and leave. I consider calling a taxi again but decide to walk around the neighborhood instead. I'm halfway down the walkway when I spot a grey sedan pulling into the driveway. I glimpse the driver—a woman—and as the car pulls up to the garage, our eyes lock for a moment. I swallow a lump in my throat and will my feet to leave—fast.

Maybe she didn't recognize me. I have to get out of here.

I manage to make it to the end of the driveway when I hear her voice behind me. "Hello? Can I help you, sir?"

I cringe and don't turn around. She still sounds the same only with a hint of wariness in her voice. "No, I was . . . I was just leaving," I say, my voice cracking. I lower my head and break into a jog—run. But my vision is blurry from my stinging eyes. There's a metallic bang, and a sharp pain shoots through my forearm. I stagger backward, the world blacking in and out. I collapse on the asphalt, my body numb with pain.

I hear hurrying footsteps, and I'm suddenly being pulled up into a sitting position.

"Oh my goodness!" the woman exclaims. "Are you all—" She breaks off and gasps.

I open my eyes and blink away the tears of shame and pain. The red flag from the light-blue mailbox at the end of the driveway now lies broken on the ground next to me and my duffel bag. There's a small but noticeable dent on the side of the mailbox, and the little pink painted-on azaleas are now crumpled inward.

I turn to look at the woman, who is kneeling beside me. Dressed in jeans, sneakers, and a brown sweater, she looks every bit the same as I remember. Her dark brown eyes are wide.

"M . . . Michael?"

I cringe, more from the pain than anything. But Mama's voice is so close. I place my hand over my left forearm and feel something warm and sticky. *Shit.*

I look up at her, hoping she hasn't noticed my gash. "Hi, Mama," I whisper.

"Oh, Jesus . . . *oh, Jesus!* Michael! You're home!" She leans in like she wants to hug me, but then she looks at my hand covering my arm. "Baby, are you okay? Let me see that." She puts her hands over mine and gently pries away my fingers.

I protest at first, but her grip is insistent. It's the same way she used to handle me when I'd skin my knee or get bruises from sparring. Once the rest of my hand is pried away, blood oozes from the slice in my arm. Who would've thought a fucking mailbox flag could be so sharp?

Mama helps me to my feet. "Come inside, baby. I'll fix that."

My throat tightens more. I can barely breathe. "N-No, that's okay. I'll be fine."

"Michael, you're bleeding. Don't be ridiculous. Now come inside." Mama hefts up my duffel bag, slinging the strap across her shoulder. She hooks her other arm around my waist to support me, and we start shuffling toward the house.

Geez, it's just a little scratch—not as if I'm an invalid or something. I want to run away, run until I bleed to death. My instincts scream that I should get the hell out of here and go somewhere else—*any*where else. Anywhere but here. The blood and Mama's horror-stricken expression take me back in time. I remember Kevin lying in a pool of blood and Mama standing there with that same look on her face.

But Mama's azalea scent hits me hard, and memories of home—the good memories of Mama reading me bedtime stories and cooking me chicken soup when I was sick—flood my mind. She walks me through the side door of the house. She moves pretty quickly for a woman of fifty-one. It's good to see that Pops didn't suck all the life out of her. As I walk through the side door and into the house, Mama starts talking to me, but her voice is a dull buzz, and I can't understand what she's saying. Azalea-scented laundry detergent and the aroma of old cedarwood—the smells of home—sock my senses as I enter the hallway leading to the three smaller bedrooms. My room looks more cramped than it used to. It's empty except for a bed and night table, from what I can see. Kevin's is across the hall and empty, too, his walls devoid of shelved vinyl records and posters of his favorite basketball stars. All that's left in Dominick's room, other than the basic furniture, is a stack of magazines sitting on his desk.

Mama leads me into the bathroom, slips off my duffel bag, and runs the cold water from the sink over my arm. She cleans around the wound with soap then dabs it dry with a washcloth. She puts the washcloth in my free hand and guides my hand to the open wound. "Hold that there," she instructs.

I do as she says while she fishes through the cabinet for a bandage. I remove the washcloth, and she tends to my arm, carefully swiping and dabbing the gash with an ointment-soaked cotton ball. Finally, she places the bandage over it and gives it a little pat.

"Thanks," I mumble, lifting my head slightly to her.

She smiles up at me, her eyes glassy. She still has beautiful brown eyes, but they have faint wrinkles in the corners. Her cheekbones are high and defined like a model's. But a solitary tear slides down one cheek, tarnishing that beauty.

"Oh, Michael, baby," Mama whispers, more tears welling up in her eyes. She pulls me into a tight embrace. With nowhere to run, I reluctantly succumb to the feel of her fast-beating heart and her inviting warmth, and I inhale her azalea smell. She pulls back and kisses my cheek gently. She places her hands on both of my cheeks and looks at me deeply, as if she's looking into my soul, searching for the little boy she lost. But that boy is gone—long gone.

"Oh, thank the Lord you've come back. I've prayed and prayed that one day I'd see you again."

I sigh. After that shit with Pops happened, Mama went and got saved and did all that other religious stuff. I was glad that she found a way to cope with the problem of our broken family.

She looks me over again and smiles admiringly, even though I still haven't said anything. "What a handsome man you've become."

"Thanks," I force out.

She takes my hands and rubs them gently. Her hands feel rough, calloused. They're small and thin compared to mine.

"I . . . I'm sorry I came unannounced, Mama . . . "

She shakes her head, takes my hand, and leads me out of the bathroom. "Baby boy, you're the most important thing to me right now. You are always welcome here."

We enter the living room area, and I halt. There's a new couch and TV as well as a new dinette set in the adjoining breakfast nook, and other odds and ends have been added too, most likely to cover up the past. But I can still see the ugliness through it all. As my gaze travels toward the kitchen, my heart pounds. I slide my hand from her grasp, and my body feels heavy. I stare at the spot between the kitchen and breakfast nook.

The same spot where I saw Kevin lying unconscious and bleeding on the floor from a neck wound. The same spot where I saw Dominick curled on the floor in a fetal position with his pants pulled down around his ankles.

My knees buckle. My lungs constrict like I'm being held underwater for far too long. I take a few steps back and bump into the edge of the couch.

Mama takes my hand again and pulls me toward a seat at the breakfast nook. "Sit down, baby."

I look at the chair with worry and try to protest, but no sound comes out. I will myself with all my strength to pull away from her. I can't let myself be dragged to *that area* of the house. "I . . . I can't," I manage to say in a shaky voice.

She looks at me, her eyes darkened with sadness and worry, and then she nods in understanding. She guides me to the couch. I sit down slowly, the unfamiliar softness of the furniture keeping me on edge.

"I just want to talk to you," she says. "Tell me what you've been doing with yourself."

Mama and I end up talking for a couple of hours about the family and about my life in New York. I mention my "job" as a fitness trainer and leave out the underground fighting, even though I have a few old scars and bruises that she questions me about.

"It's part of being a trainer. Sometimes there are a little bumps and bruises along the way."

"Adam *had* said you were traveling a lot," Mama says. "It makes sense now, being a trainer and all."

"Yeah," I say in a choked-up voice.

She claps her hands together and grins. "Oh, this is wonderful. I need to call Dominick and Kevin and tell them you're finally back!" She grabs her cell phone from the coffee table.

I widen my eyes and swipe the phone from her. "Mama, no. *No!* Please don't. I beg you, Mama, please don't call them."

Her brow furrows. "But, baby . . . "

I shake my head firmly. "Please, Mama. I don't want them to know I'm here. Please don't tell them right now. It's been a long time, and I just want to take things slow."

She purses her lips and then nods. "Okay." She gets up from the couch and goes to the kitchen. "But at least you're going to stay here, right? I'm going to make your favorite dinner tonight," she says, opening the fridge.

I get up as well and follow her, inching toward the breakfast nook. I suddenly see Dominick lying there at my feet—I'm about to step on him. I pull back my foot and take a step backward. The image of Dominick disappears. "I, um, can't stay long, but . . . wait, you remember what I like?"

"Baked chicken, collard greens, and sweet potato fries, right?" She closes the refrigerator door and grins, carrying vegetables and other cooking ingredients. "A mother never forgets."

I can't help but smile. *She remembers, all right.* Man, I especially love the way she always seasons those collard greens with bits of ham in it. "All right. Well, let's not eat too late. I'm supposed to be meeting someone tonight."

Her smile widens. "A date?"

"Uh . . ."

"Oh, baby, that's wonderful. When will I be able to meet her?"

"She's not a girlfriend or anything. Just . . . a friend." My mouth goes dry as I say this. I'm honestly not sure what Lexi and I are right now.

Mama doesn't stop smiling. "Okay." She opens the pantry door. "Do you have any transportation? Or is she picking you up?"

"I'm meeting her downtown. I'm just gonna call a taxi."

"Don't waste money on a taxi. Use my car."

I blink. "Uh, no, that's okay."

"Don't worry about it, baby. I'm planning on staying home all weekend to do some yard work. I won't need my car."

The idea of driving my mother's car to see a girl I like is all kinds of weird, not to mention embarrassing. "Mama, it's all right. Really. Besides, I don't have a license. Nobody drives in New York City."

"Oh, fine. Then at least let me pay for the taxi, so you'll have money to spend on your girlfriend." She takes out a couple of pots and pans from one of the lower cabinets.

"But she's not my—" The sudden clanking as she searches for the cooking utensils she needs makes me lose my train of thought.

"Go on and unpack and relax. You can settle into your old room."

I sigh and grab my duffel bag. "I still can't believe you haven't converted it to a storage room or office or something else by now, Mama."

"No, baby. I've been waiting for this day to come when the Lord would finally bring you back home." She pulls out a pack of chicken breasts from the freezer and turns to me, beaming. "If you need anything, let me know."

I go back down the hall to my room and drop my bag. The white walls are bare except for the Basic Striking Points poster hanging by thumbtacks next to my closet and a shelf with trophies I won at martial-arts tournaments when I was little. There's no dust on the trophies; Mama must've been in here keeping things clean and neat. My dumbbells and bench press bar are still under the bed. Smiling, I pull the dumbbells out. They were my very first weights, a gift from Uncle Adam when I was seven. They look so much smaller than I remember. I heft them and almost laugh at how light they feel—lighter than paper.

I sit on the edge of my bed, making the mattress creak and bounce under my weight. I do a few effortless curls with one of the twenty-pound dumbbells. My phone suddenly chirps. I set the dumbbell aside and pull the phone out my pocket.

hey, hope u had a safe trip :)

I smile at the text, assuming it's Lexi since it's from an unknown number, and she's the only one I know who puts emoticons in her messages.

I did. Thanks. how bout u?

It was good.

I lie back in bed and stare at the screen, envisioning Lexi lying on top of me while we talk.

Still on for 2nite?

Definitely! i invited Denise and Dom, too. Figured we can do a little celebration for their engagement

I jerk upright. My chest feels weighted as if the whole ceiling came crashing down on me. *She did what?* I can't let Dominick see me. He's got so many great things going for him. I'll just be a distraction. Like Kevin, he'll never forgive me. I don't want Lexi caught up in my drama. No, this is a very bad idea. But how the hell do I tell Lexi this?

I fumble with the phone, my hands sweaty as I attempt to type in the first excuse that comes to mind—that I think I have a stomach bug.

My fingers aren't fast enough.

k. meet you outside Chauncey's @ 9. Laterz

I hit Send and suddenly realize my text reads "tink hve a stoah bug."

lol what?

My heart thumps. It's already done. There's no turning back now. Sighing, I concede and type:

nm, cya at 9

K. <3

My mouth's gone dry, my lips chapped. *I can't do this. But I want to see her.* I stare at her last text and notice something different about it: the heart emoticon at the end of her message. She never sent me a heart before. Is she trying to say something? Or is this just her way of being cute? I wish I knew what was going through her head.

My thoughts return to Dominick. I'm going to totally ruin the moment for the two of them if he sees me. Lexi will get pissed at me for upsetting her best friend. But if I don't go, Lexi will get pissed at me for standing her up. Either way, I'm screwed.

Maybe coming home was a bad idea after all.

CHAPTER 11

I LEAN MY HEAD AGAINST THE CAB WINDOW, WATCHING cars and streetlights pass by in a constant rhythm of flashes. The faint, staticky noise of the cab driver's radio is the only thing that keeps the interior from being completely silent. But it's quiet enough that I can think about the chaos that happened earlier. It was hell just to get out that house without Mama making a scene. She kept insisting on paying for the damn cab—to there and back. Then she insisted on giving me emergency money. The smothering is getting ridiculous. I swear, after tonight, I'm getting a motel room.

But damn it, can I really blame her? I just suddenly popped back into her life. What kind of fucked-up shit is that? And now I'm in this cab, about to see a girl I like and possibly see my brother who hates me. How did I get into this mess?

The cab stops, cutting off my confused thoughts. We're parked along the curb in front of a building with a neon sign shaped like a martini glass. I'm five minutes early, but I already spot Lexi leaned up against the wall outside the bar, talking on the phone. I pay the driver and get out. Lexi looks up and waves, smiling through glossy lips. I force a smile and wave back. I'm scanning the area for Dominick. Maybe he won't recognize me.

Lexi slips the phone into the pocket of her hip-hugger pants, from which a silver chain is attached to a belt loop and drapes along the pocket. Light winks off the silver studs of her belt. She rolls up the sleeves of her black-and-white button-down shirt, which she wears under a short leather jacket.

"Hey," she says, approaching me, her feet covered in black, calf-length boots.

"Hey," I say, giving her another once-over.

"Denise and Dominick are on their way."

I tense at the mention of Dominick.

"Let's grab a table inside," she says.

I mutter, "I . . . I don't know if this is a good idea . . . "

She wrinkles her brow. "What? Having drinks?"

"No . . . " I adjust my glasses nervously. "I mean . . . "

She raises her eyebrows, looking at me expectantly.

"Never mind. Maybe I just really need a drink."

Her face softens, and she grabs my hand, leading me inside. "C'mon."

I look at our clasped hands, and my heart stutters. Suddenly, all the worry and fears are gone from my mind. I've missed her touch.

We enter the bar full of college students and some older patrons. The TVs are on, tuned to a college basketball game, but most of the activity is happening around the pool and foosball tables. We stop at the counter, where a shapely female bartender is actively tending to other patrons.

Lexi lets go of my hand, and my attention is back on her. "What do you drink?" she asks me. I open my mouth, and she continues. "Wait, don't tell me. You look like a bourbon guy."

I smile and shake my head then reach in my pocket for my wallet. "Whiskey sour," I tell the bartender, slapping down the money on the bar before Lexi can protest. I ask Lexi, "How about you?"

She puffs her cheeks in a deliberate—but cute—way, making a playful face at me. She exhales and says to the bartender, "Malibu."

As we wait for our drinks to be prepared, I scan the bar. I repeatedly tap my foot on the floor, and the back of my throat tightens. I haven't seen Dominick in years, so I probably won't recognize him, either. Maybe it'll be okay. I shouldn't stress out over this.

Carrying the freshly prepared drinks, I follow Lexi toward the back of the bar. We go through a doorway and into a quiet seating area outside that's strung with white Christmas lights along the edge of the roof. A few couples are sitting out here, but it's peaceful compared to inside. Lexi takes her drink from me, and we settle at a small table with four chairs. I sit next to her and stir my cocktail. I look nervously from her to the doorway and back to her again.

"You okay?" she asks, and my heart jumps in my throat.

"Uh, yeah, sure." I take a quick sip, hoping the liquor will calm my nerves. "It's just . . . you know . . . I'm here. With you. It's nice."

She smirks wickedly and swirls her drink. "It's just a bar. Not like we're on a date or something."

I give her a dubious look. "Then what is this?"

"You tell me." She tilts her head slightly, lifting an eyebrow.

Aw, hell. While I'm wrestling with my thoughts, Lexi suddenly pops up from her chair and waves. "Hey, girl!"

My heart pounds faster. I keep my eyes on my drink and don't look directly at the doorway. But in my peripheral vision, I can see three people standing there, and I hear their voices—one of them is a man's—greeting each other. Sweat beads on my skin, and the world around me gets all muffled and distant.

I finally force myself to raise my head enough to get a glimpse. While Lexi and her friend are hugging, Dominick stands by and watches them, his hands stuffed in the pockets of his baggy jeans. He sports a clean buzz cut, trimmed beard, and one of those confident smiles that looks as though it could easily charm the ladies. I guess that's how he's snagged that beautiful woman beside him. Denise is slightly shorter than Lexi, with smooth caramel skin and a cute face. She has a contagious smile, kind of like Kevin's girl. *Dominick did good getting her.*

I would never have recognized him if Lexi hadn't said anything. He's gotten taller but still looks a little shorter than me. And he's nowhere near as built as Kevin. He's got Mama's eyes. He always had them, but now it's even more obvious. He's been keeping himself up physically. I wonder how he's doing mentally.

Lexi and her girlfriend separate, and Lexi goes to hug Dominick, wishing him congratulations. Dominick beams, his face brighter than I've ever seen it. I don't want to fuck up his happiness if he recognizes me.

That's it. I'm leaving.

With my head down, I rise from my chair and head for the exit. I gently brush past Lexi's girlfriend and am suddenly tugged backward, nearly stumbling.

"Hey, Knox! What gives?" Lexi says, pulling on my arm.

"Gotta go," I say quickly, not looking back. I ease my arm from her grasp.

She arches an eyebrow. "Is it an emergency?"

"Yeah, uh . . . " I keep my head lowered and turned away from Dominick, who stands only a hair's breadth away.

"Is it your mom? Do you need me to drive you somewhere?" Lexi persists, concern filling her voice.

"No. I'll be all right." I can practically feel my brother's eyes on me. "Sorry, I can't stay. I gotta take care of something. Uh, congrats, you two."

I walk back inside the main bar area and push my way through the crowd. I hear Lexi's annoyed voice. "Geez, Dom. What's up with your brother?"

"Huh? Whose brother?" Dominick's voice says.

"What kind of question is that? Knox is your brother, right?"

A lady walks in front of me, and I dodge her just in time to avoid knocking her drink onto the front of her blue dress. The noise inside begins to drown out the conversation behind me, but I manage to catch bits and pieces of Dominick's reply. " . . . don't know anyone named Knox . . . got me confused with someone else."

I finally make it outside and lean against the wall and exhale. My heart's still pounding. I pull out my phone to call a cab, but my hands are shaking so bad I can hardly press the numbers.

I'm a coward. I'm a fucking coward like Pops. I grit my teeth. "No . . . " I look back at the bar's entrance and the people heading in and out of the place. *It's not too late to go back in there.* I continue staring at the entrance, part of me hoping Lexi will come out, so I can try and explain. *No. She won't understand. Why the hell did I even come here in the first place?*

"Good evening. City Cab Service. How may I help you?"

I snap alert and stare at the lit-up screen on my phone.

"Hello?" the lady's voice says again.

Looking back at the entrance, I slowly raise the phone to my ear. "Hi. I need a cab at Chauncey's Bar."

Coming to Washington was a bad idea. I sit on the edge of my childhood bed, rubbing my temples. I can't get the scene out of my head—Dominick, Denise, and Lexi together, smiling, all happy while I run far, far away. Why the hell is this so hard? *I shouldn't have come back.*

There's a knock at my door. "Michael? You okay, baby?"

I rub my hands over my face. "Yeah, Mama. Fine."

I don't bother acknowledging when the door creaks open and Mama comes in. "You're back early. It's not even eleven o'clock yet. Is everything okay? How did your date go?"

I dig my fingers into my scalp. "I told you. It was *not* a date."

I hear her approach the bed. "Baby, I'm sorry. I've just been so excited for you that—"

I lift my head, glaring at her.

"Michael? What's wrong? Please talk to me." She places her hand on my shoulder.

"Nothing." I shrug her hand off violently and pop up from the bed. "I'm going back to New York tomorrow."

She blinks. "What? Already? Oh, baby, don't leave yet. You didn't even get to see your Uncle Adam."

I shake my head and grab my duffel bag. "I can't stay here any longer," I say, tossing the open bag on the bed. "I don't even know why the hell I came back. I just need to get out of here. Now."

She spins me around. Placing both hands over my cheeks, she forces me to look at her. "Don't leave, Michael," she says, her eyes getting misty. "Please, baby, don't run away."

I swallow a lump in my throat. "Dominick and Kevin are happy. I'm just gonna screw things up for them. I'm a constant reminder of the past. I'm a disease, just like Kevin said."

Her eyes widen. "No you're not, baby. You're their brother. And my son. I love you so very much. What happened in the past . . . we can't fix that. But we can make things right now that you've come back." Her bottom lip trembles, and she bites it. "Please don't run away, baby. Nothing will ever change if you keep running. Please . . ."

Seeing the first tear fall down her cheek, I shut my eyes and sigh. I wrap my arms around her and pull her close. She buries her face in my chest and sobs. I rest my chin atop her head and inhale her azalea-scented shampoo. The sound of her crying fades as memories of *that day* come crashing down hard on me.

I was fifteen. I remember lifting my head from Mama's shoulder and looking around the empty waiting room of the children's hospital in Seattle. It was pleasantly quiet despite the scenes from that evening that continued running through my mind and giving me a feeling of chaos. I gazed at Mama's face. Her eyes were bloodshot, and dried tears streaked her cheeks. "Mama, can we see them now?"

Mama looked at me and pursed her lips. She rubbed my hair and then sniffled. "No, baby. Not yet. The nurse will let us know when it's okay."

I stared blankly at the tiled floor. "Are they dead?" I said emotionlessly. I'd seen the blood all over Kevin and heard one of the paramedics say something about Dominick going into shock when he was being wheeled away on the stretcher.

Mama sniffled and whimpered. "Oh, baby . . . " She began to put her arms around me, but I wriggled away from her and stood up from my chair.

"Tell me, Mama."

She shook her head. "N-No baby. They . . . they're not dead."

I chewed my bottom lip and looked in Mama's eyes. "What did the doc tell you?"

She stared at me sadly then covered her mouth and looked away. Her body shuddered.

I balled my fists. "Mama . . ."

She didn't answer right away, only cried silently, fresh tears streaming down her cheeks. She slowly regained her composure and focused on me again. She took my hands in hers and kissed them. "I'm sorry, Michael. I'm so sorry," she whispered.

Not retracting my hands, I knelt down in front of her. "Tell me, Mama."

She took a deep breath and then whispered, "The doctors said Dominick had large amounts of semen in his rectum, and . . . he was severely bruised on his back, arms, and legs. He'd gone into shock from . . . from the trauma. Kevin lost a lot of blood from the neck wound and went unconscious. The doctors have been scrambling all night to find enough blood to do a transfusion."

Tears welled up in my eyes, and I kept staring blankly at a button on her flower-printed blouse. My brothers were hurt—physically and emotionally scarred from what our father did. I could've stopped it if I hadn't gone out grocery shopping with Mama. I could've saved them. I was old enough to protect them—and bigger, stronger. I'd finally gathered enough courage to stand up to Pops if he mistreated us boys again. But I was too late. It was all my fault.

I can't stay here and drag them back down. "They'll never forgive me, Mama," I murmur, rubbing her back. "I am my father's son."

She pulls back and looks at me. "Baby, no. No! You are not like him. Lord Jesus, you will never be like that evil, sick man. He destroyed our family. And my heart."

"It's my fault . . . I should've been there . . . "

"None of us knew that was going to happen. You can't blame yourself for something you couldn't prevent."

I look back at her sadly. I could've prevented it because I'd seen the signs. Pops was always hard on us boys—extremely so. Especially Dominick. That day, Pops was drinking a little more than usual, and he'd been looking at Dominick strangely as we all sat around the table eating lunch. But I was too chickenshit to speak up. He would've probably killed me if I ever stood up to him. He almost killed Kevin.

"Pops was drunk," I say in a small voice, and I instinctively look to the doorway as though my father could come storming into my room at any moment.

Mama shakes her head. "You can't blame yourself, Michael. It's not your fault. That man . . . was not your father. He was not the man I once loved."

I lower my gaze to the floor. No matter how much she wants to deny it, his blood still flows through my brothers' veins and through mine.

Mama kisses my cheek softly, distracting me from my thoughts. "Michael, please stay a little longer, okay? For me?"

I sigh. How long am I going to keep running? I at least owe Lexi an explanation. I don't want her caught in the middle of my drama. I don't want to destroy whatever good thing we have going. "Yeah, sure . . . I guess. Just a little longer . . . "

Mama exhales in relief. "Oh, thank you, baby." She kisses my cheek again. "I love you."

I gently push her away, cringing from the excessive smothering. "Love you, too."

She leaves and closes the door.

I toss my duffel bag back on the floor and sit on the bed. My phone buzzes with an incoming text. From Lexi.

WTF? >:(

I'm hesitant to text back. But she deserves an explanation.

im sorry…

I wait for her to reply, but when she doesn't, I text:

can we meet somewhere? I'll explain.

She still doesn't reply. I text again:

U still there?

I receive a "message sending error" notification.

Exasperated, I toss my phone on the floor and flop back onto the mattress. *Great. Just fucking great.*

Chapter 12

I WAKE UP TO THE SOUNDS OF MUFFLED VOICES ARGUING IN the living room.

"I told you there's no Knox that lives here," Mama says.

Shit! I rub the sleep from my eyes and dig my phone from the pocket of my discarded jeans. The screen wakes up, displaying the time—12:49 a.m. I spring out of bed, struggle into my jeans and a shirt, slip on my glasses, and then hurry out to the living room.

Mama's at the front door in her gaudy flowery robe she's worn for as long as I can remember, talking to someone I can't see through the small space allowed by the chain lock.

"Move aside, Mama," I say, reaching for her arm as I rush to her side.

Mama looks over her shoulder at me, her brow pinched with concern. "She's looking for someone named Knox. Do you know anyone by that name, baby?"

My skin prickles.

"Knox!" Lexi's voice hollers from behind the door. "Get your sorry ass out here. We need to talk. *Now!*"

I pale. *Damn, what is she doing here? How did she know where I lived? Oh yeah, my phone.* "Lexi," I mutter.

Mama scowls toward the unseen Lexi. "Hey, now you listen to me, missy. Don't come around *my* house, making demands and—" She stops herself, and whips her head back to me. "Is *this* the girl you went to go meet earlier? And why does she keep calling you Knox? What's going on here, Michael?" The disappointment on Mama's face feels like a thousand needles piercing my chest.

I run my hand over my face and take several deep breaths. "Yes, Mama, I know her. 'Knox' is just a nickname. No need to get all upset about it." I gently push my mother away and say in my calmest voice possible, "I need to talk to her alone, Mama. Go back to bed."

Mama glares at me then at Lexi and shakes her head, her face full of disappointment. She turns and places her hand on my shoulder. "You're a grown man, Michael, but I don't like the way she talks to you." She mutters in my ear. "Reminds me too much of your father." She then heads down the hall.

I cringe. *No. Unlike Pops, she has a good reason to be upset.* I turn back to Lexi, who looks pissed as all hell. Her arms are crossed, and she's glaring at me sharply.

"What are you doing here?" I'm annoyed, and my mind is too jumbled to think straight.

"You said it was an emergency, so I wanted to make sure you were okay," she replies. "But now I see it was all bullshit. So, what the hell's *really* going on?"

I rub my temples, trying to find the right words. But how the hell do I explain all this without pissing her off again? I step outside and close the door behind me. It's cold, but I ignore my goose-bumped arms. "I asked you not to track me down like that."

She eyes me coolly. "I can do *far* worse."

I swallow. "So, is that it? You're gonna blackmail me until I spill?"

"I think I'm owed a little more than the bullshit you've given me."

I stare out at a black car sitting in the driveway. "What happened to your cool sports car?" I ask in my poor attempt to prolong the inevitable.

"That was a rental." She pokes me in the chest. "*Don't* change the subject."

I glance down at her slender finger with its nail a deep shade of purple under the dim porch light. Her thumbnail is painted black. "Look, it's complicated, all right?" I say, lifting my chin.

She withdraws her hand. "I didn't come all this way to hear your lame-ass excuses. Tell the fucking truth."

"You've seen more than enough of the truth."

"What? That you're living with your mother? Or your name's not really Knox?"

"It's ... I ... " I sigh. "I think you should leave now, Lexi."

She glowers, spins on her heel, and walks down the porch steps. "I knew this was a mistake," she mutters, heading for her car. "And you call yourself a man."

I pinch the bridge of my nose as I debate whether or not to follow her. *If she leaves, I'll probably never see her again. But . . .*

She flings open the driver-side door of her car, scowls in my direction, then gets in.

I can't keep leading her on like this. Lexi wouldn't come all this way out here for nothing. And to know that she can obtain and exploit my personal information on a whim is a bit unsettling.

She starts the car. I hustle down the steps. The concrete walkway is cold against my sock-covered feet. The headlights come on. I run to the passenger side.

The car begins to move. I yank on the door handle, praying that it's not locked. To my relief, the door flings open, and the car stops abruptly.

"What the fuck are you doing!" she yells.

I hurl myself into the passenger's seat and shut the door. "I'll talk."

She glares at me for several painful moments then mutters, "I'm listening."

I swallow. "Can we not talk here, please? Not in front of this house."

"You've got the balls to make demands now?"

"It . . . it's hard to talk about . . . certain things . . . when I have to look at this house." *Please, God, any place but here.*

The corner of her lip curls. "If you're fucking leading me on again, I swear, I'm done. *Done.* Understand? I don't need to put up with your shit."

I nod once. "I promise. No more bullshit." I rub my arms, trying to keep them warm.

Lexi punches the gas, and the tires squeal as the car backs out the driveway. I have no idea where she intends to go. For all I know, she might just drop me off at the nearest police station. Or maybe drive me into the middle of a forest and leave me there to fend off wild animals and shit. I don't know. I don't care.

I suddenly realize I'm without my wallet. No money, no ID, no shoes, no jacket. I'm screwed.

We ride for a while in silence, heading deeper into the city, which is pretty much dead this time of night—nothing like New York, which has constant activity no matter what time it is. She pulls into the nearly deserted parking lot of a strip mall, looks around, and then shuts off the car. Silence fills the car, making my ears ring.

"You didn't turn me in," I mutter, not looking at her.

"Maybe because I didn't want to."

"Why? I've obviously pissed you off enough."

"Maybe because I'm not the heartless bitch you think I am."

I blink. Did she really think I thought that about her? "Whoa. You got me all wrong, Lexi. I swear on my life I have *never* thought that about you. But I know you don't trust me after what I did."

She snorts. "Who said I *ever* trusted you?"

"Right." I rub the back of my head, searching for the words. "So, here goes. My name's not really Knox. It's . . . Michael."

"Yeah, I kinda gathered that from your mother."

I nod. "A lot of bad shit happened to me and my family when I was younger, and I wanted—*needed*—a new name. Dominick and Kevin don't know me as Knox, though. They're both really angry at me for what happened a long time ago." I chew my bottom lip. "That's all I can say about that."

"What happened?"

"Personal family shit involving Dominick and Kevin. I can't really say anything more about it. I hope you understand."

She tilts her head, giving me a dubious look. "Hm . . . "

"It's the truth. I swear to God."

"You never told me why you ran away."

I clasp and unclasp my hands. "Part of it has to do with the personal family shit." I look at her pleadingly. "Haven't I said enough already?"

She runs her fingers across her lips in thought. "Maybe."

"So, were you just bullshitting me about being able to get my info? I mean, if you're really a hacker, what's stopping you from getting all you want to know instead of making me tell you?"

"Just because I can, doesn't mean I do. I use my abilities responsibly. Even hackers have a code of ethics."

I snort. "A hacker with ethics? That sounds like an oxymoron."

She glowers at me and pulls out her phone, which is enclosed in a sparkling, hot-pink case decorated with stickers of anime characters. She holds the phone up, as though she's taking a picture. Then suddenly, my own phone makes a weird beep in my pocket. I've never heard it sound like that before. Curious, I take it out and look at the screen, but nothing seems to have changed about it.

"What was that?" I ask.

Not answering, Lexi types something on her phone. It makes a similar beep in response, and she reads, "Michael Anderson Junior. Also known as Knox from da Bronx. Born October 12, 7:02 a.m. at Bronx-Lebanon Hospital. Currently lives on 148th Street in a one-bedroom apartment on the third floor in Bronx, New York. Previously lived in Renton, Washington and Rochester, New York. Your father's name is Michael Anderson Senior, now deceased. Mother's name is Elouise Covington . . . " She pauses and looks up at me.

I stare at her, openmouthed and speechless.

She returns to her phone. "You were diagnosed with moderate myopia at age five, wear a size eleven shoe—"

"Stop."

She arches an eyebrow.

"I get it. No need to read off my fucking life story."

She snorts and shuts off her phone. "That was hardly your whole life. I can dig a little deeper if you want. Like trace everywhere you shopped, every grade you got in school, your favorite food, your favorite color, where your grandma was born—"

"No."

She sets the phone in the console. "Lighten the fuck up, will you? I don't dig that kind of dirt unless I absolutely have to."

I scan the darkened strip mall, thinking. "I don't know why the hell I decided to jump in this car and ride with you out here like this."

"And I don't know why the hell I decided to drive to Renton to find you," she says.

I smile. "Well, it's only a twenty-minute drive, at least."

"Twenty minutes of my life wasted."

My smile falls. "Was this really a waste of your time?"

She rolls her eyes. "Kidding, Knox." She puts the keys in the ignition. "I'll take you home. To your *mother*." She smirks.

I cringe. "I don't live with her, you know. I'm just spending a few days there. I haven't seen her in over ten years."

"Mhmm."

"I'm serious."

"*Mhmm.*"

I'm not sure if she really believes me or is just pulling my leg, so I let the matter rest. I don't want to go back home, but it's nearing two in the morning, and I could use a nice soft bed right about now.

Lexi starts up the car, and I look over at her. She reaches for the gear selector, but I put my hand over it. "Wait."

She looks at me expectantly.

"So, once you take me home, will I ever get to see you again?"

She shrugs. "I don't know."

"Can I at least get your number this time?"

She looks thoughtful about this. "Okay. Give me your phone."

I hesitate then dig my phone from my pocket. I unlock the screen and hand the phone to her.

Lexi takes it and chuckles. "Nice wallpaper." She begins typing her info.

"Thanks," I say, thinking about the night of one of my fights, when the picture was taken. I'd delivered a solid roundhouse kick to the side of my opponent's head. Dante had captured the perfect moment when my foot connected.

Lexi finishes typing and hands the phone back. "Don't share it with anyone."

Our hands briefly touch as I take the phone from her. But that touch alone is enough to send an electric pang through my body. I look at her number, smile, and return the phone to my pocket. "Of course not. I would never do that."

Her gaze briefly drops downward, perhaps to my lips. "I'll find out if you do."

"Lexi, I'll do whatever it takes to earn your trust."

The corners of her mouth tug upward. "Yeah, I somehow believe you would."

My smile broadens. "Yeah? Well, that's a good start then." I lean my head ever so slightly toward her, wondering if she'll pick up on the hint.

She doesn't move but continues watching me. I lay my hand atop hers and caress it gently. She looks at our hands, and I can practically see the wheels turning in her head.

"You're a cool girl, Lexi." I bring her hand to my lips and plant a gentle kiss on the back of it. I inhale a whiff of bubble gum and strawberries coming from her skin. I tilt my head up, and she looks back at me with a soft smile.

She pulls her hand back, flips the console up, and leans closer to me. She pulls off my glasses and sets them on top of the dashboard. She leans her face close to mine and caresses my smooth jawline down to the small stubble along my chin. "You piss me off, and yet, I don't know why you fascinate me so much."

I lick my lips in anticipation of kissing her once again and feeling that lip ring. "I've been fascinated by you for a while now."

She brushes the pads of her fingers across my moistened lips, and I kiss them. She watches me carefully then presses her lips to mine. The touch of cold metal gives me goose bumps. I kiss her back earnestly, devouring those wonderful-tasting lips. The small, nearly inaudible moan that escapes her doesn't go unnoticed.

God, I want her so bad.

"Wow," she whispers. "That was . . . kinda hot."

I smile slightly. "Kinda?"

Her lips crash into mine again, and she kisses me with a little more force. A little more need. I feel her hands on my shirt, drifting lower, lower. Then she runs her hands under my shirt and caresses my abs.

I shiver. Her hands are cold, but that doesn't stop me from getting hard. I deepen the kiss. I hope she never stops touching me. *I wish she were on top of me right now. Maybe we can go back home and fool around.* But then I realize I'm not in New York, where we could just jet off to my apartment.

Lexi's purple-and-black nails graze my pecs, and I become a wreck. I groan. "You keep doing that, and I won't be able to let you go."

She chuckles against my lips, and I silence her with another eager kiss. She finally pulls back. "Damn, I need to stop. This is getting way too hot."

I laugh and kiss her forehead. "You're hot."

She looks up at me, smiling.

"Can we do something tomorrow—er—later today?"

"Sure. I get off work at eight, so maybe we can do something after that."

"Shit. I didn't know you had to go to work. Sorry. I should let you go home and sleep. I'll walk home or something."

"Don't worry about it. It's my first day back from vacation. I don't have to be in till twelve. It's only"—she retrieves her phone from the console, and the screen flashes on—"2:10."

"Where do you work?" I ask.

"Ratty's Parlor. You should come check it out sometime."

A tattoo parlor? If so, that would explain all her lovely ink and piercings. "Definitely. I need to hit up a gym first."

"Plenty of them around Seattle. Actually, there's a gym one block over from Ratty's. I'll text you the address later."

"Sweet."

She drives me home, and we kiss a final time goodbye before I get out of the stuffy car and into the biting cold. I watch her drive off, and I make my way to the front door, but to my dismay, it's locked. *Great.* Lexi's already gone, and I don't want to wake my mother up and have to endure whatever lecture she'll most likely give me. I shiver. My feet are like ice as I glance down at my socks, thinking about how ridiculous they look against Mama's azalea-printed welcome mat.

Welcome mat? I wonder . . .

I squat and take a suspicious peek under it. There's an old, rusted key. *Holy shit.* I can't believe Mama still keeps the spare key under the mat. She used to do that for my brothers and me in case one of us lost our keys when we came home from school.

This key looks as if it's been under there for the past ten years. I can't believe I still remembered. Some things never change, it seems.

C HAPTER 13

THE SMELL OF BACON, EGGS, PANCAKES, AND BISCUITS rouses me from my deep sleep. I open my eyes to the morning light, which casts bright streaks through the closed blinds. Yawning, I sit up in bed and rub the sleep from my eyes. It's after ten in the morning, according to my phone. I slept like a log, and damn, did I have an awesome dream. I still can't stop thinking about last night.

Lexi and I making out in a car. The touch of her beautiful, silky skin. Me kissing that cold metal lip ring of hers.

Just those thoughts alone have worked up a serious case of morning wood. Groaning, I take several minutes to ease it back down. God, I can't wait to see Lexi again. But first, the gym.

I slide out of bed and put on some sweat pants and a faded T-shirt with XL Westside's logo on it. I open my bedroom door. The smell of breakfast hits me even more strongly now, making my stomach growl instantly. I hear the TV on in the living room and see the top of Mama's head at the couch. Yawning, I make my way to the living room.

Mama's watching the morning news while sipping some coffee. I lean over the back of the couch and plant a kiss on her cheek. "Morning."

She starts, turns her head, and smiles. "Oh, good morning, baby. Did you sleep okay?"

"Yeah," I reply, leaning back upright. I follow my nose to the kitchen. "What's all that awesome food I smell?"

Chuckling, she hops up from the couch. She's as spry as ever. "I didn't know when you were going to get up, so I kept breakfast warm in the oven. Eat as much as you like."

"Don't have to tell me twice." I peer into the oven at the covered dishes and start filling a fresh plate with lots of everything. My entire daily calorie limit is probably on this plate, but damn it, there's no way in hell I'm going to pass up a free home-cooked meal. I'll make an extra effort to burn it off at the gym. I take my mountain of food to the dinette. I'm a little hesitant to eat here, but not as much as yesterday, when I had dinner at this table for the first time in years. Each time I sit down with Mama, the wound mends a little more. Maybe one day, I'll be able to face my brothers, too, and heal the scars and gashes that have torn us apart.

Mama refills her coffee cup and joins me at the table. I start wolfing down my breakfast as if I've not eaten in weeks.

"So, who exactly was that ridiculous-looking girl that came by the house so early in the morning?" Mama asks.

I frown. "Just a girl I know," I say, not looking up from my food.

"Girlfriend?" She arches an eyebrow.

I stop eating and finally look at her, mortified and still not sure what exactly Lexi and I are right now. "Just a girl I know," I repeat.

She takes a sip of coffee. "She was extremely rude."

"She was just angry at me."

"What did you do?"

"I don't want to talk about it."

"Baby, I don't want to see you being mistreated. I've seen enough of it from your father."

I drop my fork on my plate, and it makes a loud clang. "Mama, I'm a grown man. I can take care of myself. Stop worrying about me. And stop comparing Lexi to Pops, who, last I checked, is dead."

"I'm sorry, baby. I just . . . I want you to be happy."

"I am happy. Lexi makes me happy. She's not a bad girl. Don't let the tattoos and Mohawk fool you." I pick up my fork and resume wolfing my breakfast.

She nods and slowly spins her coffee mug with her fingers. Her face brightens. "Oh! Dominick called early yesterday while you were out. Guess what he told me?"

I look at her dubiously, waiting for her to continue.

"He's getting married next year! He and his beautiful girlfriend Denise are going to tie the knot in June after he graduates. Isn't that exciting?"

I swallow a forkful of scrambled eggs. My stomach turns at the thought of last night, when I made a complete ass of myself in front of Dominick. *Because I'm such a coward.*

"Yeah. That's cool, Mama. I'm happy for him," I say in a small voice.

"Dominick is going to be interning at a pharmaceutical company in Redmond this spring," Mama continues. "Something to do with developing medical devices."

"Wow, sounds like he's gonna be making the big bucks if all goes well."

"I hope so. I'm so proud of him."

I force myself to finish the rest of my breakfast. The food seems to taste more bitter than it did when I started eating.

"Your Uncle Adam called earlier this morning, too. He's going to come over in the afternoon," Mama says. "He's been anxious to see you."

I frown. I'm not sure I'm ready to face Uncle Adam right now. I just know he'll keep pestering me about shit I don't want to talk about. Like whether I've talked to my brothers yet, or if I've told Mama about my fighting. "I'm gonna go to the gym in a bit. I don't know when I'll be back."

The excitement drifts from her face. "All right, baby. Do what you have to do. I hope you'll be back later to be able to see him, at least. He's going to stay until tomorrow."

"I won't make any promises," I say bluntly.

She stares down at her coffee mug. The brief silence unnerves me, so I get up and return to the kitchen to wash my plate. When I finish, I leave the kitchen and still see Mama sitting at the table, staring at her mug. *Damn it.*

"Mama." I place my hand on her shoulder. "I'm sorry."

She makes a light sniffle. "I've missed you, baby."

Scowling, I pull her out of the chair and hug her tight. "No crying," I say, my eyes starting to burn.

She buries her face in my chest and sniffles a little more. "I wish you'd understand how much I love you. How much your family loves you. You don't have to run away anymore, Michael. You don't have to hide from what happened in the past."

My throat tightens. "I do what I have to do to protect this family. To protect you. I wish you'd understand."

"Please, let's talk more about—"

"No, there's nothing to talk about," I say.

"But—"

"No, Mama."

She breaks the hug and looks at me sadly. "Okay, baby." She stands on her tiptoes, and I lean my head down so that she can kiss my forehead. Afterward, Mama returns to the living room, curls up on the couch with her coffee mug, and continues watching the news.

With a sigh, I head to my room.

The taxi pulls up in front of a well-kept building in the heart of Seattle. I'm kind of glad I let go some of my pride and let Mama give me cash to pay the cab fare. I really should get out of Renton as soon as I can. The transportation alone is going to suck the life out of my wallet.

Seattle looks amazing. Clear skies, clean air, clean streets—not at all the dreary, rainy, depressing place people think it is. Or maybe I just happened to come at the perfect time of year. I've only recalled coming to Seattle a handful of times when I was little, and I don't remember much other than when I was seven and our parents took my brothers and me to visit the Space Needle.

I shoulder my duffel bag and stand before the front doors of a three-story building, which looks more like a ritzy hotel than a gym. There's a sign above the door that reads: "Your Way Fitness." I watch as an elderly couple dressed in brightly colored spandex exits the frosted-glass double doors of the building and a muscled, tattooed guy with a buzz cut strolls in.

This must be the place. I enter the building and halt as the doors close behind me. The interior reminds me of some sort of eclectic, futuristic work of art. One of the walls is crafted of tin in various designs, and the other walls are brick. The floors are wood, polished to a shine. I *love* wood floors. The place reminds me of Master Rho's *dojang*. The air in here is cool, and the smell of new rubber equipment smacks me hard. Two teenage girls dressed in loose workout shorts and T-shirts head my way, chatting like crazy. They notice me then slow their walk. Their eyes widen, and their mouths drop open.

I tip my head at the girls and brush past them. "'Scuse me, ladies," I mutter, keeping my eyes focused straight ahead. I pick up their low voices even as I get farther and farther away.

"Oh my gosh. He called us 'ladies'!" one of them says and then giggles.

"He's so hot," the other says.

I roll my eyes and fight down a smile, not at all impressed. I hope there aren't a lot of clingy teenage girls who hang out around here. I'd like to work out in peace.

The reception area is at the end of the short hall, and a young, attractive, red-haired woman sits behind the desk in front of her computer, chewing gum. She looks up from her computer screen and smiles brightly at me. "Good afternoon. How may I help you?"

Looking past her, I peek at the rest of the gym, which has weight machines, treadmills, elliptical machines, and more. Many of the machines are occupied. I notice Buzz-cut Guy heading toward a set of stairs in one corner, going down.

I turn back to the receptionist. "Hi. How much is it to use this gym?"

Twisting a red lock of her hair around her finger, she gives me the once-over. She chews her gum in a sophisticated kind of way—at least, she tries to, but she's trying so hard it looks more like a cow chewing curd. "You don't look like you need to use the gym."

I smile back. "Trust me, I do."

"Well, we have a three-day free trial for newcomers. After that, it's fifty bucks a week." She retrieves a piece of paper from somewhere on her desk. "You'll need to sign a waiver first, and you get a fancy wristband to wear during your free trial. So? Interested?"

"Yeah, sure," I say, filling out the waiver. I just want to pump some iron. She writes my name on a neon-green rubber wristband and then punches a star-shaped hole in the band with a hole puncher. I hand the waiver back to her, and she gives me the band.

"Be sure to wear that when you come back next time. You'll get another star punch. When you get three stars, your trial is over."

"Got it." I slip on the wristband.

"We're open from six in the morning till eleven at night. Have fun."

Like a kid in a toy store, I'm overwhelmed by the amount of equipment—many of it foreign looking—in this gym. Hell, it doesn't even look like the gyms I'm used to. This one is way nicer, like a posh "studio" where rich people go.

I feel my phone vibrate in my bag, and I quickly retrieve it. There's a text from Lexi.

> Hope u found the gym okay. ;)

I grin widely.

> sure did! this place is NIIIICE! thx.

> yw! <3

There's that heart emoticon again. My own heart beats as I stare at it. I wish I knew what she was thinking. But why the hell am I getting all worked up over a damn text? It may not mean anything. Maybe it's just Lexi's way of telling me it's her.

Or I could be a fool and think she might've enjoyed last night a little too much. I know I did. I think I'm starting to fall for this girl—dangerously so.

Two hours pass, and I've not even hit all of the machines in this place, but I'm sweating like a motherfucker. I head over to the group of water fountains sitting amid the sea of equipment. While I'm drinking, my eyes cut to the back corner of the room where more rough-looking people are heading up and down those stairs. I have a strange feeling about what might be down there, but I'm not entirely sure.

I rummage through my duffel bag for a banana, which I packed along with other fruit from Mama's house. I meander toward the stairs as I wolf down my snack and then descend through the darkness. I begin to hear voices and the slapping of canvas and vinyl when I'm halfway down. I quicken my descent, and the room below opens up to a large, grungy basement, lit by five strategically placed fluorescent ceiling lights. It's in stark contrast to the posh gym above and feels more like what I'm used to. Men and women, young and old are scattered throughout, hitting bags alone or with partners who hold up hand targets. Some do extreme weight-training exercises, and others gather in the center of the room watching two people engaged in some ground-and-pound sparring. I wander over to an unoccupied hanging bag, unsling my duffel bag, and pull out my gloves. Not long after I go through some of my usual sets of punching and kicking drills, someone approaches me.

"Hey, man. Mind if I join you?"

I turn to look at a fair-skinned younger guy with light-brown dreadlocks who looks about nineteen, maybe twenty. He's shorter than me and has a small frame but is built for someone his size. The grey tank top he wears is soaked, and sweat beads on his skin. Carrying a pair of boxing gloves, he looks to me with determined green eyes.

Catching my breath, I glimpse the rest of the room. All of the hanging bags are occupied, and there are even more people down here than before. Most are gathered in the center of the room, where another makeshift ring has been created. The crowd shouts and cheers; it's starting to get a little rowdy.

I turn back to the kid. "Sure." I step to one side of the bag, and he situates himself on the other side.

"Thanks. I'm Jesse, by the way," he says, putting on the gloves and securing the straps.

"Knox," I say, practicing some combinations on the bag. I end the combo with a back-spinning hook kick, the impact sending the bag swaying side to side between us.

Jesse whistles. "Holy shit, man. That was a sweet move. You do kickboxing or something?"

"Nah," I say, bouncing on my toes, waiting for the bag's swaying to lessen. "I've fought kickboxers before, though." I do another combination then give Jesse a turn at the bag.

"That's cool." Jesse pummels the bag with all power and little accuracy, causing the bag to swing every which way. "I'm training hard to fight in the amateur circuits. Hopefully I'll get picked up by some scouts."

I cringe. *He's not gonna go very far with that sloppy technique.* "Well, keep practicing, man."

We take turns practicing our drills for about half an hour then take a break.

"Thanks for sharing the bag, Knox," Jesse says, out of breath.

"No prob." I wipe sweat from my forehead.

Guzzling from his water bottle, Jesse walks off toward the noisy crowd in the center. I wander over to a group of people who are just finishing up on a set of raised pull-up bars. They leave and head upstairs. I grab the highest bar and pull myself up effortlessly. Then, I begin doing three sets of thirty reps. I love working out on these. I wish we had some at XL Westside. When I finish, my abs are burning like hell, but I know it won't change much, unfortunately. I've worked these muscles like crazy, and they just won't respond.

The crowd in the middle has grown, and there only seems to be one match going on, so I finally go over and see what all the noise is about. I peer over people's heads and make out two women on the ground, tangled up around each other like a pretzel. They're rough-looking, as if they've taken one too many shots in the face in their fighting careers. And damn, the woman on top looks more ripped than me. *All the more reason to not take off this fucking T-shirt.*

The woman on the bottom shifts just enough to get part of her leg hooked around her opponent's neck, and the woman on top taps out. The spectators clap and congratulate the winner, and the two women are escorted out of the makeshift ring.

Two guys jump in; one of them is Jesse. He adjusts the strap of his gloves and bites down on a bright-orange mouthpiece. His opponent is taller than Jesse and stocky. His shirt's off, and part of his chest is bandaged. But the injury—at least, that's what I think it is—doesn't seem to faze this guy.

The two of them touch gloves, initiating the match. The crowd shouts and cheers, but I stand there quietly, watching the two of them. Jesse's opponent looks like a seasoned fighter by the way he stands and counters Jesse's attacks. Jesse's all over the place. He stands like a street brawler, every target on his body fully exposed. His opponent unleashes a clean punch at Jesse's solar plexus, and Jesse doubles over, spitting out his mouthpiece.

"Ooh!" the crowd says in unison. Some of the spectators high-five Jesse's opponent, though he doesn't look all too proud. He goes to Jesse, who stands up slowly, holding his midsection. He pats Jesse's back and says something to him, and Jesse nods. The guy smiles, pats his back again, and Jesse picks up his mouthpiece and leaves the ring. He collapses in a corner of the room, his head down.

I wait to see if Jesse's trainer is possibly here, so he or she can take care of it. But after a few moments of watching people pass the kid by, I finally approach him.

"Hey, man, you all right?" I ask, kneeling against the wall beside him.

He looks at me, scowls, and turns his head away. "Fine." He coughs.

"You shouldn't sit down when you get hit there. Your diaphragm contracts, as will your lungs, and you'll start cramping up when you sit. You need to stand with your hands on top of your head and take deep breaths to stretch those muscles."

He looks back at me then furrows his brow. "You a doctor or something?"

"Nope. I've just been hit there more times than I can count." I smile.

He cracks a small smile as well and stands, putting his hands on his head. He leans against the wall and takes deep breaths. "Thanks. I feel a little better."

"You got a trainer? He or she should know these things."

"Nope. I started training on my own. I can't afford a personal trainer."

I stare blankly at the group of spectators, and I suddenly hear Dante's voice in my head. *Consider it, kid.*

Jesse sighs, and I'm brought out of my thoughts. "That match totally sucked," he says.

I stand, fold my arms over my chest, and slowly bounce my body on and off the wall. "You just need a good foundation."

"What are you talking about, man? I stayed on my feet the whole time."

"You did, but you took a bad shot. Your entire body was wide open for the pickings. Give your opponent half of a target instead, and it'll be harder for him to hit you there again." Seeing the confusion on his face, I pop off the wall and demonstrate with a simple fighting stance and put my hands up. "There's a reason why many seasoned fighters stand like this."

He nods understandably. "Oh! I get it now." He pushes off the wall and mimics me. *The kid's a fast learner—I'll give him that.*

"I'm going back in for a rematch," Jesse says, bumping his fists together anxiously.

"Whoa, hold on. You need to learn a lot more than just stances."

He shakes his head. "I got this, man."

He returns to the circle for a rematch and, as expected, ends up losing again. But it wasn't as bad this time, and at least he didn't get another solar-plexus hit. The other guy is just too strong and experienced. But the kid's got heart. That'll take him far.

It's nearing four in the afternoon when I finally hit the showers and leave the gym. I've been having so much fun here, I forgot I promised Lexi I'd stop by her job before she gets off. Finishing an apple, I walk up the block in the direction of the tattoo parlor.

"Knox! Wait up!" Jesse's voice yells from behind me.

I stop and turn around, and the kid runs up to me, his backpack slung over one shoulder.

"Hey, I . . . I just wanted to . . . tell you . . . tha . . . thanks for helping me," he says between panting breaths.

I raise my eyebrows. "Huh?"

"With my fighting. You fixed me up all right! I have a long way to go before I should think about fighting in the amateur circuits."

"Just keep practicing. You'll get there eventually."

"You live around here? Maybe we can meet up sometime and train like that again."

"Uh, no, I'm just visiting. Sorry."

"Damn." Jesse's shoulders slump.

I swallow. This kid's starting to get a little attached. But I didn't do that much for him. "I'm sure there's someone you can hook up with locally."

He shrugs. "Yeah, I guess. You just make shit so easy to understand. Like, mind-blowingly understandable."

"Ehh . . . " I look up the street. The neon lights of the tattoo shop glow welcomingly several hundred feet away. I look back at Jesse. My throat tightens. I can't just give this kid the cold shoulder. *No, I won't.* I've already brushed off one person who needed my help. And now she's dead.

My eyes well up at the thought of Bonita, and I wipe my eyes with the back of my hand, holding my glasses up with the other hand.

"You okay, Knox?" Jesse asks.

I clear my throat and reset my glasses. "Yeah, sure. I just . . . uh . . . got sweat in my eye." I take out my phone. "Tell you what. I'll give you my contact info. Call or message me whenever you have a question about something with your training, and I'll try and help."

His eyes light up. "Seriously? That's awesome, man! Thanks so much!"

We exchange info, and he leaves. *There, Dante. I've done my good deed for the day.*

CHAPTER 14

The bells over the door jingle as I enter the tiny tattoo parlor. The place is lit up with multi-colored Christmas lights and bright neon signs, which reflect off the polished, black-and-white-checkered floor. Fantastic, detailed framed drawings of intricate designs cover the walls. Rock music plays from unseen speakers, blending with the buzzing of needles and the light chatter of employees and customers.

Two women sitting on a retro-style blue vinyl couch look up at me from their fashion magazines. They're sporting a poor attempt at the classic California-girl look, with their too-blond hair, tanning-spa skin, and artificial curves. But their wolfish gazes are more than genuine.

I leave them to their ogling and scan the place for Lexi. Three customers are being tended to, but there's no sign of her. A guy with a green-spiked Mohawk sits at the front desk with his feet propped up, drawing something on a sketchpad.

I walk up to the desk, and the graphite pencil he holds stops moving.

"'Sup, man? What can I do for ya?" he asks.

I glimpse the sketchpad in his lap and can make out an elaborate drawing of a black crow. "Is Lexi around?" I ask, looking back at him.

He arches an eyebrow, which is covered in piercings, and then his expression hardens. "Who's asking?"

"Knox."

At that moment, Lexi comes through a beaded curtain at the back of the shop. An older man follows, leering at her from behind. A deep scowl is etched on her face as she rummages through a drawer at an empty workstation.

"Thanks, Alexis. You're a doll," the man says flirtatiously then heads to the front counter. I clench my jaw. She doesn't respond, nor does she look up. *What happened back there?*

The man stands next to me, casting a small, condescending glimpse my way before turning his nose up and plunking down a wad of cash on the counter. "Be sure Alexis gets *all* of my tip." He emphasizes the latter with an obvious hint of sensuality.

Mohawk Guy swipes the cash and counts it, his eyes becoming wide as saucers. "Yeah, sure, man," he says, not looking up.

The man smiles, casts Lexi another glance, and then leaves.

"Damn. I think this is the most he's ever tipped you," Mohawk Guy mutters. "You flash your tits at him or something?"

The girls on the couch go into giggle fits.

Lexi slams the drawer, and the entire workstation trembles. She glares at him. "No, asshole. Now, put that shit in the community bucket."

"Hey, you heard what he said. 'Make sure you get *all* of his tip.'" He mimics the guy's sensual tone and then snickers. The other employees join in.

She storms to the front counter. "Look, Nash. I don't want anything to do with that creep or his dirty money, understand?"

"He's our best customer, Lex. Roll with it. Sheesh."

"*Hell* no."

She finally focuses her attention on me, annoyance still riddled on her face. "Hey."

I smile. "Hi, Lexi."

Nash looks from her to me then pops up from his chair. "Hold the fuck up. You know this guy?"

"What's it to you?" she says.

"Oh, shit. You mean that vajayjay's finally out of retirement, and you didn't tell me?" Nash says.

I stay silent. The conversation is turning all sorts of awkward.

Lexi turns beet red. "Shut the fuck up, asshole."

The employees and customers break into laughter. Two employees whistle and make catcalls.

"I heard that!" one of the female workers yells, not looking up from her work.

Nash throws his head back and laughs. "It's about damn time. Anyway, you can't leave yet. You got three minutes left."

"Whatever." Lexi rolls her eyes and flips him off then spins on her heel and heads for the back of the shop. She beckons me to follow.

Nash smirks and sits back down.

Lexi and I enter the back room area, which has long tables made for lying on. She grabs her jacket off a hook by the back door and heads outside. I follow her. The outside rear of the building opens up into a tiny area with Dumpsters and a couple of parked cars. Lexi stops in front of her car and leans on the hood.

"Sorry about that," she says, running a hand over her purple, slicked-back Mohawk.

"About what?" I ask, leaning next to her.

"Nash being a douche. He's all right for a boss, though . . . I guess."

"He's your boss?"

"Yeah, can't you tell?" She smirks, light glinting off her lip ring.

"I hope I didn't get you in trouble for leaving early."

She shakes her head. "No, he enjoys fucking with me like that sometimes. He's like that annoying sibling who won't stop flicking your ear or something, you know? He's never gonna let me live this down for as long as I live. And I thought my girlfriends were bad."

"What do you mean?"

"The 'me suddenly leaving with a guy' thing. They're always trying to play matchmaker. And now, Nash knows there's something going on between us."

I look at her carefully. "Is there?"

She meets my eyes and lifts her head a little. "Sure . . . why not?" she says after some delay.

I tug my lips into a smile. "That's cool, Lexi."

She pushes up from the hood and opens the driver-side door. "Wanna grab a bite to eat?"

I'm already at the passenger side before she can finish the question.

The sun's setting as we zoom out of the heart of the city with a bag of groceries in the backseat. We settled on cooking dinner at Lexi's place rather than eating out. I still can't believe she's letting me come over. I mean, she seemed like quite the ice queen before, but now I think she's starting to trust me. We drive north to Shoreline, and Lexi parks along the curb in front of an eclectic-looking apartment complex. Some kids are playing in the gated playground on the side of one of the buildings while couples sit on stone benches scattered around the center of the complex.

"Grab the food."

Lexi's voice snaps me out of my thoughts. I carry the bag and follow her to a building across the street. It's not as big as the main one. She taps her keycard on the reader attached to the door and lets us both in. The inside of this place is done up with a contemporary flair—carpeted flooring, bright-red and pastel-green walls with matching modern geometric furniture. Colorful track lights shine on framed artwork depicting coffee, music, and other images related to Seattle. We take the elevator up to the seventh floor and go a short way down the hall. It's quiet—totally the opposite of the twenty-four-seven chaos in my apartment building. Lexi's keys jingle as she fiddles with the lock on her door, but then she doesn't open it right away. She turns to me.

"I need you to promise me something," she says in a low tone.

I look at her seriously. "What?"

"Promise me you will keep what you see inside a secret."

I furrow my brow. *What else does she have to hide?*

"You promise?" Her expression hardens.

Smiling, I step up to her and kiss her lips softly. I hope I don't get slapped for it, but damn it, it just feels like the right opportunity. "I promise."

She tenses at the initial contact, and as I release the kiss, her face is full of fluster. She licks her lips and nods. "Okay," she says in a whisper.

A whoosh of ice-cold air hits me as she opens the door to a small studio apartment that looks like something straight out of a sci-fi movie. Atop two six-foot-long tables in the middle of the room is a spread of five computer monitors. Wires are snaking everywhere across the floor toward two big boxes set up near outlets on either side of the place. Set against one of the walls is a futon, which is made up of pink, anime-girl bedsheets. Sitting on the futon are two closed laptops and a tablet computer. Against another wall is a shelf of disassembled computer cases, electronic parts, and wires. The rest of the walls are covered with posters of tattooed, half-naked rock stars and giant road signs, which I assume were stolen. There's even a construction barrel with a working blinking light posted in one corner. It brings back memories of doing that shit with some of my friends years ago.

"Wow . . . " I say under my breath.

"You promised," she says in a normal volume.

"Yeah, I did. I just . . . wow, Lexi. You actually live here?"

"Yup." She takes the bag from me and totes it to the kitchen, where more electronic parts and another tablet computer sit on a countertop.

I rub my arms. "It's cold as fuck in here. Can we get it just a little bit warmer?"

"No can do, Knox. The servers will overheat."

I walk around to the long tables, under which six computer towers sit. They hum and blink, lively with multi-colored lights. "So, this is what a hacker's pad looks like, huh?"

"No, this is what *my home* looks like." She grabs some pots and pans from one of the cabinets. "Are you gonna help or what?"

I join her in the kitchen and begin unpacking the food. "I figured you were a tech geek, but holy shit, I think this place would give any tech geek an orgasm."

She laughs and washes her hands. "What's to say I don't get an orgasm every time I wake up in the morning?"

I raise my eyebrows.

"Kidding, Knox. Geez." She playfully flicks water from her wet hands at me then dries them.

"Hey." I grin and wash my hands. I don't flick her back, though.

She hands me a knife. "You peel the potatoes. I'll do the chicken."

I pick up a potato and start peeling. "So, who was that weird guy who was eyeing you like fresh meat today when I stopped by?"

She chuckles. "You sound jealous."

I stop peeling and look at her. "What? No, I'm not jealous. That guy looked old enough to be my father." I scrunch my face. "Do you have a thing for old guys or something?"

"Oh my God." She laughs out loud. "No, Knox. I don't have a 'thing' for old guys. That guy you saw is a fucking pervert. Comes to the shop almost every month to get me to 'touch-up' some of his old ones." She cringes. "He's got a fucking monkey on his left ass cheek. Grossest thing I've ever seen. He always says he needs an ink touch-up there, but I know what kind of *touch-up* he really wants. Ugh."

I look hard at her. "You don't really give that guy the satisfaction, do you?"

"If you mean getting off on mindlessly touching his ass cheek, then *hell* no. I touch up his ink like he wants because he is a paying customer, and I need money to eat. I charge him out the ass—no pun intended—for every job he wants me to do, though. I hoped I would overcharge him right out of his business, but he seems to be coming *more* now. Seriously, I think he's made of money."

"What does he do?"

She purses her lips and lays out some foil in a pan, not answering right away.

I look at her carefully. "You know what he does?"

"He gambles," she finally replies. "I know about him and some of his other friends."

"Okay. So, that's why you didn't want to take his tip money, right?"

"Pretty much."

"Do I need to teach this guy a lesson for harassing you?"

She chuckles. "That's adorable, Knox, but no. I don't need a knight in shining armor. He has his uses."

"What kind of uses?"

She shakes her head. "After dinner, Knox."

I roll my eyes, finish peeling four potatoes, and then rinse them off in the sink. Lexi adds spices to the raw chicken breasts and puts them in the pan.

"Cut the potatoes up into wedges," she instructs while she sets the pan in the oven.

I do so without a word. She stands beside me, watching as I carefully slice the potatoes up the way she wants.

"So, since you're Dominick's brother, does that mean you're also a master chef?" she asks.

The knife slips in my hand, and I nearly slice my thumb. "What?"

Smiling, she takes the knife and finishes cutting the potatoes. "I take that as a no. Dominick is an *amazing* chef. Denise gets specially cooked meals regularly. She even gets breakfast in bed, that lucky bitch! I swear that girl is spoiled rotten. I'm *so* jealous."

I smile weakly and watch her, the subject of Dominick leaving a bitter taste in my mouth. "Sounds like he really loves her. That's what loving couples do, right?"

She shrugs. "I guess."

"Do you like it when a guy cooks for you?"

Lexi blinks several times and looks dubiously at me. "Uh, *yeah*? I think every girl likes it. Of course, finding a guy who can *actually cook* is another thing. But it's the thought that counts, right? Last boyfriend I had—long, long ago—made me a peanut butter sandwich as an apology for forgetting to heal me during a raid on SwordCraft Online. Of course, I couldn't help but forgive him." She scowls. "Then about a week later, I caught him at the club, cheating with some dirty whore, talking about buying her a year subscription and shit."

I gawk at her.

"Sorry for rambling."

"Uh, it's all right."

She falls silent as she wraps the potato wedges in foil and sticks the whole thing in a toaster oven next to the stove. She wipes down the countertops and then brews some coffee. "Want some?"

I wrinkle my nose. "Nah, I don't drink coffee."

She looks at me, wide-eyed. "How the hell can you visit Seattle and not drink at least one cup of joe?"

"I never could get used to the taste."

She shakes her head. "You're weird." She heads to the desk chair in front of the computer setup and plops down with a sigh.

I smile and follow her.

She switches on the monitors, and the screens come to life, each displaying something different. She takes off her sneakers. I do the same and stand behind her chair, my hands resting on her shoulders.

"So, will I have the honor of watching you 'work'?" I ask.

"Yes, but only because you promised to keep this to yourself." She looks over her shoulder at me, her expression stern. "Don't make me regret it."

"Hey, you know stuff about me that I don't want others to know, so I think we're even."

She smiles at that and turns back around.

"By the way," I continue, "you haven't told Dominick, Kevin, or any of your friends about me, have you?"

"I haven't told them who you *really* are, if that's what you mean. For all my friends know, I finally got my vajayjay out of retirement." She snorts a laugh.

Smiling, I begin to give her neck and shoulders a gentle massage. Her body relaxes. I have no idea what I'm seeing on the screens. One of them is blue with crazy scientific and mathematical words and numbers written on it. Another is black with similar text, and another screen displays some kind of program while the two screens on the end display a 3D massively multiplayer online game.

"Talk about multitasking." I laugh.

She types commands and a bunch of numbers on the black screen, and more computer gibberish pops up.

"What are you doing?" I ask.

"Checking to see who else has been on the website."

"I haven't been able to get any fights scheduled because of cops sniffing around."

"Yeah, the organization's put things on hiatus till the smoke settles. Sucks for me, because it makes it all the harder to find my targets."

I'm about to ask her who her targets are when a message pops up on the screen with the strange program.

She grumbles. "Damn it. What does he want now?" She clicks over to the screen and types her reply.

"Is that Nash from work?"

"Yes. And I really shouldn't be letting you see this. This shit's confidential."

"I told you I wouldn't say anything." I glimpse the screen, where another message pops up from someone named Bianca. "Have any of your friends been at your place before?"

"Only once. But they don't like coming here because they say it's too cold." She replies to Bianca and closes the box. I laugh.

Nash replies in his message box with some complex computer code. Lexi transfers the code to the black screen and initiates it. Her eyes light up as more code is displayed in response. She whistles and mutters, "Thank you, Nash. You haven't lost your touch."

I furrow my brow, trying to make sense of it all. "Wait, is Nash a hacker, too?"

"He used to be. Then he decided to open up a tattoo parlor instead. I'm his protégé, if you can imagine. He still has access to a lot of stuff I need to crack this case."

I suck in a breath. *What case? A cop case?*

"Monkey-butt's in cahoots with the organization running the gambling business. But he also knows me on a personal level."

"How?"

She bites her bottom lip. "I just . . . have had personal encounters with him. *Not* in the suggestive way it sounds."

I frown and watch as she types more code, and the black screen starts continuously scrolling up with more and more text appearing. Occasionally, a message outputs on the blue screen. Lexi picks up a game controller from the table and clicks over to the two screens at the end.

I begin to smell the coffee brewing, so I go to the kitchen and pour her a cup. I bring it and the cream and sugar to her because I have no idea how she likes it.

"Hey, think you can do me a favor?" I ask.

She sets the game controller aside and prepares her coffee—a little cream and lots of sugar. "That depends. What's up?"

"Think you can get me in on another fight somewhere? My trainer's sorta given up on that."

She takes a long sip and relaxes in her chair. "I could, but why do you want to fight so bad?"

I rub the back of my head. "Well, I could use the money, for one, and I . . . I just need to do something to beat out the bad shit I've had to deal with recently."

"Bad shit, huh?" She arches an eyebrow. "You seem to be overflowing with baggage. What's eating you now?"

I feel as if I can talk to Lexi about this. I mean, she seems like a good listener. Besides, she's trusted me enough to let me into her apartment and see things that the FBI would probably have a field day with. But I need to sit down for this, because just thinking about it makes me weak in the knees. I sit on the futon, lean forward with my elbows on my knees, and clasp and unclasp my hands.

Lexi spins around in her chair and faces me.

"A friend of mine committed suicide the other day," I say in a low voice. "She was only twenty-three."

Lexi's face falls. "Whoa, I'm sorry to hear that."

"What really sucks is that I could've prevented it."

"What are you talking about?"

I sigh. "It was my fault . . . "

"What!" She gets up from the chair and approaches. "You can't take the blame for other people's instability."

I say nothing and stare at my hands.

"Was she your girlfriend or something?"

I shake my head quickly. "No, though I think she wanted something to happen between us. But I wasn't interested in her like that."

She touches my face and lifts my chin up. "Hey, it's not your fault."

I swallow. "But you don't understand. I saw the signs. I knew the road she was treading, and I ignored it. I don't know why. I just . . . *chickened out.*"

"Fuck that. You're not a coward."

"No, Lexi, I am. That's one of the reasons why I came out here. That's why I ran away at fifteen. That's why I fight."

She lets go of my face. "What the hell are you so afraid of?"

Becoming my father. Taking the easy way out. Because my life is a fucking mess right now. "Lexi, I really like you. But I don't want to hurt you."

"What? You think I want to fight you?"

"I mean *emotionally*."

Her gaze hardens. "Why the fuck would you do that?"

"Because I'm damaged goods." *Really damaged.*

"And you think I'm sunshine and rainbows? Get a grip, Knox. You're not the only one in the world with a sob story."

I bury my face in my hands, my glasses getting pushed to the top of my head. "Find me a fight, please. I don't care who or where."

One of the computers makes a strange sound, and I uncover my face. Lexi returns to the monitors. She starts typing furiously on the keyboard. "Oh, fuck yes. This is good," she mutters.

"What?"

"I found the evidence I need to end this shit." She spins back around in her chair, facing me and grinning like a fool.

I wrinkle my brow, still confused.

The smile fades, and she gets up and goes to the kitchen. "I don't like the underground fighting, Knox. Not when there are people like Monkey-butt supporting it. I've been tracking the website—the organization—for some time, trying to find clues to the evidence I need to shut it down."

Her tone is serious, almost a little scared. Is she jeopardizing her life with all this hacking she's doing?

I get up and go to her with long strides. "Whoa. Hold up. What organization? Who are these guys? Are you in danger?"

Not responding right away, she checks the potato wedges still cooking in the toaster oven. "You think it's just a site that does a little illegal gambling with the fights. But there's far more than gambling going on. It runs deep. I'm talking drug dealers and gunrunners and other lowlifes. The owner is being strung along like a fucking puppet while things happen behind his back. But I can't reveal anything to the cops until I've gotten enough clear evidence. And no, I'm not in danger. Not directly. No one knows what I'm up to. Nash taught me well." She grins wryly at me.

I'm not sure what to say. I can't understand why she's playing digital detective and snooping around a dangerous bunch of people like this. She opens one of the cabinets and reaches for some plates, but I grab her arm—gently—and stop her. "Hey. Who's the owner?"

She averts her eyes. I pull her close to me, spin her around, and tilt her chin to force her to look at me. "Lexi," I say softly.

Scowling, she jerks her head, and my hand slips from her chin. "My father."

Chapter 15

Surely my ears must be deceiving me right now, because I thought Lexi said her father was the man behind the underground fighting organization. Which would mean she probably kept tabs on me for years. And I can only guess what her father might have done.

I stare at Lexi in disbelief, releasing her from my grip. Silence fills Lexi's studio except for the low hum of the computers. "Wait. Hold up. Say that again?"

"Look. I'm not exactly proud to admit that."

Nope. My ears are definitely not deceiving me. "Holy shit . . ."

"You don't know the half of it."

"You mean, all this time . . . all these years . . . I've been working for your dad?"

"He's been at this a long time. Many, many years. I've only recently learned about this. How long have you been fighting?"

"About seven years. My trainer, Dante, didn't want me to get caught up in that shit until I turned eighteen."

"My dad's been all over the place. He's got money, and lots of it. Unfortunately, money makes people do stupid shit." She scowls. "It's a long story. And one I don't care to tell."

"You don't have to tell it if you don't want. I just . . . I'm just trying to understand where you're coming from."

"Enough about that. I just want to enjoy the rest of the night. Let's have dinner." She retrieves the plates and then grabs some potholders from a drawer, pulls out the pan of chicken, and sets it atop the stove.

I take out the potato wedges from the toaster oven. We fix our plates and lounge on the futon with our food.

"How about a movie?" Lexi asks. She turns on the wall-mounted TV.

I dive into my food, half listening. "Uh, sure," I say absentmindedly, hoping it was the right answer to whatever question she asked.

Lexi shuts down the MMO game that was taking up two of the computer monitors and loads up another application. A list of thousands upon thousands of movies scrolls endlessly across one of the screens. "What kind of movies do you like?"

"Fantasy, sci-fi, and action. But not in that specific order." I smile. "I am a sucker for martial-arts flicks, though. Admittedly, I skip to the fight scenes."

She laughs. "You too? I thought I was the only one who did that. Of course, there are always exceptions. Case in point . . . " She selects a movie, and it appears on the TV.

I didn't get a good look at the title on the monitor. However, once the movie starts, I immediately smile. "You didn't! *The Last Dragon*?"

Lexi grins as well. "It's a fucking cult classic! I totally fell in love with it when I first saw it as a kid. I think I've practically memorized every line."

I laugh. "Me too. This movie was what inspired me to take up martial arts when I was little."

"C'mon, what kid wouldn't want to be badass like Bruce Leroy?" She nudges me in the arm.

We enjoy the movie over dinner—and an awesome dinner it is. Lemon-pepper chicken and steak fries. Lexi continues to surprise me with her skills.

It's eight o'clock by the time the movie is done, and Lexi and I are curled up on the futon under a blanket. Her body's so warm against mine. My arms are around her, my hands gently massaging her midsection. I don't ever want to move from this spot.

"Do I need to take you back to Renton?" Lexi murmurs, her head resting against my shoulder.

"No, I brought my stuff with me. I'm thinking about getting a hotel." *Though I'd rather stay here.*

She sits up, breaking my embrace, and faces me. "If you want to stay here, you can, you know." Whoa, is she psychic?

I nervously push my glasses up the bridge of my nose. "Well, uh, I didn't want you to think I was trying to force my way in or something."

She rolls her eyes and leans her face close to mine. "Fuck that. I think we've established that there's something going on between us, right?"

Can't deny that. "Yeah, sure."

"Well, I don't know about you, but I wanna know what the hell it is."

"Yeah," I say, idly caressing the side of her face with the backs of my fingers. "But I don't want this to be some cut-and-dried relationship or for us to ever hang out because we feel obligated. I . . . I like you, Lexi. I just hope you don't get turned off by my baggage."

"I'm no stranger to baggage, Knox." She pauses and frowns. "Knox. I'd rather call you Michael. The name Knox reminds me too much of the underground shit that Monkey-butt sponsors."

I blink several times then laugh. The expression on her face is priceless. "Only my family calls me Michael," I say.

"So, is calling yourself Knox your way of running from your baggage?"

Yes. "No."

She looks at me skeptically. "Why'd you run from Dominick last night?"

I bite my bottom lip. "He's upset with me, Lexi. It's difficult to explain. Just know that I'm pretty much estranged from my brothers."

"I had a stepbrother. We were really close, but he hates his mom and kinda keeps his distance from my dad. I hate his mom, too. He left as soon as he turned eighteen, and I haven't heard from him since. I miss him. But he wanted nothing to do with the family."

"I'm sorry," I say.

"Yeah, so am I. I just hope he's not dead somewhere. He had anger issues while he was at home."

"I'm sure you'll see him again."

"Are you ever going to tell me why Dominick and Kevin hate you so much?"

It's nothing she couldn't just dig up on the Internet, with her skills. Part of me wonders if she already knows everything and she just wants me to validate it. But I don't want to believe that she'd stab me in the back like that after she told me to my face that she doesn't snoop unless she has to.

Then another thought hits me. What if her father knows about my past? If Lexi's a hacker, he might very well be, too. Someone in his position would be more dangerous than her because he also has money to throw around. I shudder to think how much he could ruin my life, as well as my family's.

"Well?" Lexi says again, interrupting my thoughts.

My phone buzzes before I can reply, and I reach down next to the futon and pick it up. Uncle Adam's calling. I look at Lexi apologetically. "Sorry, I should take this."

"Whatever." She gets up, taking the blanket with her and leaving me with a sudden chill from the room. Wrapped in the blanket, she sits at her desk and begins typing away on the keyboard.

I answer the phone. "What's up, man?"

"Junior, are you coming home tonight?"

Pursing my lips, I look over at Lexi—or rather, the back of her. She's steadily typing away at one screen. Another screen shows the website for Kevin's online radio station. There's a countdown on the page for when the show starts live in a few hours. "I dunno, man. I'm in Seattle."

"I'm here at your mother's house. I was hoping to see you before you went back to New York. She said you were going to stay for the weekend."

I clench my jaw. "I didn't tell her that."

"Okay." He sighs. "I miss you, son. I wish you'd stop running."

"I'm not running."

"Will you at least come home for your birthday next week?"

Ugh, I totally forgot my birthday was next week. I *must* be getting old. "Maybe. We'll see. I gotta go, now."

"Son . . . "

I close my eyes.

"You can't keep running. If you call yourself a fighter, then damn it, be a man. Stand up to those demons, and fight. Don't let what happened in the past control your future."

I swallow a lump in my throat and don't reply.

"Hey," he continues.

I stay silent.

"You're *not* your father. And you never will be. Understand?"

I take a deep breath.

"I love you, son. Your mother loves you. Please try and see your brothers and find a way to mend this rift between you three."

My eyes sting, and I end the call, unable to reply. I lift my glasses and wipe my eyes, but they won't stop burning. Before Lexi can turn around and notice, I head into the bathroom and shut the door.

Chapter 16

Sunday afternoon, I'm punching out my frustration at the gym. I woke up before Lexi and left a small parting gift of eggs and toast waiting in the oven for when she got up. I've checked my phone periodically throughout the day for any texts or missed calls from Lexi, but there are none. Maybe she's busy. Or maybe she's upset I left without a word.

But what do I say to her? How do I say it?

The heavy bag thumps and sways with each punch and kick I deliver to it. I feel eyes on me, and I've no doubt acquired some spectators as I go all out on the bag, sweating like a pig. My arms and legs are numb from hitting so hard, but the numbness seems to calm the rage and frustration from Uncle Adam's call last night.

And Lexi . . . *God.* I don't know how long I stayed in the bathroom last night, but by the time I came out, the lights were off, and she was asleep on the futon. I kept my distance and slept on the floor, using my duffel bag as a pillow. It was cold and uncomfortable down there, but I'm still not entirely sure whether it's okay for me to be sleeping with her like that. She's just now starting to trust me. I don't want to fuck up again.

I deliver an uppercut to the bag. The blow puts a dent in the black vinyl, and then the spot disappears. I take a deep breath and steady the bag.

Damn it. Uncle Adam's right. I need to stop running. I'm going to be twenty-six in two days. For once, I'd like to enjoy a year of my life and not worry about those fucking demons.

Man up and fight. I stare long and hard at the bag, which is about a foot taller than me. Thoughts of ten years ago suddenly flood my mind. *Mama and I return home from the grocery store, and I help her unload the car and carry the bags through the side door that leads into the house.*

I deliver two jabs and a cross punch to the hanging bag.

Mama and I discover Dominick and Kevin's bodies laid out on the floor in the breakfast nook.

Jab, jab, cross, uppercut.

Dominick's pants are down. He's totally exposed. There's blood on him, and bruises and semen. He's not moving.

Jab, jab, cross, uppercut, hook punch, hook punch.

Kevin's body is crumpled. There's a small dent in the wall by his head. He's covered in blood, and more blood is smeared on the wall behind him and on the floor around him. There's a deep wound on one side of his neck.

Jab, jab, cross, uppercut, hook punch, hook punch, spinning back fist.

Mama screams. She cries. She yells for my father to come, but no one answers.

Jab, jab, cross, uppercut, hook punch, hook punch, spinning back fist, double roundhouse kick.

I notice the front door is open. The door handle is covered in blood. I look outside and realize Pops is gone, along with his car.

Jab, jab, cross, uppercut, hook punch, hook punch, spinning back fist, double roundhouse kick, back-spinning hook kick.

I pant as I watch the bag swing and sway every which way. My face and arms are slick with sweat.

"That was intense, man."

I look toward the source of the familiar voice. Jesse stands nearby, his hands all wrapped up like he's ready to go into the ring. He grins and salutes me.

"Hey, Jesse," I say.

"I love those moves. Think you can give me a few tips before I spar?"

I raise my eyebrows. "You're sparring?"

"Yup." He points to the circle of people spectating a sparring match. "Gonna try my hand at a Jiu-Jitsu guy. What do you think?"

"I think you're gonna get your ass kicked unless you know how to ground fight."

"I can stay on my feet." He grins and bounces around. "I've been working on my foot movement. I think I'm getting quicker."

I shake my head. "No, you need to start with someone who also fights on their feet before you do that ground-and-pound shit."

He stops bouncing and frowns.

I take off my gloves, stuff them in my duffel bag, and retrieve my hand wraps. "I'll spar with you."

Jesse blinks. "What? You serious?"

I nod and look toward the circle of contenders. The two guys in the middle look winded. It won't be long till that sparring match is over.

"Don't kill me, man," Jesse says with a nervous laugh.

I slap him on the back. "Relax. We're just having fun."

Cheering erupts from the crowd, cuing the end of the match. I step inside the ring of people and adjust my hand wraps as I wait for Jesse. He enters the ring nervously and takes a short fighting stance. I smile. *He's learning.*

I take a matching stance and wait for him to make the first advance. He's young, he's eager, he's liable to make mistakes, but he also wants to impress.

Just like me. *Holy shit.* I notice that fierce look in his eyes, and suddenly, I see myself looking up to my teacher. Master Rho would tell me to gear up for sparring, and I'd be in my foam gloves and footpads and biting down on my mouthpiece in no time.

Jesse fakes a jab then lunges in with a cross punch. I weave my body effortlessly and block his incoming fist. I counter with a double roundhouse kick, first to his ribs then to the side of his head. My foot's too quick for him. Both strikes connect, and they rattle him. He slowly shifts into a brawler's stance, leaving his entire front open for the pick-ings.

"Half of a target," I remind him.

He shifts his feet, looking unsure of himself. He's still a little open, and his hands are down, so I tap him on the nose—not too hard—with a back fist. He grunts.

"Hands up," I say, and he quickly complies.

We spar a solid thirty minutes. Jesse is learning quickly, and by the end, he's already starting to get hard to hit. Pant-ing and soaked in sweat, we collapse on the floor by a wall and guzzle from our water bottles.

"Thanks for the lesson," I say to Jesse.

Jesse stops drinking and looks at me with raised eye-brows. "What lesson? You taught *me* a lesson, man!"

I chuckle. "I'm always learning, just like you. Every spar-ring session I engage in is a new lesson."

"That sounds so . . . philosophical."

"In my stage of training, it's all about the knowledge and philosophy of the art."

"Are you a Karate master or something?"

"My style is Tae Kwon Do, and no, I am not a master." *Not yet, anyway.*

"Well, you sure fight and talk like one."

I smile and pat him on the back.

We hit the showers and leave the gym. It's after five o'clock, and I'm starving. Jesse walks beside me, his hands stuffed in his jacket pockets.

"When do you head back to New York?" he asks.

I shrug. "I don't know. Soon, I guess."

"Bummer. I guess I'm gonna have to find myself a new trainer soon."

I raise my eyebrows slightly. "You thought I was your trainer? All we did was munch around."

"Fuck that. You showed me how not to get my ass kicked. You know your shit. I wish you could train me. I really want to enter the next amateur fighting competition."

I look away toward the busy streets. His words are flattering; I sure as hell have never had anyone say something like that to me before. "Just keep working hard. You'll go far."

He grins and presses the button to cross the street. "I'm gonna head home. Maybe we can do it again tomorrow night after I get off work?"

I nod. "Yeah, sure. Take it easy, man."

When he leaves, I check my phone. Lexi still hasn't called or texted me. I decide to call her instead.

"What do you want?" she answers, flatly.

I chew my bottom lip as I idly walk toward the tattoo shop she works at. But the sign says it's closed on Sundays. I don't care. I lean against the wall of the shop. Just being here makes me think of her more. "Hey, wanna get a late lunch somewhere?"

There's a brief silence. "You've gotta be out of your fucking mind, Michael."

I cringe. "Knox, remember?"

"You run from the world and run from your own fucking name. Maybe you're right. You *are* a coward."

My palms get sweaty, and I almost drop the phone.

"I don't need to hear any more of your bullshit excuses. Don't call me anymore. Hell, don't even text me. I have enough drama in my life. I don't need you adding to it."

"Lexi, I'm sorry . . . "

The call suddenly ends.

I stare at her number on the screen. "Damn it!" I growl, slamming my fist against the wall. *Fucked up again. What the hell's wrong with me?*

I try to calm my mind. Hunger overtakes me, and I manage to push aside my troubles with Lexi for now. I take the bus to the University District, where there are bound to be plenty of choices for food.

The bus stops on the corner of a strip of businesses, and I get off, the cold air hitting my face, replacing the comfortable warmth from the bus's interior with a chill throughout my body. I stuff my hands in my jacket pockets and wander down the sidewalk, taking in the sights and smells of the various restaurants and food trucks. I walk past shops selling clothing, some of it with the University of Washington's "W" logo. Some of the people I pass wear purple sweatshirts and hoodies with that logo on the front, showing their college pride. I feel so out of place here, being a high school dropout.

Something in the distance catches my eye, a sight I've not seen in over ten years. A neon red-and-green PIZZA sign blinks steadily over a weathered green awning. It's Loriano's, where my parents used to take my brothers and me as kids whenever we visited Seattle. It was the only place in town that made truly authentic, New York-style pizza like what we used to get in the Bronx.

I can't believe the place is still here after all these years. My stomach growls just thinking about biting into one of their famous big-as-your-head slices. Diet? What diet? I'm in fucking heaven right now.

I head to the restaurant, which is on the corner of Brooklyn Avenue and Fiftieth. A few cars and a red motorcycle are parked along the curb. The building's green paint is peeling, giving it a grungy, rustic look.

The wooden glass door gives a familiar creak as I enter the restaurant. It's not very busy. There's a large family sitting at a table in the front and a few people in a booth in the back. I order a slice of pepperoni, and—

"Oh, man. You guys still have Italian ices?" My eyes widen when I notice what's sitting in the display freezer. Pleasant memories of my childhood come to the forefront. I used to crave those little cups of lime-flavored ice, which I'd eat with a tiny wooden scraper.

The woman laughs as I swipe a cup and set it with my pizza and lemonade. "They're a bit of a hit, especially in the summer."

These ices taste good no matter what time of the year it is. After paying for my food, I find a booth and enjoy my meal in peace. A nearby TV hanging from the ceiling is tuned in to a pro football game.

Finishing the last of my pizza and ice, I'm left with a bittersweet feeling in my mind. It's not often I recall something positive about my childhood and spending time with my family. My brothers and I were closer back then, especially when we'd go on family outings to Seattle. We went to the

Space Needle one day. Pops took lots of pictures. It was cool to be so high up, as if we were flying, looking down on the city. Dominick, Kevin, and I pretended we were superheroes. Life was great.

No wonder Mama wants her family back. I sigh as my mind returns to the present. With my straw, I play with what's left of the ice in my lemonade cup. *I need to stop running and help Mama get her family back.*

Laughing erupts from a booth in the back, drawing my attention to the group of people—three in all. I notice the top of a purple, slicked-back Mohawk. Adjusting my glasses, I squint at the other two people sitting on the other side. *Dominick and Denise.*

Denise is bundled in a light-brown sweater and a yellow scarf. Her hair is cornrowed in a cool design. It's the first time I actually get a good look at her face. She's got beautiful, exotic eyes, a little button nose, and an amazing smile.

Sitting next to her, Dominick wears a purple hoodie with "WASHINGTON" on the front. He smiles and laughs at something Lexi says then rubs the back of his head in the same habit I've always remembered him doing whenever he's embarrassed. I haven't seen Dominick smile like that since we were kids—before the bad shit happened.

My heart suddenly pounds. *No, damn it. You're not running away again.* I get up from my seat, dump the garbage from my tray, and head toward the back of the restaurant. My footsteps slow as I draw nearer to the group. Denise is the first one to notice me, then Dominick.

I nervously push my glasses up the bridge of my nose and stuff my hands in the pockets of my hoodie. My eyes linger on Denise then rest on Dominick. He narrows his eyes slightly then tilts his head as though he's trying to recognize me.

I lick my dry lips. Suddenly, time seems to go slower as I stare at my little brother for the first time in years. "Hey, Li'l D . . ."

Dominick blinks, and his mouth hangs open.

Lexi snaps her attention my way. She glowers. "Michael?"

"Michael . . ." Dominick says in almost a whisper.

Denise scrunches her brow. "Michael?" she says as if wondering who the hell I am.

It takes everything I have to not have a mental breakdown over that damn name. I tighten my fists in my hoodie pockets.

"What are you doing here?" Lexi says. "I told you to leave me alone. Get the fuck out of here."

I look at Lexi sadly then over to Dominick, whose expression has hardened. "I just wanted to see my brother," I say, not taking my eyes off him.

He frowns. "You heard her. Get the fuck out of here."

I sigh and lower my head. "Right . . . well, I missed you, little brother." I turn to leave. "And I'm sorry again, Lexi."

Lexi doesn't respond.

I take a step, pause, and look over my shoulder. "By the way, congrats on your engagement, Li'l D." With that, I leave without another word.

CHAPTER 17

I WAKE UP AND STARE AT THE GRUNGY CEILING OF AN apartment. It takes me a moment to realize where I am, but then I move around on a couch and suddenly remember: I shamelessly called Jesse last night asking if I could crash at his place in exchange for doing a little extra training with him. Of course, he didn't mind, nor did his pothead roommate, Brandon, whom I only met briefly.

I stretch and yawn, the sunlight beaming on me from the bent-up blinds. It's Monday. *Damn.* Where did the weekend go? A lot of shit's happened in these past few days. Yesterday was a complete disaster. But what the hell was I thinking would happen? Of course, Dominick would tell me to fuck off. And Lexi, too. But there was definitely no excuse for what I did to Lexi. I don't want to give her any more ammunition to dig up the bones of my past. It's still bugging me that I pissed her off so much—twice. I'll make it a point to go down to her job and talk to her one last time.

I check my phone. It's not even nine o'clock yet. The apartment's quiet. Jesse's already gone to work at the coffee shop. Who'd have thought a tough kid like him was a barista? Brandon is gone, too. He's a maintenance worker for a small business in town.

I spot a key sitting on the coffee table with a sticky note that says, "Make yourself at home. -Jesse."

Holy shit. They left me the spare key to this place and everything. These guys really trust me. That's much more than I could say about Dominick or Lexi.

Dominick, I'll have to deal with later. But Lexi . . . I owe her an explanation even though I should probably leave her alone. Then I think about that guy, "Monkey-butt," who's been harassing her. I should do something to help her—even if she tells me to fuck off afterward.

After what she told me about him—that he's affiliated with the underground fighting organization I was involved in for so many years—I've finally decided to give up that shit. I feel a lot better training Jesse for the amateur circuits. Dante was right. This was what I needed. It's a breath of fresh air. Dante will think I've totally lost it when I return to New York.

I decide to forego the gym today and do a light workout here in the apartment. I pump out five hundred push-ups, do all of my Tae Kwon Do forms, and practice a little shadow boxing before heading to the shower. The water pelts my back as I think about what I'm going to say to Lexi. I hope she gives me a chance to explain. This time, I'm not running away.

By noon, I'm stepping off the bus, which stops a few blocks from the tattoo parlor. The cold, dry air makes my face itch. I pull my beanie farther down on my head, stuff my hands in my pockets, and walk in silence. The city's busy during the lunch hour, with almost every eatery filled.

The bells of the door jingle as I enter the parlor, which is comfortably warm inside. Business is slow, it seems, with only two customers being worked on while Nash and another male employee are at the front desk shooting the shit. I don't see Lexi anywhere.

I remove my beanie and unzip my jacket.

Nash peeks around the other guy. "Hey, it's Lex's booty call. 'Sup, man?"

Booty call? I cringe. "Naw, it ain't like that."

Nash throws his head back and laughs. "Riiiight."

His colleague snickers.

"Is she around?" I ask.

Nash smirks. "Yeah, she's with a customer right now. Sorry, I can't have her leaving work early again, as much as I'd love for her to get some. Business is business, y'know."

"She's just a friend, man. Nothing serious."

"You shitting me? After the way she looked at you and tugged you along like a puppy on a leash the other day?" He leans back in his chair and props his feet up on the counter. "'Nothing serious' my ass."

I slump my shoulders. It's useless trying to convince him of anything. "I really need to see her. When does she get off work?"

"Keep your dick in your pants, man. She gets off at five. Now, unless you have an appointment with her, then—"

"You guys do walk-ins?" The words are already out of my mouth before I realize what I just said.

Nash and the other guy stare at me dubiously then look at each other. "Uh, yeah, if we're not busy, we do," Nash says to me. "But—"

"Can you fit me into her schedule today?"

Nash hardens his gaze. "You gonna get some ink?"

I chew my bottom lip. I'm not sure about getting a new one, but I guess she could just touch up the ones I already have. "Yeah, sure."

Nash gives me one last skeptical look and then checks his tablet computer. "She's got an opening at one thirty if you can wait that long."

I glance at the artsy-looking clock on the wall. It's about twelve thirty. "Sounds great. Pencil me in."

"You better not be bullshitting, man." Nash taps the screen and types some info. "Your name is Knox, right?"

I nod. But somehow, when he says my name, it doesn't sound quite right. Maybe this is what Lexi meant about not liking that name. Her voice remains in my head as I fill out paperwork and then sit in the waiting area.

You run from your own damn name. I'm a coward of the worst kind.

I try to clear my thoughts by flipping through a music magazine. But then I stop at an article about some Asian gothic-punk star. The picture of her decked out with spiky, dark purple hair, a face full of makeup and piercings, and a sexy black studded-leather outfit with silver chains and buckles makes me think about Lexi.

I toss the magazine back on the leather ottoman with others and pass the rest of the time playing a game of spades on my phone. Out of the corner of my eye, I notice the curtain in the back of the shop moving, and a woman wearing a tight halter top, a painted-on blue skirt, and three-inch pumps emerges. The light-brown skin just above her right breast is a shade of red from where a white bandage is partially visible. As she passes by, she sneaks a look in my direction, smiles, and heads to the counter.

Moments later, Lexi comes through the curtain. She relaxes in an empty chair in the back and sighs, looking exhausted. She doesn't seem to notice me right away.

"Yo, Lex, your boyfriend's here to get some ink," Nash calls from the front counter.

Lexi rubs her face then suddenly stops and looks toward Nash and then at me. She lowers her hand from her face and pops up from the chair. "Oh, *hell* no."

I get up as well, trying to smile, but the anger in her voice keeps me from doing so.

She storms over to the counter and slams her hands on the top, causing Nash to jump in his chair. "First of all, he's not my fucking boyfriend. Second, I'm *not* gonna ink him. Let someone else do it."

Nash rolls his eyes. "Geez, you guys oughta get married, the way you go on with this melodrama."

I let out a sharp breath as though I've been punched in the gut. *Did Nash just say that? Holy shit—what an asshole.*

Lexi's eyes widen. She raises her hand as if she's about to slap him but controls herself and balls her hand into a fist instead. "Fuck. You."

Nash smirks. "Look, Anna and Blaze are booked solid for the rest of the day. You're the only one with free spots. Unless you want me to call up Mason Engle and ask him if he wants another *retouch*." He laughs darkly.

Lexi scrunches her face. "Don't you fucking dare, Nash. I swear, I'll kick your ass if I see that fucking pervert today."

Mason Engle . . . is that Monkey-butt?

Nash raises his eyebrows expectantly.

Lexi sulks and approaches me, glowering. "What are you getting?"

I half smile. Man, she looks hot when she's angry. "Think you can touch up my back?"

She looks horrified. "Fuck. No."

"I heard that, Lex," Nash says from the counter.

She gives him the finger, but Nash ignores it.

"Either you're getting new ink, or you're getting the hell out of here," she says to me.

I swallow. If I leave now, I'll probably never see her again. I won't be able to surprise her like this again, and she'll most likely warn Nash about me. Nash doesn't seem to understand what's really been happening between us.

Well, tomorrow's my birthday, so what the hell. New ink for a new person.

"Fine. I want one right here." I trace a circle on the left side of my chest, over my heart.

Lexi arches an eyebrow then purses her lips. She spins on her heel and marches toward the back of the shop. I follow her through the curtain. We enter another curtained-off room with a table that looks like something you'd find in a doctor's office. The top of the table is covered in white tissue paper. Next to the table is a chair and another small table with various tattooing instruments and bottles of ink, all covered in small plastic baggies. She grabs some more items from the wall shelves and sets them on the table.

"Take off your shirt and lie down," she says coldly.

I remove my jacket and pull off my shirt then hang them over the back of another chair. I hop up on the table and watch her get set up. As she turns back to me, she pauses, her eyes traveling the length of my bare chest and back, and she looks rather awestruck for a moment, but then her features tighten again, and she clears her throat.

"You better not be wasting my time, Michael," she mutters.

I flinch at the name. "I'm not. I want a tattoo."

"You don't sound very sure of yourself."

"Because I'm not sure where or how to begin to tell you how sorry I am."

"Yeah, you are a sorry excuse for a man."

I sigh. "I wouldn't come here like this, letting you ink me, if I wasn't serious."

She eyes me coolly. "What kind of tat do you want?"

I think for a moment. I spot her necklace, the one that's been etched in my mind since I first saw it. "That." I point to the skull and rose design.

She looks amused. "A bit feminine for you, eh?"

"I don't care. It'll remind me of you."

The amusement quickly lifts, and she's annoyed again. "Look, don't take this the wrong way, but this is just business. There's nothing going on between us."

"Funny, I thought there was . . . " I gaze at her intently.

She looks back at me for a few moments then breaks the stare. "So, you want this over your heart?" She traces a small circle around the area.

Her touch is soft yet electrifying. I close my eyes briefly. "Yeah . . . "

I suddenly feel her touch the side of my shoulder, where one of my old tattoos is. I shiver a moment and then open my eyes.

"What's this symbol?" she asks.

"It's Chinese for 'tiger.' I have another one on my right shoulder for 'dragon.'"

"When did you get them?"

"When I was nineteen. I visited a Wing Chun school one day and got to train with the students there and even talk with the master. He reminded me a lot of my late Tae Kwon Do master in that he told a lot of philosophical stories and applied them to real life. One of his stories, which I never forgot, was about the tiger and the dragon."

Lexi's face softens, the annoyance in her eyes fading. "So, what's the story?"

"The tiger is strong, brash, and powerful. He is fearless and relentless. The dragon is sneaky, cunning, and smart. He looks for the opportunity to strike. The tiger will attack in a headstrong way, creating the opportunity for the dragon to slip in unnoticed and make the kill.

"The Wing Chun master's philosophy about smart fighting really stuck with me when I started doing underground fighting. Because I was—still am—a little guy in a big man's world. I've always gotten underestimated. But I have to remember to be like the dragon and fight smart, and be like the tiger and fight hard. Applying those two concepts together, I become a deadly weapon.

"So, I got those tats as a reminder of who I am. My left side is my power side, and my right side is my speed side."

Lexi's mouth is slightly open when I finish. "Whoa. That's actually pretty cool."

I smile.

She pats the table's headrest. "Lie back and relax while I draw up a quick template."

I do as she says, and she turns and goes to another table, out of my line of sight. I hear paper rustling.

"You're a man of mystery, Michael."

"It's nothing you couldn't have just found out online, I'm sure," I say bitterly.

"Yeah, if I really want to be a bitch. Or is that what you want me to be?"

"I want you to be yourself."

The chair rubs against the linoleum floor. She approaches my line of sight and scowls. "Are you saying I'm a bitch?"

I blink. "What? No! *Hell* no! You're the most amazing girl I've ever met."

"Right." She holds up a paper, which has an image of her logo on it. "How's this?"

That's her logo, all right, and it's done pretty well for a quick sketch. "Wow, you're a talented artist."

She rolls her eyes. "I sure hope I am since it's my job, dork." She sets the paper aside, washes her hands, and puts on a pair of latex gloves. She returns to me with a bottle of alcohol, petroleum jelly, skin cleaners, and some prep pads.

I stare at her face while she begins cleaning the designated area of my chest with the cool liquids, the strong odor of the alcohol and chemicals assaulting my nose.

"You can ignore what I'm about to say, but I just feel like I have to tell you," I murmur while she works. "I meant what I said before—that I'm sorry."

She says nothing and rubs some sort of lotion on my skin. She then takes the paper and presses it firmly onto the area, holding it there for several moments.

"I should've not just up and left like that. You're right. I was a coward. You made me see that. And you made me reconsider what the hell I'm doing with my life." I lick my lips, which begin to feel dry from my nervousness. "I've given up the underground fighting. I'm gonna be a legit trainer instead. I've already taken a kid under my wing, teaching him some stuff. It's great."

She still says nothing and removes the paper. A clear outline of the logo is stamped on my skin. She holds up a mirror, allowing me to check the placement of the design. I give her a thumbs-up.

"I'm gonna turn my life around, Lexi. Because of you. Yeah, that sounds corny, but whatever. You've given me a reason to rethink my life. I mean, after seeing Dominick yesterday, I realize that's what I gotta do. And I'm not going to run away from myself. My name . . . " I pause. My heart begins to pound. "My name is Michael."

Still silent, Lexi dabs some petroleum jelly on a small area of the outline, reaches for the dreaded plastic-covered needle, and finally looks at me. "This is gonna sting a little."

"Yeah, I know the deal. Just get it over with."

Her face softens. "Do you want this tat or not?"

I think about her question. "Yeah."

"Once you get it, there's no turning back."

"In case you forgot, tomorrow's my birthday. What better way to start a new life than what I'm doing right now?"

Her brow furrows. "You're weird." She turns the needle on. "All right. It's your body. Don't say I didn't warn you."

The sound of the buzzing needle makes me cringe. *I want to do this.* "Hey . . . "

She shuts off the needle and looks at me questioningly.

"Are you still mad at me?"

She huffs. "Yes, I am . . . but I accept your apology. I've never had a guy begging for me to ink them just to say they're sorry."

I manage to smile. "I like you, Lexi. I'm sorry I weirded you out before. I wanna give things another shot. What do you say? Round two?"

She twists her lips into a small smile as she stares, then she leans over and kisses my lips. God, how I've missed those lips. I devour her kiss and flick my tongue over her lip ring as she slowly pulls away.

"Maybe," she murmurs. "But I'm still mad at you." She says that in a much more relaxed tone.

I smile. "Story of my life."

She turns the needle on again, and I shut my eyes.

Chapter 18

THE NEXT MORNING, I WAKE UP TO THE BUZZ OF AN incoming text. I fish for the phone, my hand shoving aside empty beer cans and an ashtray with one of Brandon's blunts on the coffee table. A sharp, burning pain suddenly sears my chest as I move, and I cringe. I slept shirtless last night, and my skin is still tender. Lexi insisted that I needed a bandage to cover it after she finished, but I refused. Well, now I'm paying the price.

I locate the phone, and Uncle Adam's message lights up the screen.

Hey son. Happy Birthday… hope youll come home today.

I rub my face. *Birthday.* Holy shit—I'm twenty-six today.

I scroll through my phone and find birthday messages from Dante and the rest of my friends in New York, and one from . . .

Lexi. I smile, staring at her message, which was sent from her actual phone number and not the secret one.

Happy Birthday, Michael. Hope it's good. <3

The little heart emoticon doesn't go unnoticed. I type a reply.

It's even better now, waking up 2 that message.

She replies back:

LOL

can I come see u at work today?

nope. Im booked. Waiting for my second client to come. Then Denise & I are doing stuff after work.

Her mention of Denise makes me think about Dominick, and I wonder what would be the best way to mend this trouble between us. If Lexi is waiting for a client, then she will have a few minutes to spare. I quickly dial her number.

"Don't call me while I'm working," Lexi says, foregoing the greetings.

I raise myself up, the sharp pain continuing to throb in my chest. "Sorry, but you said you were waiting for a client, so I figured you had some time to talk."

There's brief silence. "What do you want?"

"What do I want? I want to see Dominick, but I don't know how to find him."

"He doesn't want you to find him, obviously. You should quit while you're ahead."

"Yeah, I kinda figured that much. But it's about time I try and make amends with my brother."

She sighs. "Denise has been bummed out about Dominick. She said he's been acting all moody and shit. I think they just spend too much time together. I mean, seriously, they're attached at the hip."

"They *are* getting married soon."

"Yeah, well . . . Dominick needs to know what's up before I kick his ass myself. He's stressing out my friend."

I purse my lips. *Because of me, I bet.* "He and I are past due for a talk."

"Oh, geez. 'The Talk.' You know nothing good will probably come out of it."

"No, I'm not giving up. I have to do this. I'm twenty-six. It's about time I clean up all the messes I've made."

"If you say so."

"I do. Now, where's Dominick?"

"He's probably at class now. Then he goes to work in the afternoon. Tonight's his motorcycle club meeting, so he probably won't be home till nine."

"All right. Where does he live?"

"You're really asking for it, aren't you?" When I don't reply, she continues. "Whatever. Don't say I didn't warn you. He and Denise live at Emerald Gardens Apartments in Laurel Hurst. I'll text you the address."

I take mental notes. I'll have time to drop by Mama's for a bit before I go to see Dominick. "Great, thanks."

When we hang up, I stare longingly at her name and number on the screen. My phone suddenly switches to an incoming call from Uncle Adam.

"Hey, man," I answer.

"Junior. How're you doing today?"

"I'm awake, I'm alive, and I'm twenty-six." I laugh lightly. "What's going on, man?"

"I'm leaving Everett now—on my way back to Renton from a car show. I was wondering if you got my text this morning."

"I did. Thanks for the birthday wishes."

"Did you think about coming home?"

I sigh and stare out the window, which is half-covered by the blinds. "Yeah, maybe I'll come by for a bit, but I got some things to take care of tonight."

"That's fine, son. Well, I'm on the road now, so I can head down there and pick you up. How's that?"

I swallow. "Now?"

"I should be in Seattle in about thirty minutes or so. You going to be ready by then?"

"Uh, sure." I give him directions to the apartment, and we hang up. My chest burns again as my heart pounds as if it's about to beat right out of it.

Around eleven thirty in the morning, I notice a white SUV pulling up in the parking lot of the apartment complex, and a big, stocky man gets out the driver's side. *That's Uncle Adam,*

all right. He hasn't changed a bit. He's still the big bear of a man I'd always remembered.

I leave the spare key on the coffee table, grab my duffel bag, and head out the front door. Outside, I discover Uncle Adam in a black leather jacket, leaning against the hood of his SUV with his arms crossed. He occasionally checks his watch. He looks in my direction and waves, and I hustle over.

Uncle Adam's even stockier close up—like a brick wall. But he used to wrestle in high school, so it's no wonder. His frame is the total opposite of my father's, which I've inherited.

Uncle Adam extends his arms, smiling crookedly. "Hey, son."

I hesitate then inch forward and embrace him. His body is rigid, and he still smells like motor oil and sweat, as if he's been working on another one of his beloved antique cars.

He pats my back, we break the hug, and he looks me over. "How're you doing?"

"Good, man." I nod and pick up my duffel bag. "We leaving or what?"

He chuckles and walks around to the back of the SUV and opens the hatch. "Yeah, sure. Put your things in the back."

I do, and we hop in afterward and speed off. I watch the city pass me by as we zoom through the streets, making our way to the interstate.

"I'm glad you decided to come this time, Junior," he says, breaking the awkward silence. "I've missed you."

"Missed you too, man."

There's another moment of silence as we swerve around the sharp bend of the ramp leading onto the interstate.

"Dominick called me last night," he says. "Said he saw you over at Loriano's."

"Yeah, I was there. Totally wasn't expecting to see *him* there, though."

"He was pretty upset. Did you two talk?"

"Nope."

He frowns. "That's a shame. I wish you two would finally mend this rift."

"I want to. But I think it's too late. I've been gone for so long. I'm gonna try anyway, though. Just once. I'll talk to him man-to-man."

"That's smart. And if he still refuses to accept you, then, well . . . at least you can say you tried."

I nod. "A lot's happened since I've come out here, man."

"A lot of good, I hope."

"Sort of. I've given up underground fighting to be a trainer, for one."

His face lights up. "That's great news, son."

More silence. This time, my ears ring from the awkwardness. I keep my gaze focused out the window, away from Uncle Adam.

"You know," he says, "Kevin's first pro basketball game is in a week. Your mother and I got two courtside tickets in the mail yesterday from him. He even booked plane tickets and a hotel room for us."

I look over at him, surprised. "Hey, that's awesome, man. So, are you two gonna go?"

He nods. "We plan on it. It was definitely a surprise, I'll tell you what. Kevin also sent some tickets to Dominick and Denise, but Dominick won't be able to go because of school."

"That sucks."

"Eh, it is what it is. But I'm sure he'll check it out on TV." He glances over to me. "Hey, maybe Dominick can give you those tickets instead."

I guffaw. It would be awesome to attend Kevin's first pro game, but I'd rather not be the bringer of bad luck, showing my face where I'm not wanted. "Fat chance of that ever happening. Dominick wants nothing to do with me. Besides, I don't think Kevin would like it very much if he looked over and saw me sitting in Dominick's seat."

"I think you guys just need to talk it out."

"Easier said than done," I mutter.

By twelve thirty, we've arrived at Mama's house. Uncle Adam pulls into the driveway behind Mama's car, and we unload. We're not even halfway up the walkway when the front door flings open, and Mama pokes her head out. She's looking bright and cheery today.

"Hi, you two!" she says then looks at me. "Happy birthday, baby."

I approach her and give her a kiss on the cheek and a hug. "Thanks, Mama."

She and Uncle Adam hug briefly, and the three of us go inside. I join Mama in the kitchen, where slices of bread, a tomato, and an open bottle of mayonnaise sit on the counter. Uncle Adam remains in the living room. He switches the TV to the classic movie channel and plops down on the couch.

Mama hands me the tomato and a knife then rummages in the refrigerator for the lunch meat. "I'm glad you came home for your birthday. I was beginning to think that you weren't going to come back."

Frowning, I carefully cut the tomato into thin, even slices. "Sorry. I just . . . I needed to take care of some things in Seattle."

Her lips thin a moment. "I understand. But sometimes a mother just can't help but worry."

I half smile. "Hey, you need to stop worrying so much about me. Stop worrying about everyone else around you, and worry about your own health and happiness. You deserve to be happy, Mama."

She stands beside me with packets of deli-sliced ham and salami. "I'm happy, baby. And praise the Lord I'm in good health."

My smile falters, and I grab several slices of bread. "So, Uncle Adam said Kevin sent you and him some tickets to his game," I say, changing the subject.

Mama takes two slices from me and smears them with mayonnaise. "Oh, yes! I'm so excited! Did you know his team plays Chicago on opening day? That means Kevin's going to play against Fresco Davis!"

I stare openmouthed. "*The* Fresco Davis?" I'm not much of a basketball fan, but even *I* know about the greatest pro basketball player in our lifetime.

Mama nods.

"That'll be some game."

"Kevin said tickets to this game sold out within three hours of going on sale a couple months ago."

I whistle. "You and Uncle Adam will have to take a picture with Fresco."

She laughs. "We'll try."

We finish making the sandwiches, and the three of us gather in the breakfast nook to enjoy it. My nerves stay calm, even though we're eating in here. It's weird how quickly I've been able to overcome that fear.

Now, if only the same could happen between my brothers and me.

Chapter 19

The rest of my day is spent with Mama and Uncle Adam, catching up on their plans. They'll be leaving for New York this Sunday. Mama made all my favorite foods for dinner, including a vanilla cake. I swear, the smothering is annoyingly excessive, but she only means well.

Still, I've stayed here longer than I wanted to. It's almost eight thirty, and Lexi said Dominick would be home by nine. The evening news cuts to a commercial, and I get up from the couch. "I gotta go now, Mama."

"Oh, you have to go so soon?" Mama says, getting up as well.

Uncle Adam stays put on the couch. He looks up at me.

"Yeah, I got some things to take care of in Seattle," I reply.

"Again?" She sighs. "It's that girl, isn't it?"

I don't respond.

"Baby, as long as you're happy, that's all that matters. That's all I've ever wanted for you and your brothers. I would love to get to know the girl who's stolen my oldest son's heart." She smiles at that then moves in to hug me.

I smile as well. There's no hiding anything from Mama. As we hug, Mama presses right against my tattoo, which is hidden under my pullover hoodie, and I wince.

She kisses my cheek, seemingly oblivious to my pain. "I love you, baby."

"Love you too, Mama," I say hastily then pull out of the embrace.

Uncle Adam finally gets up. "Need a ride back to the city?"

The offer's tempting, but I don't want him to know my plans. Chances are he'll call Dominick beforehand or try to interfere. I know how much he wants us together again, but I don't think he realizes how delicate the situation is. Sometimes he can be a little too ambitious.

"Uh . . . " I say slowly.

"Of course he does, Adam," Mama says. "I'm not letting him spend money on a taxi again."

He smiles and nods then swipes his keys from the coffee table.

Not wanting to argue, I grab my duffel bag and head to the door.

"Oh, wait! Take some food with you," Mama says, rushing to the kitchen.

I turn away and sigh. "That's okay, Mama."

Uncle Adam notices my expression and smiles, patting my back reassuringly.

"There's plenty of food left. Just take a plate, okay?" she says from the kitchen. Moments later, she appears with a foil-wrapped paper plate.

I gingerly take it. "Thanks."

She sees Uncle Adam and me to the door. "Take care, baby. Call me sometime, okay? I love you."

Cool air sweeps across my face as I step outside. I head for Uncle Adam's SUV while he and Mama say their goodbyes. Soon, we're back on the road again. I search on my phone for a place near where Dominick lives so Uncle Adam can drop me off there.

"When do you go back to New York?" Uncle Adam asks, breaking the silence.

I look up from my phone and realize we're already on the interstate. "Next week, probably. I want to get back to Dante and see how things are holding up with him."

"Dante's your trainer, if I remember correctly?"

"Yeah." *Among other things.*

"I hope he doesn't persuade you to fight illegally again."

"He won't. He's been trying to get me to quit that shit for years."

He smiles. "That's good, son."

Half an hour later, we pull up in front of a shoddy-looking motel. We say our goodbyes, and I get out with my things. Once Uncle Adam drives off, I cross the street and begin walking in the direction of Dominick's apartment complex. A red sport bike sits by the door, and a tricked-out hatchback sedan is parked in a space in front of his apartment.

I reach his door and hear rap music. But there aren't any lights on, from what I can see. My hands suddenly get clammy. I swallow, my throat constricting. *This is it. My last chance. I can't run away this time.* I ring the doorbell and wait. After a few moments, I ring it again. I hear the music get turned down a notch, so I ring the bell again.

The door opens, and Dominick appears, wearing a Washington Huskies sweatshirt and baggy jeans. He looks me up and down and scowls.

"Hey, Li'l D," I say with a small wave.

Dominick narrows his eyes. "How the hell did you find me?"

"Uh . . . " I nervously push my glasses up the bridge of my nose. "A little birdie told me."

Dominick begins shutting the door. "Get the fuck out of here."

I wedge my foot in between the door and the frame. "Wait."

His nostrils flare, and his face grows darker.

"Can we *please* talk?"

"There's nothing to talk about, you son of a bitch. Your actions speak louder than words."

I sigh and lower my head. "Yeah, I've been a real coward running away from the problem. But I'm turning my life around now, man. I want to mend this shit with you and K. Please, just hear me out."

He glowers at me for several long moments. "Fine. Five minutes."

"Great. Uh . . . it's cold out here. Can I come in?"

He hesitates then opens the door all the way and steps aside to let me in. Warmth immediately spreads through me. I glance around at the place. It's small and quaint, with white walls that are mostly bare and sparse furniture placed here and there. But little touches—a floral centerpiece on the coffee table, cute fuzzy frog slippers by the front door, and a decorative pink throw blanket on the couch—tell me a female has been here.

I look back at Dominick, who crosses his arms and watches me expectantly.

"Nice car, by the way," I say, breaking the silence.

"Thanks. Kevin gave it to me before he moved to New York."

"That was generous of him." I set down my duffel bag and hold out the covered foil plate. "Here."

Dominick arches an eyebrow. "What the hell's that?"

I smile slightly. "Food from Mama's. She made a kickass dinner for me today."

He pauses then takes the plate and peeks beneath the foil. His face softens, and his eyes widen. "Holy shit. Are those . . . collard greens?"

"Yup."

He re-covers the plate. "Okay, so why were you at Mama's?"

"The same reason why I'm here, little brother. To fix my shit."

His expression goes rigid again.

"Look. I know a simple 'I'm sorry' is not gonna cut it. It's been years, and all that time, I thought running away from the problem would help things, but it only made them worse. I realize that now."

"You knew what happened, and you ran off like a scared bitch. Like *him*."

I shut my eyes a moment. "Yeah . . . it serves me right I have to bear his fucking name."

Dominick's face falls, and instead of replying, he turns and heads to the kitchen. I consider following him but instead detour to the living room and sit on the worn leather couch. It looks as though it's seen better days, but it's still comfy.

Dominick returns with a can of beer in his hand and sits in the recliner adjacent to the couch. I don't blame his needing a drink over this. I scoot to the edge of the couch, my elbows resting on my knees, and I continuously crack my knuckles.

"All I wanna know is why," Dominick finally says.

I push my glasses up the bridge of my nose. "Sometimes *I* don't even know why." I sigh. "That day it happened, I had this weird feeling I should've stayed home instead of going grocery shopping with Mama. But I figured if anything happened, K would be able to handle it. I'd shown him a few self-defense moves. Then when Mama and I returned home and saw you and K . . . "

I bite my bottom lip. "And then I heard the news about Pops's suicide and . . . " I take a deep breath. "I was so fucking angry with myself. You two got hurt because of me. I failed you both. And Mama. I couldn't take all that guilt. I was only fifteen. What the hell was I supposed to do? Well, I thought about it. I thought about taking my own life. It would've been better for you guys if I was gone."

I hold my fingers like a gun and point it to my temple. "One bullet to the head would solve everything. *Bang.* No more Michaels in the family. His fucking legacy would die right there. That would erase what had happened. It would erase *him* forever. Yep. That's what fifteen-year-old me thought that night."

Dominick stares at me, wide-eyed, but stays silent.

I continue. "But then I realized I'd be no better than Pops if I did that. So I ran. The farther away I could be from the problem, the better. I guess Mama put out a missing-child report on me or something, because I had cops on my ass for a while. But I didn't want to go back home. I couldn't. Not without having that scene of you and K playing through my head over and over." I crack my knuckles again. "So, I scrounged up enough money to buy a bus ticket to Rochester. I left and never looked back.

"Around that time, I met Dante, my trainer. He was the first one I told this story to. But instead of turning me in to the cops, he sort of adopted me as his son and taught me how to cage fight. I fought underground for years. All the anger built up in me ended up breaking someone's jaw or arm or leg. Fighting was therapy for me. It was the only thing that helped me keep my sanity.

"I got older and a little wiser and finally realized I couldn't keep running anymore. And here I am now, on my twenty-sixth birthday, back where I started, telling you this story, hoping you'll find some way in hell to forgive me for fucking up." My heart is pounding as if I've run a marathon. I wipe my sweaty palms on the tops of my thighs. There's a tightness in my throat that won't go away.

Dominick just sits there, drink in hand, and stares at me blankly. I'm not sure what I'm really expecting him to say. I practically spilled my guts to him, so now the ball's in his court.

He sets the can on the coffee table and runs his hands over his face. Peering between his fingers, he stares at the floor. There's pain in his eyes, and I know he's probably remembering things . . . bad things.

"I'm sorry, Li'l D. Sorry for all that shit. I'm a terrible big brother. I wish I could've been there to save you. I would've killed Pops myself for what he did. I fucking wish I could've just listened to my gut instinct and stayed home."

"No," Dominick says in almost a whisper.

I furrow my brow.

"You were just being responsible and helping Mama, like you always did."

"What are you saying, man?"

"I'm mad you ran away from the problem. But . . . maybe it was for the best. I think Mama would've died of grief if you committed suicide, too. You were always her favorite."

My eyes widen. "What? Hell no, I wasn't her favorite. She loved us all the same."

"Trust me, Mike, you were. Always helping her with chores and shit. Doing everything you could to keep her happy. The most I'd ever done was help her in the kitchen. But you were the real man of the house when Pops was too lazy to take up that job."

I shake my head. "Whatever."

Dominick shifts in the recliner. "You know, last Thanksgiving, Kevin got into a run-in with some drug gang. He was held up at gunpoint but ended up defending himself from the attacker and saved his girlfriend and her family as a result. He said it was because of what you showed him when we were kids."

I sigh and think about his text that I'd missed, which was now saved on my phone. "I'm glad he's okay."

There's a long, awkward silence. Dominick looks at his feet while he fidgets with his hands.

"I . . . I missed you, Li'l D," I finally say.

He stops fidgeting, looks up, and cracks a smile. "I missed you too, bro."

I hear the clicking of a lock on the front door, and two muffled voices beyond. The door creaks open, and the voices become clearer.

"Trust me, you're gonna look hot at the club in that, girl."

"I'm only doing it 'cause you're my BFF. But I sure as shit don't wanna have a bunch of piss-drunk pervs grabbing on me."

Denise and Lexi come in, and I pop up from the couch in surprise. The two girls stop and look at me, then Dominick, then each other.

Lexi steps forward. "So, I see there aren't any bloodstains on the floor. Does this mean you two kissed and made up?"

Dominick and I exchange glances. I wait for him to speak up, but he seems to be waiting for me.

"Uh . . . " I scratch the back of my head. "I don't know about kissing, but we talked."

"And?" Lexi puts her hands on her hips, looking from me to Dominick, glaring.

"And what?" Dominick says. "We talked. Why does there have to be an 'and'?"

Lexi approaches Dominick and pokes her finger into his chest. "Why? Because I want to make sure you're done with your male-PMS mood swings around Denise. I mean, shit! She didn't even get any for a week! What the hell kind of man are you, huh?"

"Oh my God! You didn't have to say that out loud!" Denise's caramel face turns a shade of red.

Dominick cringes and holds his hands up in surrender. "All right, Lexi. Jesus! Are you gonna be like this when Denise and I get married, too?"

"I just might have to in order to keep your ass in line," Lexi says, narrowing her eyes.

I gently clear my throat, wondering if they all forgot I was in the room. Lexi snaps her head to look at me, glowering.

"This, uh . . . sounds like a private conversation, so I'll see myself out, now. Bye, Li'l D." I head for the door, ignoring the stares and gawks from Denise and Lexi.

I shut the door behind me, the cold air hitting my face and making me shiver. I pull out my phone and am typing in

Jesse's address on the GPS when I hear the front door open behind me.

"Where do you think you're going?" Lexi asks.

I look over my shoulder at her. She's bundled up in a chic leather jacket and loose black pants with chains around the pockets. "Nowhere in particular. Just going for a walk," I say, looking at her hopefully. Jesse's cool, but I'd rather spend the night with her—even if she is pissed as hell.

She smirks a little, seeming to catch the hint. "It's too damn cold to be going for a walk." She fishes in her pocket for her keys, accented by a decorative anime-girl key ring.

I laugh. "I'm from New York. I'm used to the cold."

She rolls her eyes and walks to her car. I follow her and get in the passenger side.

We ride without talking for the first ten minutes or so, with only the sound of the radio blaring the melodic guitars and guttural, screaming, have-no-fucking-idea-what-they're-saying voices of death metal music. I glance sidelong at Lexi, who's bobbing her head to the beat.

"You actually understand what they're saying?" I ask with an arched eyebrow.

She smiles and cranks the volume down a notch. "Most of the time, no. But a lot of death metal isn't meant for you to know what the lyrics are."

"Is that why they growl like animals?"

"The growling is part of the music. It brings out the aggressiveness of the song. Gives it a lot more feeling."

"You like listening to aggressive music?" *And people think my taste in music is weird.*

"It's not a matter of like or dislike. Death metal helps me to channel my own aggression and anger in such a way that it relaxes me. It's kind of like a drug, only there's no smoking or snorting involved." She chuckles at that.

I try to make sense of it, but it all seems way over my head. She cranks the volume back up, a little louder than before, until the bass makes the car vibrate. My head pounds from the distorted guitars and screaming voices. I think about some of the things that make me angry—my mistakes in life, Pops—and try to let the music help me "channel that aggression," but it doesn't do shit for me. Maybe this is just her way of dealing with her problems, just as fighting is my way of dealing with mine.

I'm relieved when we reach our destination, and she shuts off the car—and with it, the music. But I can still hear the pounding guitars and growling voices in my head. Glancing out the passenger-side window, I realize we're outside the now-closed tattoo parlor. The streets are empty, save for the occasional car driving by. We're the only ones parked in the area other than a white utility van that's sitting by the curb across the street.

She looks toward the van, frowns a little, then says to me, "I need to run in and get my sketchbook real quick. I'll be right back."

I've half the mind to follow her, but it'd be pretty pathetic of me to supervise her getting her sketchbook, so I watch her go inside, instead. My phone buzzes in my pocket, and I pull it out. It's Jesse.

"Hey, man, what's up," I say, laying my head against the seat's headrest.

"Hey, Knox. Great news! I signed up for an amateur fight in December!"

I blink several times. "What?"

"Yeah, man. A bunch of guys at the gym are going, and I couldn't pass it up. It looked like it could be my big break. Gonna train extra hard for it from now till then."

"Where is it going to be held?"

"At the . . . convention center down in Santa Monica." He sounds a little hesitant when he says that.

"You sure you'll be ready?" I ask.

"Yeah. I mean, I gotta start somewhere, eh?"

"You *do*. That means start local and *then* work your way up to the big leagues."

"I got this, man. I've been applying all that stuff you taught me about my fighting, and I feel better. Cleaner. Faster. I'm ready for this."

He sounds too eager to prove a point. He's liable to get his ass kicked with an attitude like that. Ironically, I talked the same way until reality gave me a wake-up call in the form of a solid knockout to the temple, resulting in the first loss of my career. Nothing I can say will likely stop him. Dante tried to stop me, but I didn't listen. Now I know how Dante felt. Damn, I really gave the old man a hard time.

I'm about to respond to Jesse when I notice two figures getting out of the utility van across the street. It's dark, and the only thing I can make out with their silhouettes is that they are men. My eyes follow them as they casually cross the street and walk toward the tattoo parlor. *One of them must be Nash.* But there's a weird feeling in my gut that something's not quite right.

"You still there?" Jesse says, distracting me from my thoughts.

"Uh . . . yeah. Hey, I gotta go. Call you later." I end the call without even waiting for a reply. My eyes remain fixated on the two figures, who now stand outside the parlor. The lights go off inside, and I wrap my fingers around the door handle. The two figures haven't moved from their spot. They almost look hidden in the shadows outside the door, but I can make out their outlines.

I squeeze the door handle.

The parlor's front door opens, and Lexi appears, her sketchbook cradled under one arm. She locks the door. As she's walking toward the car, the two men jump out from the shadows. One of them grabs her wrist, while the other confronts her. I recognize the guy talking—it's Monkey-butt.

I scramble out of the car and rush to her just as she whips her hand out from the other guy's grip and kicks him square in the nuts with black, studded, steel-toed boots. *Ouch.* The guy crumples to the ground in a fetal position.

"That was your first warning," Lexi says, pointing a finger in Monkey-butt's face. "Don't you or any of your goons fucking touch me again. Got it?"

"Are you going to finally give me those files so we can stop doing this?" he says.

What files? I march over and stand between them, my gaze focused on Monkey-butt.

"Michael! What the fuck? Move!" Lexi tries to shove me aside, but I stand rigid.

Ignoring her, I say to the guy, "Leave her alone."

He looks me up and down and sneers. "You again. So, you're her boyfriend, huh? Sorry to say, but you picked the wrong girl to get yourself involved with."

"Yeah?" I grab two handfuls of the guy's leather jacket and shirt and shove him until his back slams against the wall. "And you picked the wrong girl to fuck with."

He grunts.

"I know about you, you son of a bitch. And you better leave her the fuck alone, or you and your friend will get more than just a kick in the balls." I give him a final shove. He grunts again. I let him go and stand back.

Glowering at me, then Lexi, he fixes his clothes and hastily gathers his disabled friend. They lumber back across the street to the utility van and drive off. I keep an eye on the taillights until they're gone.

Lexi shoves me in the back, and I lurch forward, my glasses nearly falling off my face. "What the hell's wrong with you?" she says.

Fixing my glasses, I whip around and scowl. "A simple 'thank you' would've been nice."

"You have no idea who you're messing with, Michael. And I'm this close to stopping them. If you fuck this up . . . "

I look at her in disbelief. "What? So, you're saying you *wanted* to be grabbed and possibly kidnapped by those guys?"

"Hell, no." She shuts her eyes and rubs the bridge of her nose a moment then turns and walks toward the car. "Come on . . ."

I hesitate in following her. She obviously has some motive that I'm not meant to know—and perhaps I don't *want* to know. She starts the car and sits in the driver's seat, staring straight ahead.

She's waiting for me. I take a deep breath and slowly climb in on the passenger side.

Chapter 20

THE TRIP BACK TO LEXI'S APARTMENT IS SILENT. I DON'T even look at her. She's mad—at me, no doubt—but I don't care. It's not in my nature to see her—or any woman for that matter—get mistreated by a couple of assholes. This is what I get for caring so damn much.

She gets out the car and heads to her building. I grab my duffel bag and follow her. She walks quickly, and I have to take longer strides to catch up with her.

Inside her icy-cold apartment, I shut and lock the door behind me. I remain at the door and watch her throw off her jacket, plop down on her futon, and bury her face in her hands. The computer monitors are the room's only source of illumination. I drop my duffel bag and approach her.

"Mason works for Diamond-Sapphire Promotions," Lexi suddenly says, breaking the silence. She slides her fingers off her face and looks up at me expectantly.

I rub my chin. "Diamond-Sapphire? The guys who promote the big fights on TV?"

"Among other places," she says flatly. "Anyway, the company is owned by Lacie Laughton."

"Who's that?"

She makes a sour face. "She's technically my stepmother, but I don't consider that bitch part of my family."

"Right. So, what does her company have to do with all this?"

"They have a bunch of small affiliates. One of them being EBBF—Extreme Blood and Bone Fighting. When she married my dad, she somehow coerced him to sign his name to the illegal business."

I sit down in the desk chair and roll closer to her. "He didn't know?"

Lexi shakes her head. "He was—and still is—too pathetically love struck over her to know or care. When my mom died, he was desperate to find love again in order to stop the pain of her loss. He ended up marrying one of the richest women in Santa Monica, though I don't think he knew that at the time. And I had no idea that she was up to this shady shit until very recently."

"Does she have any kids of her own?"

"One son. He's pretty cool. Nothing at all like her. He and I were pretty close, went to the same high school and all that. But I graduated two years before he did, and I never saw him again. He probably couldn't wait to get out of the house. I know *I* couldn't with that bitch around."

"I'm sure one day you'll see him again."

"I'm not holding my breath."

Leaning back in the chair, I swivel back and forth in it as I think about her story. "Okay, so, what does all this have to do with tonight? And why the hell are you pissed at me for saving you?"

She rolls her eyes. "Because I don't want you involved in my problems. Mason is the network admin for her company. In other words, he keeps an eye out for people like me. The time I first hacked into the illegal fighting website, I managed to acquire a bunch of data that pointed me to Diamond-Sapphire Promotions before Mason caught me and shut me down. But I found another way in, which was in the form of the little beacon you accidentally found on the page. Mason's been none the wiser ever since, but he knows I still have the info from the first breach. So, he's been harassing me about it, coming to my shop and trying to get me to break down and give him what he wants. He knows I don't have enough to go to the authorities, but he still feels threatened that I know more about this shit than he wants. And now that you've interfered, he'll most likely find a way to use you against me as blackmail."

I stop swiveling in the chair and glare at her. "Fuck that. Why can't you go to the authorities with the info you have?"

"Because I need more concrete evidence. Like I said, the illegal business is under my dad's name, thanks to Lacie. She can put my dad away for a very long time with how she has things set up. The underground fighting thing is her real cash cow, but she hides it under the guise of her legit company, Diamond-Sapphire Promotions."

"There has to be a paper trail somewhere that documents the company transfer."

"Yeah. The question is: *where?* That's what I've been trying to figure out for the past year." She gestures to her computer setup. "That's what all that's for. And that's why Nash is helping me."

I lean forward in the chair. "Let me help you, too."

She looks up at me dubiously then laughs. "No, Michael. This is my problem. Not yours. It's been my problem since before we met. Let's keep it that way."

"Look, I'm not gonna sit and watch another random guy grab you on the street like what happened earlier."

"As you saw, I can take care of myself. Stop trying to be a white knight."

I throw my hands up, exasperated. "Oh my God! Is it so wrong for me to be concerned about you? That maybe I actually care? That maybe . . . " I bite my bottom lip, the words on the tip of my tongue.

She looks at me carefully then narrows her eyes. "That maybe *what?*"

I pause, my brain unsure of what I'm feeling but my heart speaking otherwise. "That maybe I love you," I say in a single breath.

Her eyes widen slightly, and her mouth is half-open.

My heart pounds against the tender skin of my chest. I leave the chair and close the distance between us. I draw my face close to hers. "I love you, damn it."

Her gaze flutters down then back up to my eyes. She takes off my glasses and sets them on a side table next to the futon.

I touch her lips with mine. She responds with a more forceful kiss. Man, I've missed her taste.

She pulls back from the kiss, and we lock eyes again. I caress her cheek with my hand. She closes her eyes and tilts her head toward my touch.

I move backward, toward the chair, and begin to pull her to me. She gets up from the futon and follows. I sit in the chair, and she straddles me, facing me. I wrap my arms around her waist and enjoy her nice, tight ass resting on my lap. Her tits, soft and squishy, press against my chest, agitating the tender spot. She looks at me apologetically and then lifts my shirt. She examines the new tattoo a moment, gently runs her fingers along it, and feathers it with soft, tantalizing kisses. I suck in a breath, watching her.

"It looks good on you," she murmurs, looking back at me.

"Of course it does. You did it." I smile and kiss her lips. I savor her taste and enjoy the warmth of her body, which eases my own body's chills. She moans softly, sending tingling waves of pleasure to my dick.

Closing my eyes, I run my hands along her back, fantasizing the sexy things I want to do to her. My dick is ready to burst from these jeans. She starts grinding me with her ass as I continue to caress her. I can smell a hint of her musk and can safely guess that she's most likely wet.

I reluctantly break the kiss and look at her with half-open eyes. "Do you want me?" My words come out ragged and husky.

She glares in response. Then, without warning, her lips are on mine again. Her kiss is fierce, violent, and she teases my mouth with her tongue. I happily join her with my tongue while I shift in the chair to gain access to my wallet. It's a balancing act, keeping her steady on my lap as I fumble around, and she giggles. Finally, I hold up my wallet in triumph and grin.

As I fish for a condom, Lexi stands and wriggles out of her pants and underwear. The light from the computer monitors winks off the liquid trailing along her inner thighs.

God, I was right. I undo my jeans, freeing my erection, and sheath myself. I admire the smooth skin of her thighs in the dim light. I inhale her mind-blowing scent again, and my dick becomes harder than steel.

She undoes the silver buttons down her black shirt, revealing a sexy, fuchsia-colored bra beneath.

"Hell yes," I mutter, reaching out to her with both arms.

Smiling, she situates herself atop my dick, and I wrap my arms around her waist. I slide into her with ease.

I run my hands under the back of her shirt and undo the clasp of her bra. Smirking, she wriggles and moves, doing that weird bra trick that girls do, and manages to get the thing off without taking off her shirt. I love watching a girl do that.

I take in the rest of her body. Her arms and upper chest are riddled with tattoos—way more than I have. Hers are a unique work of art. I wonder what some of the designs mean to her. It's like she's a living book of infinite stories. I trace my hand down her sternum, running my fingers along some of the designs. "You are so beautiful, Lexi."

Her smile broadens. "Thank you."

I peel back her shirt, revealing more of those beautiful tattoos down her biceps and forearms. My hand finds its way to one of her tits, and I squeeze it, my fingers sinking into its softness. She exhales and yields to my touch, her hips grinding harder against me. I respond with a heavy thrust, burrowing deeper into her core. Her whole body trembles. She moans loudly, desire spreading across her face. I take her breast in my mouth and suck her until she lets out a ragged sigh. That dark-pink nipple hardens against my swirling tongue. I close my eyes and moan, my hips grinding into her with a faster rhythm. She meets my tempo, rocking harder. My lips trail up her cleavage, to her chest, and then across all those tattoos. I lick every bit of that ink, tasting her skin.

I throb inside her. Her wetness pools on my balls. I cup her ass, groping those cheeks, and grind into her as deep as I can go.

"Oh fuck . . . oh fuck . . . " she chants.

I kiss up to her neck, where more tattoos spiral like vines. I flick my tongue along the side of her neck, and I suddenly feel my dick get clamped tight. Harder and faster I thrust, my breaths ragged, and I get lost in the moment.

She shudders. "M-*Michael!*" A pang of warmth surges from her.

At the sound of my name on her tongue, I come undone. I explode into her, groaning.

She exhales and collapses on me. I hold her, my body every bit numb but wholly satisfied. Closing her eyes, she rests her head on my shoulder, and she pants. I can feel our heartbeats racing.

"In . . . credible . . . " I say between breaths.

She smiles, not responding.

I kiss her forehead and whisper, "I love you, Lexi." Each time I say it, it gets a little easier.

She opens her eyes and looks at me deeply, as though she's wrestling with her thoughts. Her face softens, and she whispers back, "I love you, too."

CHAPTER 21

IT'S FRIDAY, AND FOR THE PAST THREE DAYS, I'VE BEEN helping Lexi find the answers she's been seeking about her stepmother's company. Unfortunately, I haven't been able to do shit in the technical department. But I did call up Dante and ask him about it. Apparently, a few of his crooked-cop friends are aware of the company but don't believe there's anything suspicious going on. Dante promised me he'd look into it more and will hopefully have some answers by the time I return to New York on Saturday. It was a hard decision to make, but I need to go back home. I'm running out of cash the longer I stay in Seattle, and I need a new job since I gave up the fast cash of underground fighting. Dante apparently landed a new place for a gym, and he and a bunch of his friends have been working since Tuesday getting it all fixed up to open for business by this coming Monday. I hope Dante still wants me to work for him as a personal trainer.

But damn it, I don't want to leave Lexi. Long-distance relationships suck, as I've learned many times from all the places I've traveled during my fighting days. I can't think about not being able to wake up every morning beside her, hold her in my arms, feel her warm body against mine . . .

Like now. We lie together on the futon under layers of blankets, naked, Lexi's body nestled against mine. A sliver of sunlight peeks through a small break in the closed curtains and hits the side of Lexi's cheek. She continues sleeping peacefully, looking every bit as beautiful now as she was last night. I think about the way we fucked between these sheets, the way she said my name, the way she kissed me . . . the way she told me she loved me.

It's amazing how three little words hold so much power. I've said it so many times to her these past few days, it's become a habit—a good habit I have no intention of breaking.

I kiss her closed eyes gently. She stirs and moans then buries her head in my chest. I smile at her.

With my free hand, I grope around our discarded clothes and condom wrappers on the floor, just under the futon, and retrieve my glasses and phone. I slip my glasses on and scroll through the list of missed messages, stopping at a text from Jesse.

hey knox. Are we gonna get to train one last time before u leave?

It's weird now, seeing him call me 'Knox.' The name feels foreign to me as if I've totally forgotten that I've been called that for the past ten years by all my friends. Man, this trip has done all sorts of crazy shit to me.

I read the text again and half smile. Jesse reminds me so much of me that it's a little freaky. When I was seventeen, I used to bug Dante about training all day and all night. I thought for sure the old man would be burned out by this point in our lives. But Dante's still as energetic as a toddler loaded up on sugar. I can only hope I'll have a quarter of that energy when I'm his age.

I text Jesse back:

> yea sure. How bout tonite?

He replies not a minute later:

> Sounds good. Cya @ the gym.

I set the phone aside and carefully wriggle myself free of Lexi's warm, inviting cuddle. She's still fast asleep as I quietly get out of bed, slip on a pair of sweats, and head to the bathroom. After doing my business, I return to the main room, flip on the TV and settle on the floor in a plank position. I remain in that position even as my abs start to ache. I stare at the TV—or rather through it. My whole body's burning now, so I let my mind go to another place.

It sucks having to leave Lexi alone out here with guys like Mason, who might do hell knows what to her. Sure, she was able to defend herself from being grabbed the other night, but what will happen if Mason brings more friends next time?

I don't want to go home—not without her. But with my wallet's current state, I don't have a choice. My body is numb now. I finally collapse on my stomach and exhale. Then I move into a push-up position. I'm burning—the good kind of pain—as I begin to pump out a hundred reps. I actually start breaking a sweat despite how cold the room is.

"The hell are you doing down there?"

I pause at my thirty-eighth push-up and look at Lexi's feet. Her toenails are painted alternately purple and black. My gaze travels up the length of her perfect creamy legs, the oversized nightshirt that still manages to show off her luscious curves, and finally, her face. She smiles coyly at me.

"Hey," I say, resuming my push-ups.

"Geez, when are you *not* working out?"

I smirk, not faltering from my reps. "When I'm in bed with you."

"Oh, really? So, you're saying you're not getting a workout in bed with me?"

"No, it's a different kind of training—the sexy kind."

She snorts, plops down beside me on the floor, crosslegged, and looks toward the TV. "Um, you *do* realize this is an infomercial for menopause medicine?"

"Yep," I lie, because I have no idea what's showing on TV. I continue pumping out the last twenty or so reps.

She smiles and then shifts positions and hugs her knees to her chest. "I totally wanna call in today so I can try and do more searching. I feel like I'm so close right now."

For the last five reps, I go slowly. Finally reaching one hundred, I exhale and relax. "You should. I think this is more important, anyway. I'm sure Nash would understand."

"Eh, but I could use the cash. Fridays tend to be the busiest time at the shop. Besides, Monkey-butt might stop by."

I cringe as memories of the other night take over. "If he touches you again . . . "

" . . . then I'll fuck him up good," she finishes. "I'm a big girl, Michael. I can handle myself."

"I'm not saying that you can't, but . . . "

"Then drop it."

I frown.

She gets up and heads to the kitchen. I watch her a moment then get up as well.

She rummages through the cupboards for her coffee items and then starts the coffee maker. Her back is turned to me. I approach swiftly and grab her arm from behind.

Her body goes rigid, and I tighten my hold. "What the fuck are you doing?" she asks.

"Do something."

"Let go of me."

In any other case, I'd let go in a heartbeat. But this is important, for her—and my own sanity's—sake. "You said you can handle yourself? Then do it."

She spins around, and as I see her foot lift from the ground, I deftly dodge the incoming groin shot. Her eyes widen. While she still looks dumbfounded, I pull her to me and lift her arm up behind her back in a tight armlock. My other hand comes across her body, holding her tight. "You're in a bad situation now."

She squirms and struggles in my arms. "Oh my God! Stop! You're going to break my arm!"

I release her. "No, I'll never hurt you like that. But people like Mason and his guys might. I just wanted you to see that you shouldn't rely solely on that one move to save you all the time. I know you can hold your own. But you should also have a few backup plans. Incorporate other moves with that groin kick. I want you to be ready for anything."

Frowning, she rubs her arm.

I grab her wrist. "Do you know how to get out of this?"

She looks thoughtful a moment. Her foot comes off the ground, and I dodge the groin kick again. But what I don't anticipate is the palm of her free hand headed straight for my nose. I loosen my grip. Shutting my eyes, I tense, bracing for impact and excruciating pain, but I don't feel anything. I slowly open my eyes and notice her hand so close to my face I can feel the heat from it.

"Holy shit. That's some pretty good accuracy and focus. Definitely effective. I never expected you to follow up with a palm strike to the nose."

She smiles and lowers her hand. "I saw that in an old Kung Fu flick."

I spend most of the morning teaching her more basic self-defense techniques—the same ones that Master Rho first taught me, and the same ones I taught Kevin when we were kids. Lexi catches on fast. I only hope that she'll remember some of them if she ever gets in a pinch again. At least when I leave Washington tomorrow, I'll know she has a few more options in her back pocket. But it still won't remove the fact that I will always worry about her.

CHAPTER 22

Stepping off the Jetway of LaGuardia Airport, I'm swept up in the sea of commuters and travelers and follow the crowd toward the ground-transportation level. A metro bus is already waiting outside, about to head into the city, and I hop aboard. I slump down in a seat in the back and set my duffel bag between my feet. Leaning the back of my head against the wall, I heave a huge sigh. I miss Lexi already. I've missed her since we said goodbye at the Seattle airport. When I got a signal on my phone again after landing in New York, I noticed Lexi had texted me a cute little note about tuning in to Kevin's show tonight. Of course, I texted her in reply, but it bounced back with an error message.

I get back to my apartment around four in the afternoon. I open a window to air out the place and then make a beeline for the bathroom for a nice, long shower. Even as I'm in here, I wonder what Lexi is doing and if she found any more answers.

After the shower, I start on dinner. While the food's cooking, I do a light workout of crunches and leg lifts in the living room. My phone buzzes, and Uncle Adam's number flashes on it.

I sit up and scoot back until I'm resting against the couch. "Hey, man."

"Hey, son. You back in New York yet?"

"Yeah, got back a few hours ago. Sorry I forgot to call."

"It's all right. Your mother was worried. We'll be flying out that way on Monday for Kevin's game on Tuesday."

"Cool."

"Did you talk to Dominick before you left?"

I sigh and think about our little conversation. It was the most we'd talked since we were kids. "Yeah, everything's cool."

"That's great, son. Did he give you his tickets?"

I blink. "Uh, no. Why would he?"

There's a moment of silence. "Never mind. Anyway, your mother and I will be staying at one of the hotels downtown near the arena. I'll text you the info when we get there."

"Okay, thanks."

Silence again. "It was really good to see you again, son. And your mother still can't stop talking about you."

I swallow a lump in my throat. "I wish she *would* stop, so she'd get on with her life. I don't want my visiting to keep reminding her of the past."

"I don't think she worries about it as much anymore. Now that she knows you're well, she can finally have some peace."

I hop up and return to the kitchen to check on the food.

"But you know what she really wants more than anything?" he continues.

"What?" I ask.

"To see the three of you together."

I stop stirring the pasta. "I don't think that'll ever happen."

"Maybe, but she's not giving up hope."

This conversation has suddenly taken a sour turn. "Look, I gotta go."

"Okay, I hope to see you soon. I love you, son."

"Love you, too."

That night, while I'm sprawled out in bed listening to Kevin's show, I get a call from an unknown number. I hesitate in answering it. "H—Hello?"

"Hey, it's me," Lexi says in almost a whisper.

I lower the volume on my laptop as Kevin's music keeps going. "Lexi? What's wrong? Are you okay?"

"Yeah, everything's fine. I had to call you and tell you what I found."

"Are you sure it's okay to talk about that like this?"

"Yeah. I'm calling from an untraceable number. I'll be quick about it, though, just to stay safe."

I suck in a breath. "I'm listening."

"I tapped into some police databases and learned that the EBBF network has been recently under investigation. That explains why they halted the fights for a while."

I exhale. *Dante.*

"The website went down again for a couple days, but it's back up under a different network address," she continues. "Mason came in today for another *retouch*. I casually asked him if he was going on vacation, and he hinted that he was probably going to be playing the slots and hitting up the bars in SoCal."

"You think he's going to be in Santa Monica?"

"I'm almost positive. The Holiday Showdown is coming up in December. This is a big deal for Diamond Sapphire. It's their largest event of the year. What better way to cover up their dirty business?"

I stroke my short goatee as I think. Jesse's supposed to be fighting in that event, too. He was really hoping I'd come see his first fight. And I'd love to. "So, you're going to go Cali?"

"Hell yeah, I'm going! If Mason's going to be there, he'll be overseeing all the fights going on in one place. The few digital documents I managed to check out clued me in that I'll probably find what I'm looking for on one of Mason's secure servers. I just need to figure out how to tap into them undetected."

I nearly drop the phone. "Whoa, wait. You're going to confront Mason by yourself?"

"I'm going to corner him, Michael. I'll either get what I want, or I'll wreak havoc during Diamond-Sapphire's big event." I can practically hear the smile in her voice. "How do you think that would look for business, hmm?"

"You've got this pretty thought out, don't you?"

"People like me need to be several steps ahead in this game. I'm going to see if I can get Nash to help with some of this. This is going to be big, Michael. I'm going to finally be able to save my father and put that bitch in jail where she belongs!" She says this so confidently as if nothing—and no one—is going to stop her.

I can't—I won't—let her do this alone. I check the calendar on my computer. Maybe if things go well at Dante's new gym, I'll have some money for a flight. "I'm going to try and come out there, too."

"Don't come out to help me. Seriously. Unless you know computers like the back of your hand, you're just going to be in the way."

I chew my bottom lip. Of course, I don't want to screw up her plan, but I wonder just how far she's thought this out. Mason will most likely have tons of bodyguards around him during the event. "No, I'm not going to come there to get in your way. The kid I've been helping to train is going to be fighting in that, and I wanted to come out and support him."

"I see."

"But, I *do* want to see you again, Lexi. I miss you."

There's a brief pause. "I miss you, too."

"And . . . " I close my eyes. "I love you."

"I love you, too," she says in almost a whisper.

I grin, and my heart beats faster as her whispered words continue to echo in my mind. "So, will you get mad if I come out there?"

"And get in the way? Yes."

My grin broadens.

"I should go, now," she says. "Oh! Did you get your belated birthday present?"

"Huh? What present? Where?"

"Don't tell me you didn't even unpack yet."

"Uh . . . " I glance at the unopened duffel bag sitting on the floor. Unpacking was the last thing I wanted to do when I got home, and as the day went on, I'd completely forgotten about it.

"Check your bag," she says. "Dominick stopped by the parlor yesterday and told me to give it to you."

I blink. "Dominick?"

The line goes dead.

I get out of bed and unzip the duffel bag. I pull out a mass of dirty and clean clothes, and come across a letter-sized envelope addressed to me. I sit back on the bed and slowly open it. My heart races as I pull out two tickets to Kevin's basketball game. A note is wrapped around the tickets, written in Dominick's handwriting:

Happy Birthday, Mike.

— Love, Li'l D

I'm up bright and early the next day, following Dante's directions to the new gym, which he dubbed "Steel Power Athletics." It's about a thirty-minute run from my apartment to Tremont, where the gym is situated in a unit beside a pawnshop. Inside, the place is much smaller compared to XL Westside. But Dante has made things work, having places for hanging bags, free weights, machines, and even a small version of a caged ring. There are a few people working out on the weight machines and a couple of fighters in the cage. I spot Dante with a couple of other guys through the open doorway of a closed-off room, which looks like an office of sorts. I pause at the doorway, and the men stop talking and look toward me.

Dante's face brightens. "Knox!" He looks to the other two men. "Hey, let's talk later, eh? Thanks for the update."

"Sure, man. Let's get some drinks later on," one of the men says. He takes his leave and tips his head at me as he brushes past.

I step aside for the other man to pass. He gives me a small nod then follows his friend.

"More of your cop friends?" I turn back to Dante.

He rolls his eyes. "They're not cops anymore. Anyway, how're you doing? What do you think of the setup, eh?"

"I'm good. And the setup is great. You're living your dream, man."

"Damn right I am. Took a lot of blood, sweat, and tears to get this far, and I'd do it all again if I could."

I smile. "How's business so far?"

"Good. Growing slowly. And . . . " He raises his eyebrows. "You've been getting some inquiries."

"Huh?"

"I've been advertising that there will be traditional martial-arts classes starting up soon. I've had four people today asking about it."

I blink. "You want me to teach martial arts here?"

"No, I want you to bake cookies." He rolls his eyes. "For fuck's sake, Michael. Get your head out of your ass. This is what you wanted, right?"

I'm still stunned at the fact that people are interested in learning traditional martial arts in a place like this. That's so unreal, but awesome. "Yeah, I guess."

"Good. I told them classes will start in two weeks. Figured I give you some time to get acquainted with your new home a bit more first before you dive in."

"Gee, thanks."

"In addition to that, I want you to be one of the personal trainers. I plan to have four of them on-site. You'll be great with the younger crowd."

And here I thought working for Dante was going to be a piece of cake. "Wow, so I'll have two jobs here? You're really working me like a dog, man."

He arches an eyebrow. "Don't want it? I can easily find someone else who could use the money."

I wave my hands dismissively. "No, man! I'm not complaining, I'm just . . . surprised."

Dante slaps me on the back. "Don't be. I've been wanting to do this a long time. Now, I think we've bullshitted long enough. Let's train."

I set down my backpack and fish through it for my gloves. He grabs some hand pads from the wall. Today, he has me working on my foot movement and timing. He raps out a pattern, and I execute it while dodging his counter hits with the pads. He moves around, making hitting the targets a little more challenging. I bounce on my toes, staying as light as possible as I follow him.

"Think you can keep drilling me hard like this for a while?" I ask while I continue punching and moving.

"Why? You're not gonna train for another damn fight, are you? I told you I was done with that shit."

"No, I'm not fighting—at least, not underground. I'm just . . . preparing."

He glares. "What's going on?"

I dodge an incoming counter punch. "Long story short, I may need to go to Cali in a couple months to look after my girlfriend . . . " I fall silent a moment as I work in another rep. *I've never referred to Lexi as my girlfriend before.*

He stands there, wide-eyed. The hand pads lower a little. "Holy shit. Girlfriend? What the hell did Seattle do to you?"

"Lots of crazy shit, man." I smirk. "But seriously, remember what I told you before about that company? Well . . . " I tell him about the fight in Santa Monica and Lexi's plans.

"So, they're at it again, huh? That explains why Kurt and the others came up with the cold trail." He holds the targets back up, steady.

"Hey, don't tell your cop friends this, please. I don't want them trying to probe the website. Mason's going to notice, and that might fuck up everything."

"Yeah, I'll stay quiet. I only hope your girlfriend's plan works."

"Me too," I say. "That's why I need to get ready for this, man. There's gonna be guards all over that place, I'm sure. Lexi won't be able to get through there so easily. But if I can clear the way for her . . ."

"You've been watching too many movies, kid."

"I'm not going to let her do this alone."

He nods and lowers the mitts. "Take five."

I huff, pull off my sweaty shirt, and stuff it in my backpack. I plop down on a wooden bench with my water bottle.

"Holy shit," Dante says, sitting beside me. "You got new ink, too?"

"Yup," I say and then guzzle some water.

He shakes his head. "Maybe you need to take vacations more often. You're practically a new man now."

I laugh.

"For the good, I hope." He leans his back against the wall and stares out toward the rest of the gym. "I'll get you ready if that's what you really want."

I stop drinking and look sideways at him.

"If it means it'll end that underground network for good, then I'll make sure you train your ass off."

"It's not just about stopping the network, man," I say. "Shit's about to go down on the other side of the country, and I have a girlfriend who's gonna be in the middle of it."

CHAPTER 23

I WAKE UP LATE TUESDAY MORNING AFTER ANOTHER wonderful dream about Lexi. Still not quite out of my dream, I reach beside me, expecting her to be there, but the sheets are empty. I roll over in bed and check the time—11:51 a.m. *Damn.* Dante's going to chew me out for missing my morning training.

Still, I smile as I think about my dream—about Lexi and the way we fucked all night. The way my body responded when she called my name. Only she could have ever done that. I wish it wasn't just a dream.

My phone buzzes. With my thoughts still on Lexi, I assume it's her and reach for it, not bothering to check the screen.

"Hey, Lexi . . . " I answer with a smile, my eyes drifting shut.

"Huh?" says a male voice.

My eyes shoot open. I pop up in bed. *This can't be . . .* "K?"

"Mike?"

Holy shit, it is! "Uh . . . did you mean to call me?"

There's a slight pause. "Yeah."

My throat feels dry, so I swallow a few times. My mind goes blank. Silence returns on the other end of the line.

"Dom told me what he did with those tickets," Kevin finally says.

I chew my bottom lip, recalling my conversation with Dominick. I wonder what else he told Kevin? "I didn't ask for them or anything."

"No problem. It sucks he won't be able to make it though."

"Yeah . . . look, if you don't want me to come, I'll understand."

"No. I . . . I want you to come."

I blink. *Did I hear that correctly?* "Say that again?"

Kevin heaves a deep sigh. "Dom and I talked. A lot. So, you got to see Mama and Uncle Adam again?"

My throat tightens, and I let out a hoarse "Yeah" before closing my eyes. "I . . . I'm kinda glad I did."

"Me too, man."

"Hey . . . " I swallow again. "No hard feelings, right? I mean . . . I'm a new man now, K. Seriously. I gave up all the underground fighting. I'm a trainer, now. It's good, honest work."

"Yeah, man. That's cool."

"I'm sorry, K—for everything. I know my apologies don't mean shit now."

"I accept your apology, but you're right. It doesn't mean shit. We can't change the past."

"Yeah . . ."

"But I'm glad you're back now."

I raise my eyebrows. "Really?"

"Really. We have a lot of catching up to do, man."

The corner of my mouth twitches. "We do."

"So, you coming to tonight's game?"

My smile grows. "I wouldn't miss it for the world."

That evening, I'm swept up in a sea of people wearing orange and blue, decked out in all types of hats and headpieces, giant number-one fingers, and homemade poster board signs.

"You sure you know where you're going, kid?" Dante says from behind me. He touches my shoulder to keep from getting lost in the crowd.

"Yeah, the ticket guy said it's this way."

"But this is the way to the courtside seats—the thousand-dollar ones."

I purse my lips. "Look man, I'm just going where the guy said."

I had two tickets, and no one to share them with because Lexi was all the way on the other side of the country, so I thought of the next best person who might be appreciative. It took some effort to pull Dante out of his gym, even just for a time, but fortunately, he had some reliable friends who could keep an eye on it.

Finally, we make our way to the seats, which are right behind the home team's bench. Wow, we literally *were* courtside. Both teams were already on the floor in their warm-up clothes, shooting around and doing drills. I look for Kevin but don't see him.

Dante settles into his seat and crosses his arms as he stares out onto the floor. I stay on the edge of my seat, continuing to look for Kevin.

"This brings back memories of boxing here back in the day," Dante says. "Used to be a sold-out crowd every time. I fought some of the greats in this place."

I smile at him. "That's cool, man."

I feel a presence nearby as two people fill the empty seats beside me. I get a whiff of azaleas and whip my head around. My smile widens at Mama and Uncle Adam, who are both wearing blue jerseys with Kevin's number, four.

"Hey, guys—you made it," I say, wrapping my arm around Mama's shoulders.

She starts, looks at me, and gasps. "Oh, Michael, baby!" She gives me a full-on hug, though it's awkward doing it while sitting in a seat. She kisses my cheeks and hugs me again.

"Hi, Mama," I say, gently pulling away from the excessive smothering.

"This is such a surprise. Did Kevin send you tickets, too?"

"Uh . . . something like that," I reply then look over at Uncle Adam, who's grinning.

"Good to see you, son," he says with a tilt of his head.

I nod back and introduce them to Dante. "Hey, Dante, this is my mom and uncle. Mama, Uncle Adam, this is my gym trainer and boss, Dante."

Mama extends her hand across me to Dante. "Hello, I'm Elouise. Nice to meet you."

Dante returns the smile and takes her hand as gently as if she were a frail old lady. But she's anything but that. "Hi. I must say, many congratulations to your son Kevin."

Her face lights up. "I'm so excited for him. His very first professional game, and he's playing against Fresco Davis!"

"Speaking of Fresco, look!" Uncle Adam points toward center court, where Fresco's stretching in his red warm-up outfit.

"Wow, I have to get a picture," I say, taking out my phone. I'll probably never get to see Fresco this close ever again except on TV.

Uncle Adam retrieves his camera from his bag and snaps several pictures.

As I'm about to take a picture, I notice that Lexi had sent me a text message.

I'm looking for u on TV!!! ^_^

Fortunately, it's not from one of her temporary numbers, so I text her back:

We r sitting courtside. Wish u were here …

Mama suddenly squeals and taps my shoulder. "There's Kevin! There's Kevin!"

I look up from my phone and follow the direction she is pointing in to look at Kevin, who runs out onto the floor and joins the rest of his teammates shooting layups. He's in his blue warm-up uniform.

Mama jumps to her feet, yelling and cheering and waving like a stoked teenage fangirl. I laugh and stand, too. We're all making noise at this point, and Kevin eventually looks our way. He grins and waves back. I take tons of pictures of him. He looks great in that uniform. I feel so honored to be his big brother.

The game is over, and despite New York being ahead of Chicago at halftime, they end up falling short, 94–88. It was such an intense game, though. I know I'm going to be hoarse, come tomorrow, from all the yelling and cheering I was doing. Mama will be, too. Kevin was amazing in the three minutes that the coach put him in for. He got a steal and scored four points, including a dunk right in Fresco's face that made the crowd go wild. Uncle Adam and I got great pictures.

I stare out at the center floor as the teams and coaches line up and give each other high fives. Kevin and Fresco stop in front of each other, and they not only give a high five, but they hug, too. I fumble for my phone and snap as many pictures as I can. Kevin must be in heaven right now. I bet he's never going to wash that jersey.

My phone vibrates with a text from Lexi.

Kevin was AWESOME!!!! :D

I grin and text her back:

yeah but not as awesome as u.

LOL! ur a dork.

As the floor begins to thin of players, coaches, security, workers, and newscasters, I notice Kevin remains. He leans over to his coach and says something. The coach looks up at him and pats him on the back, nodding. Kevin heads in our direction and says something to the scorekeepers and announcer. Kevin shoots a glance our way, smiling and giving a short wave. We all wave back, yelling our congratulations.

"May I have your attention please," the announcer begins, and the buzz in the arena begins to quiet. "We have a special announcement from our very own Kevin Anderson." He hands the microphone to Kevin.

My butt's barely touching the edge of the seat—I might as well be standing at this point.

Kevin stands in the middle of the floor. The lights dim, and a spotlight shines down on him. "First of all, I want to say, thank you, New York, for your welcome and support as I made my debut tonight in my hometown, playing alongside a legend and my childhood hero, 'Fresh' Davis." He pauses as cheers erupt throughout the building. "I also wanna thank my mom, my uncle, and my brothers, Dom and Mike. I love you guys."

It's Mama's turn to scream and cheer. "We love you, too!" she yells back.

I look up and notice the Jumbotron panning right on us.

"And," Kevin continues, "I want to thank a very special woman, my number-one fan, who captured my heart from the very beginning. Trinity Brown."

More cheering ensues, and a security guard emerges from the crowd of people on the sideline, escorting Kevin's girl toward center court. She's decked out in a blue number-four jersey and a big orange hat. She's all smiles as the Jumbotron zooms in on her.

Kevin takes her hand and looks at her. "Trinity, baby. I love you. I wouldn't have been able to do this without you. This has been the most memorable night of my life, and I want to make it memorable for you, too—for us." He pauses, retrieves a small box from his pocket, and gets down on one knee.

Holy shit! The crowd goes wild. Mama gasps, and her eyes get teary.

Trinity covers her mouth in shock. Her legs look wobbly, and her body sways. The Jumbotron zooms in on her face, and distinct tears roll down her cheeks.

"Trinity Brown," Kevin says, presenting the shiny ring, "will you marry me?"

More tears flow from her eyes, and all she can do is nod repeatedly.

Kevin smiles, slips the ring on her finger, then stands and hugs her tight. They indulge in a deep kiss.

The cheering in this place is deafening—almost as loud as it was during the game. The teammates and coaches from both teams clap as they gather around Kevin and Trinity.

Fresco is the first to offer his congratulations to Kevin with a hug and a pat on his back. Then, one by one, the other teammates do the same.

Mama is bawling on Uncle Adam's shoulder while he comforts her. "Oh, Kevin. My baby. My baby's getting married. Oh, Jesus, it's so beautiful. Praise God!"

My eyes burn, too, but I try not to cry in front of her. Or Dante.

"Well, I'll be damned," Dante says. "So much good news all around. Congrats to your brother, man." He slaps me on the back.

I smile, rubbing my eyes of stray tears with my fist. "Thanks."

My phone buzzes like crazy with texts from my friends saying that they saw me on TV, but right now, I'm only interested in the text from Lexi, which is full of smiley and heart emoticons.

OMFG!! KEVIN & TRINITY!!!!!!!!! ^_____^ YAAYYY!!! <3 <3 <3 <3 !!!!!

I chuckle and text back:

yea. That was awesome.

I SAW U ON TV, TOO!!!!! :D :D :D!!!!

lol. I hope they got my good side.

All ur sides are good and sexy >;)

I smirk. Damn, I wish she was here right now.

I love you.

I <3 u more.

My smile widens. That's the first time she's said it that way. Maybe it's getting easier for her to say it, too. I sure hope so.

Chapter 24

My first day at work at the gym two weeks later was nerve-wracking but fun. I love martial arts, and I especially love teaching it. It's always rewarding to see people interested in learning the art and not dismissing it because of whatever bad rumors they might've heard. So far, my two-hour Tae Kwon Do class has three students—two teens and one adult. After class, I'm scheduled for four hours of personal training with clients. Yeah, I could definitely learn to enjoy this.

After my second week on the job, I've already made enough money to last me a good while. On top of that, I've been frugal with my spending since I'm planning to go to Seattle in December. Lexi hasn't mentioned any bad news so far—thank God—but I still miss her.

"Pay attention, kid."

I shake myself out of my thoughts and stare at the two focus mitts Dante holds in front of his face. He raps out a punch-kick combo pattern and moves the targets around as I execute the drill. It's the end of the day. My work is over, so I'm spending time training myself.

"Again," he says.

My heart pounds, and sweat pours down my face as I repeat the combination. We do fifteen hard reps.

During the three-minute break, while I'm quenching my dying thirst with water from a bottle, Dante gets a phone call. He ends it rather quickly then sits beside me on the bench. His face is solemn, the same way he looks after talking to his cop friends.

"What's up, man?" I ask.

He rubs his temples and sighs. "There's a fight coming up next Saturday over in Brooklyn. Gowanus."

I straighten. "No shit?"

"Yeah, ol' buddy of mine's gonna be fighting in it. He wants me to bet on him."

I guffaw. "Your cop friends fight in the underground?"

"He's not a cop. We used to train in boxing together back in the day. Anyway, I really don't want to go watch that shit, but . . . "

"Hey, it's worth investigating at least. Could be one of Diamond-Sapphire's sanctioned fights."

"Could be. That's why I'm considering going." He grabs the mitts and gets off the bench. "All right. Break's over. Back to training."

I gulp down more water and hop off the bench. It's even harder for me to focus on the rest of the drills when I may find some answers to Lexi's dilemma in only a week.

Later that night, after dinner, I'm scrolling around on the EBBF website, checking out the roster of fighters slated to attend Saturday. The option to place bets isn't live yet, but that will happen within an hour of the event starting. I have no idea which fighter is Dante's friend. They all look menacing and ready to crack some skulls. It's hard to believe that I was on that roster only a few months ago. It's hard to believe how easy it was for me to quit the underground fighting scene cold turkey. Who knows if I'll go at it again in the future? For now, though, I'm going to concentrate on training others—the right way.

My phone buzzes on my night table, and as I reach for it, I pause, noticing the name that's lit up on the screen. *Kevin!*

I smile. He's never called me this frequently before. It's Thursday night, and there's no basketball game scheduled, as far as I know, so he'll be doing his radio show in two hours. "Hello?" I answer.

He doesn't answer right away, and I wonder if he hung up already. I'm about to speak again, when he says, "Hey, Mike."

I blink. Several times. It's definitely Kevin, though he sounds very reserved, as if he regrets calling me. It's nothing like the way he sounded a few weeks ago at the game, or even when he called me before then. I miss my brother. I miss my *family* and that closeness we had so long ago. I've become isolated, and the more I think about it, the more I hate it. "Hey, what's up, K."

There's another brief pause, and I think I hear him sigh. "Hey, uh, I know it's a couple weeks late and all, but thanks for coming out to the game."

My smile widens just a little. "No problem, man. You were great. I wouldn't have missed it for the world. You and Fresco Davis playing together like that . . . I wish Li'l D could've come, too."

"There will be plenty more games. You going home for the holidays?"

I freeze at his mention of home. From the way he spoke, it's clear that I'm welcome. He's welcomed me back into the family. My eyes burn from the thought that Kevin might no longer think of me as the estranged big brother—a *disease*. "Yeah . . . probably. Mama still didn't get her wish yet, after all."

"Trinity and I are going to spend Christmas at Mama's. Dom and his girl are coming, too."

I smile. Maybe I should talk Lexi into coming with me. She, Denise, and Trinity are best friends, after all. "That's cool. Hey, speaking of which, congratulations again on your engagement—and Li'l D's."

"Thanks."

"When's the date for you and Trinity?"

"Not sure yet. I'm thinking about coordinating it with Dom, so we can all have a wedding together."

The thought of them doing a double wedding leaves an empty feeling in my mind. Kevin and Dominick have always been close—kind of like the way Kevin and I were close when we were kids. "Oh, that'll be awesome. You should do it," I say, a bit halfhearted.

"Gotta go now, bro." Kevin says. "Show begins in less than an hour."

"And I'll be tuned in."

During Kevin's show, Lexi and I text each other back and forth. I tell her about my earlier chat with Kevin and my holiday plans:

> it'd be cool if u came to the house too, Lexi.

> I'll think about it… I'd love to be able to hang out with denise and trinity at least! ^_^

I snort.

> Oh? and not spend any time with me???

> Dont worry. Ill spend PLENTY of time with u ;-)

I'm about to ask her what she means by that when I hear Kevin's voice over the flowing house music from my laptop speakers. "Hope you guys are enjoying the show. I got a request from a friend of a friend, who wanted me to play this for someone special. She added a note: 'To Michael. Didn't think I'd listen to nonaggressive music, did you? Right now,

I'm feeling more lovesick than aggressive because I'm missing you. Maybe one day we can dance to this at the club. Or in the bedroom. Only time will tell. With Love, from Lexi.' So here's to you, Mike, aka Big Bro. Sounds like you've snagged yourself a good woman. She's definitely got herself a good man."

The melodic, old-school-sounding guitars and mellow beats of "Get Lucky" start playing, and Kevin mixes, scratches, and works his deejay magic on the song, making it even more upbeat and cool than the original. My phone vibrates with a text from Lexi, probably wondering if I heard the request shout-out, but right now, I can't even reply to her. My eyes sting, and this time, I can't help but let the tears fall. Kevin's words repeat in my head. *Sounds like you've snagged yourself a good woman. She's definitely got herself a good man.*

Likewise, little brother.

Chapter 25

Dante and I step off the bus that stops in front of a supermarket on the east side of Gowanus. The bitter cold hits me hard in the face, light, powdery flakes of snow tickling my nose. I adjust my beanie, tugging the edges down over my ears, and pull the collar of my thick sports jacket farther up around my neck, nearly covering the bottom of my chin. Shoving my hands in my pockets, I follow Dante down the street. I've no idea where this fight's taking place, but I assume it's somewhere off the grid. Being an ex-cop, Dante knows the boroughs inside and out. We turn down a less populated street that looks half-residential, half-industrial. It's early but already dark. Dante's breath is visible from the nearby streetlights. We head down an alley, where the snow hasn't yet penetrated. Graffiti's scrawled all over the wall, garbage litters the area, and it smells like piss. Dante raps on a rusted side door of a building, and moments later, it swings open slowly. A lean, chiseled, tattooed guy wearing a backward cap, hoodie, and sunglasses pokes his head out. He says nothing and looks our way, raising one of his eyebrows slightly from behind his black shades.

Dante leans in toward the guy, taking out a wad of cash from his back pocket. "Lemme get a couple g's o'them rocks," Dante says in the street slang he hardly ever uses, stuffing some bills into the guy's hand.

The guy takes the money, flips through the bills briefly, then passes Dante two small baggies. He tips his glasses down at me. "Your boy fightin'?"

I swallow and remain silent as I watch the exchange.

"Nah," Dante says, passing me one of the baggies, which contain a small amount of tiny, white crystalline rocks. I promptly stuff it in my jacket pocket. I did my share of drugs back in the day when I was on the suicidal route, but after Dante found me, he got me cleaned up, and I haven't turned back to that shit since. The thought of smoking crystal meth right now leaves a bitter taste in my mouth.

The guy opens the door for us. "Downstairs, first left, second right."

"C'mon, kid," Dante beckons me with a tilt of his head.

I hold my breath and follow him inside, brushing past the tattooed gatekeeper, whose gaze I can feel from beneath those shades. There doesn't appear to be any power in this old, run-down building, and strategically placed tea candles in mason jars illuminate the dark hallways. Old white sheets hang from the peeling popcorn ceilings, and steel beams run between busted, graffiti-covered walls. It looks like it's been years—decades, maybe—since this building has been out of commission, and a gang of thugs or druggies—or both— have since taken up residence. My feet occasionally crunch small plastic needle covers and pill-bottle tops that litter the ground.

Downstairs, we follow the candles and crowd noises. The hallway opens to a large room full of people dressed in business suits and some dressed ruggedly like thugs. Blunts and wads of cash are being happily passed around. The crowd circles an area in the middle where two generator-powered spotlights shine down on the combatants. The room is hazy with pot and cigarette smoke. Dante and I stand on the side among the rugged spectators since we're underdressed compared to our more professional counterparts. Dante cranes his neck around the crowd in front of him, but I couldn't give two shits about what's going on in there. Instead, I search around the area for clues—cameras, flyers, important-looking people in charge. Perched a few feet above us on a balcony is a small red blinking light in the darkness. *Probably a camera.* If I can get closer to the person behind it . . .

I nudge Dante in the arm, lean my face close to his, and say over all the noise, "Look up behind you."

Dante starts, glances sideways at me, then turns his head. He returns his attention to the fight in the center. "You gonna check it out?" he asks, not looking at me.

"Yeah."

"Good. I'll keep an eye out on things down here. Careful."

There's a sudden roar from the crowd as one of the combatants gets knocked out and collapses, bloodied. The winner raises his hands triumphantly, marching around the circle in victory while he yells and growls like an animal.

Two people rush out and drag the loser out of the circle. Another person wearing a black hoodie with a strange diamond symbol emblazoned on his heart runs out and announces, "Nichols versus Leonard in ten! Place your bets!"

Dante sucks in a breath.

"That your boy?" I ask.

"Nichols, yeah," Dante says.

The crowd disperses as people gather around some similarly dressed guys who take the bets. Amid the commotion, I take the opportunity to slip away unnoticed. I walk nonchalantly away from the crowd while I backtrack out of the main room, back into the candlelit hall. I pass by several well-dressed people on their way to see the fight. The hallway splits off, and after a quick glance at the area to ensure I'm alone, I take the unlit detour.

Judging by how far I've traveled, there should be a stairwell somewhere around here that goes to the balcony. I graze one of the walls with my hand, feeling for a doorknob. I try each knob I come across until I encounter one that is unlocked. Quietly, I open the door and stick out my foot, hoping to feel stairs going up. I hear the crowd again, so I must be on the right track. I feel sturdy steps beneath my foot and slowly ascend. There's a faint light at the top, perhaps coming from the generated ones in the main room. Reaching the final step, I notice the silhouette of a person hunched over the railing, moving slightly. The stranger holds up an object that gives off a blinking red light. There doesn't seem to be anyone else up here, so I stand beside the person and casually lean over the railing. It's a young guy about Jesse's age. Bundled in a coat, scarf, and snow hat, he's fixated on the tiny camera in his gloved hands. A wire runs from the camera to a tablet computer sitting on the floor next to him. I study the setup, wondering what he's doing with the footage. If Lexi were here with all her technical know-how, she'd be able to tell me.

"Two minutes till showtime, folks," the guy mutters, seemingly to no one. "Odds so far are 52:3 Nichols, 48:2 Leonard. Get 'em in, get 'em in." He finally looks up in my direction. His eyes go wide, and he fumbles with the camera. "Sh—" He clears his throat and says to the camera, "Uh, quick battery swap, back in a few. Get those bets in!" He shuts off the camera and looks at me like a kid caught with his hand in the cookie jar.

"'Sup?" I say casually.

"What the hell're ya doing up here, man? Get the fuck outta here!" he says in one breath.

"Relax. I just came to observe the sights from above." I nod toward his setup. "What're *you* doing up here?"

"I'm working, all right? Now get the hell out. The fight's about to start."

"Who's your boss?"

"I'm not telling you shit. Now get. The fuck. Out."

I smirk at his obvious fluster then push up from the railing and walk toward the stairs as if I'm about to leave. I glance over my shoulder at him, and he turns the camera back on and aims it over the railing. "All right, folks, sorry 'bout that delay. Thirty seconds till showtime. Odds so far are . . . 64:4 Nichols, 59:2 Leonard. Get 'em in. Get 'em in."

I return to the guy's side, taking my place back where I was. It seems that he won't have time to do another "battery swap," and if he tried, it'd make things look suspicious to whomever he was broadcasting to.

He looks at me again, wide-eyed, and purses his lips as though he knows he's trapped. He mouths, "Go!"

I shake my head and remain in place, leaning my elbows on the railing.

He scowls and finally gives in. "All right, folks. All bets are in. Showtime."

I gaze at the circle of people below. The two combatants are already going at it. I spot Dante among the spectators, staring at the ground and pound with crossed arms and a stoic face. The guy next to me starts commentating on the fight and appears to have pretty much forgot about my presence. I take out my phone, snap a picture of the setup, and send it to Lexi with a text.

Know anything bout this?

She texts back almost immediately.

:O Holy shit! where are u?

Brooklyn. there's a fight here.

OMG, you just found one of their video sources for the live stream! Looks like he's tethering the network from his phone.

I furrow my brow.

i take it that's a good thing?

It's awesome! But how did you manage to get there without getting caught?

with a little luck. and this guy's alone & trapped since he's working the video for his boss

A few moments go by, and she texts again:

K. I'm watching the stream now. This is definitely DS. Can you try and find out where that guy is connecting the stream to?

will do.

careful Michael…

I smile at the message and shut off the phone.

The roaring of the crowd draws me back to the fight below. Nichols already has his opponent taken down in an ankle-lock submission. The fight's not even gone on for a full minute, and the other guy already taps.

There are six more fights, and then the event is over, and people start leaving. Dante hangs around with the other stragglers, talking to his friend Nichols. Camera Guy shuts off his camera with a sigh then picks up the tablet.

"All right," I say. "Show's over. Your work's done. We can have a little talk, eh?"

He glowers. "I'm not telling you shit."

I scratch the side of my jaw as I think. Then I pull out the baggie from my pocket. "Not even for some free rocks?"

He pauses and stares at the baggie long and hard then chews his bottom lip. "Look, man, he's gonna kill me if I say anything."

"Does the name Diamond-Sapphire sound familiar?"

He shakes his head.

I rub my chin. "How about . . . Mason Engle?"

He stares at the rocks again then reaches for them. "Yeah, man. Now gimme that shit and let me go."

"Hold on," I say, holding the baggie away from his reach. "Where did you connect that stream to?"

"Why the fuck you wanna know that?"

"I'm . . . interested in possibly working for your boss."

He scowls then looks around carefully, as though paranoid we are being watched. He lowers his voice. "You don't wanna work for him, man. That guy's crazy."

I arch an eyebrow. "So I've heard."

"Seriously, man, and he fucking underpaid me for filming this shit and swore he'd kill me if I ever came after him for the rest of it. Dude's got money, bro. Lots of it. Trust me, don't fuck around with them guys."

I acknowledge his warning with a nod. "I'll keep that in mind. You still didn't answer my question. Where did you connect tonight's stream?"

He hesitates a moment then takes out his phone. "This network address."

I glance at the screen and snap a picture of it with my own phone. "Great. Thanks."

"All right. Now gimme those rocks, man."

I surrender the baggie, and he swipes it and tucks it in his coat pocket. He smiles and gives me a thumbs-up. "Thanks . . . uh, you're not gonna say nothin', right?"

"I won't. Let's just say we have a common adversary." I look toward the door at the bottom of the stairs. "Are you alone? Is anyone gonna come up here to get you?"

He looks nervously at the doors, as well. "Yeah, you better not go that way." He points to the other side of the balcony. "Take that door over there."

"Thanks, man," I say quietly taking my leave.

Fortunately, the halls are empty when I open the door of the stairwell on the other side of the balcony area. With my hands in my pockets, I make my way back to the main room, where only a few people are hanging out, including Dante and his friend. But they, too, are slowly making their way to the exit. The place emptied out pretty fast. Dante spots me and waves.

"Well, you guys are taking your own sweet time getting the hell out of here," I say. "Aren't you worried about cops coming or something?"

Dante waves his hand dismissively. "Managed to pull a few strings to keep 'em out of our business for a while. We should still go, though."

Nichols, a man of pure bulk, dwarfs Dante as he stands beside him. Looking at Nichols makes me feel as if I've never worked out a day in my life. The man is forty-one, according to his stats on the website, but damn, he does not look a day past thirty. He acknowledges me with a tilt of his head, and I return the gesture.

"Oh, TJ, this is Knox, my newest employee at the gym," Dante says. "Knox, TJ Nichols."

"Hey, good fight, man," I say.

"Thanks," TJ says. He pats Dante on the back. "I'll talk to you later. Thanks for coming."

"Yeah, sure," Dante says a little absentmindedly.

TJ leaves, and Dante and I follow.

"Hey, kid," Dante mutters once we're alone and outside the building. It's after midnight. We head for the nearest subway station. "While you were gone, someone was passing out flyers about the next fight." He digs into his pocket for a folded-up piece of paper and hands it to me.

I unfold the paper and read the advertisement for Diamond-Sapphire's upcoming sponsored fight in Santa Monica—the Holiday Showdown. The ad urges people to check it out online and place bets as it's supposed to be one of the biggest payout fights of the year. "You gonna give me some vacation time so I can go out west for a while?" I ask him with a grin.

He snorts. "You've not even been on the job a month, and you already want vacation?" He rolls his eyes. "Young people these days . . . "

I laugh. "C'mon, man. It's not like I'll be having much of a vacation when I get out there anyway."

"Yeah, yeah. I just better hear some good news when you get back."

Chapter 26

Six weeks later, I'm texting Lexi up a storm as soon as I walk off the Jetway and into the Seattle-Tacoma airport. She's working today, so I catch a ride from Uncle Adam instead. When I reach the ground-transportation level, I spot his white SUV waiting among the line of taxis, buses, and other vehicles. He opens the passenger-side door for me, and I slip inside and toss my duffel bag in the backseat.

"How ya doin', son?" Uncle Adam asks, offering a hug across the console.

"Good," I say.

He puts the car in gear and maneuvers his way out of the line of waiting vehicles. We're soon on the interstate headed north.

"I wish you'd stop in and see your mother just for a brief moment," he says.

I sigh and recline my seat slightly. My head's pounding, and my ears won't stop popping as we drive through mountainous terrain. "I can't, man. I've got important business to take care of in Seattle." I missed Thanksgiving with Mama this year, even though she was hoping I'd be there since Dominick had spent the holiday at Denise's parents' house, and Kevin had a game in Atlanta. I promised Mama I'd be there for Christmas, though, and she seemed more than accepting of that offer.

"Yeah, yeah. I know. Work stuff. But don't piss away your family, Michael—especially your mother. Every time I visit her, the first thing she asks about is you."

I clench my jaw. "I wish she didn't."

"Can you blame her?" He glances at me.

We pull up to Ratty's Parlor, and I can already see a bunch of customers inside through the window. It's after seven at night, and the place is still busy. Outside, five cars are parked along both sides of the street. There are no utility vans in sight, thank goodness.

Uncle Adam casts one look at the parlor, and his expression grows serious. "You got a place to stay?"

I grab my duffel bag. "Yup. I'll be fine. Thanks for the ride. How much do I owe you for this?"

"The only thing you owe me is keeping your promise to your mother."

I purse my lips and nod slowly. "Yeah, man, I will."

He nods back. "Okay. Take it easy, son. I love you."

"Love you, too." I shut the door.

I watch him leave until the taillights are out of sight. I turn to the parlor, but something else catches my attention: the sound of car doors slamming shut across the street and two sets of footsteps approaching. My throat tightens. My pulse starts to race as the feeling of déjà vu takes hold of me. It's evening but not completely dark yet, and the streets are somewhat busy with cars and pedestrians. There's a police car parked along the curb one block down.

I head for the front door of the parlor and feel a hand on the back of my shoulder. Then a voice says, "We need to talk." *Mason.*

I glance over my right shoulder at the man behind me, who's standing way too close for comfort in his fancy button-down shirt and dark-blue blazer. I could drop this guy now, but then I'd probably be the one getting in trouble for assault, especially with so many witnesses around.

"I don't have anything to say to you, man," I say in a low tone.

"Oh no?"

There's a clicking behind me, and something hard presses against my left kidney. I glance over my left shoulder at Mason's lackey, the same guy who was with him before when he assaulted Lexi. My gaze drifts downward to the lump pinned against me, currently covered by the man's suit jacket.

"I don't think you have many options, Michael Anderson Jr.," Mason mutters, amusement in his voice. "Now, I suggest you cooperate and come with us quietly."

Of course he would know my name. He's the network administrator for a lucrative illegal operation. He's probably got tons of tabs on me ever since I helped Lexi that night. I want to drop these fuckers so bad, but this could be my chance to find more clues to help Lexi—if I manage to survive, that is. Without responding, I turn and go willingly with the men back across the street. We get in an expensive-looking white car with a diamond-shaped emblem attached to the front of the hood. I sit in the back with Mason while his lackey takes the wheel. I glance out the window in silence, watching the city pass me by.

"I've been doing my research on you, Michael," Mason says, breaking the silence. "And *damn*, you've made a name for yourself with all your winnings. Your net worth is nearly seven digits."

I arch an eyebrow. *Seven digits?* I can only *hope* to see that much money in my lifetime. "You're mistaken. I'm barely making rent."

Mason snorts. "You just need a lesson in investing."

"Whatever. I don't fight underground anymore, anyway."

"Twenty-six is too young to retire, Michael," Mason says.

I grind my teeth, realizing that he knows my age and who knows what else. The sound of my name constantly uttered by him makes my stomach twinge.

"I have a business proposition for you," Mason continues.

"Go fuck yourself," I say.

Mason simply smiles and retrieves a cell phone from a holder attached to the back of the driver's seat. He dials a number and sits more comfortably, resting his elbow on the backseat console. "It's a no-go. Where are you now? Okay, we'll be there in ten." He ends the call, returns the phone to its holder, and pulls a tablet computer from the back pocket of the driver's seat.

I continue watching the city go by, hoping—praying—I'll get out of this alive.

"I need to remind you that this is a business, Michael. When you fight in these . . . lesser-sanctioned bouts, you become an asset to us because you earn us money. And you have been earning lots of money for us. And it's convenient that you've also fallen for the boss's daughter in all this."

I clench my fists and glare at Mason. "Lexi has nothing to do with this. Keep her out of our business."

"Oh, but she has everything to do with this. The little bitch is trying to snoop around where she doesn't belong."

Gritting my teeth, I bow up to Mason, about to lunge at him. He suddenly pulls a gun out of his blazer, locked and loaded. Aiming it at my face, he shakes his head. "Don't make me do this, Michael."

I need to calm down and get the information for Lexi first. I take several slow breaths and relax my nerves. "Stop calling me Michael. You don't have the right."

He quirks an eyebrow. "Okay. Knox, then, yes?"

I cringe. That name sounds even worse coming from him.

The car stops in front of a fancy restaurant located in the heart of downtown. We get out, and I follow the men into the posh place full of patrons dressed in suits and ties and lavish, sparkly evening attire. Almost all the women are blinged-out with diamonds and pearls that glimmer in the light. Some of the patrons give me odd looks as I walk by in my sweatshirt and jeans. Mason and his goon lead me upstairs to a private dining area. It's quieter here, and there's a spectacular view of Elliot Bay and city lights below from the wall of windows.

A couple sits at a table in one corner, dining on fondue, drinking wine, and chatting. Mason ushers me forward, and the woman stops talking and looks over at us. Her wavy, too-blond hair drapes down the sides of her heart-shaped face, which looks as though it has seven layers of makeup caked on it. Her green eyes glitter as she looks me up and down. There's something vaguely familiar about her. I can't quite put my finger on it.

The man sits back in his chair and taps his mouth with a cloth napkin. He looks from Mason to me, and his brow furrows curiously. He's an older man, thin, dressed in a dark-blue suit. His hair is greying and balding slightly. Unlike the woman, he looks happy and relaxed.

But he, too, looks familiar. There's something about his dark-brown eyes . . .

Mason stands beside me. The woman takes a sip of red wine from her glass and acknowledges him.

"Ms. Laughton, this is Michael Anderson Jr.—aka Knox," Mason says.

Lacie Laughton. I sneer. That must mean the guy with her is . . . Lexi's father. It suddenly clicks in my mind. The physical resemblance is striking.

Lacie smiles smugly. "I know of you, Knox. You have quite a long list of accomplishments in the fighting world. Still scrapping away in the streets of New York?"

I lift my head, staring down at her, but I remain silent.

She clears her throat and continues. "It had come to my attention that there was . . . an incident involving my daughter recently."

"She's not your daughter," I retort.

Lacie raises her eyebrows. "Did she tell you that? Well, she is a filthy liar. How dare she disrespect her family like that." She looks across the table at the man, who has been so quiet I forgot he was there. "Aren't you going to say something, Glen?"

Glen pins me with a gaze that looks as if he's staring right into my soul. Then he breaks the stare by turning and taking a casual sip of wine. "She doesn't know any better, dear. Let her be," he says calmly.

Lacie scoffs. "I do not want her lies and foolishness leaking into Diamond-Sapphire's reputation."

"Why?" I say. "Has the EBBF network been losing money lately?"

Glen looks back at me, more thoughtfully this time, and then at Lacie. "What is he talking about, dear?"

Her expression hardens as she looks straight at me—or rather, *through* me. "Nothing. At. All."

Glen furrows his brow, appearing perplexed.

So, Glen doesn't know a thing about what's going on. Lexi was right.

"I have a business proposition for you, Knox," Lacie continues, sitting back in her chair and swirling her drink.

I growl in my throat. "Not interested."

"Huh." She picks up her phone and types something. "I wonder how Mr. Coleman will look in stripes once the feds get ahold of him."

I lick my dry lips. "Dante has nothing to do with this."

"Oh, but doesn't he? He's been signing you up for all the fights, hasn't he? He seems to be doing quite well for himself with his new gym, now. Maybe he will train more fighters for Diamond-Sapphire. Won't that be nice?"

I look around and notice Glen sitting a little straighter in his chair, his movements stiff and his face pale. He seems deep in thought. *I need to talk to him, somehow. Alone.*

"Well?" Lacie says, and I snap my attention to her again.

I have no idea what she's been blathering about, so I simply answer, "Whatever."

"I'll assume that's a yes and that you will agree to fight in the Holiday Showdown next Saturday. Remember, when you win, we all win."

I grit my teeth. I may have accidentally agreed to participate in the fight, but that doesn't mean I'll let her plans go accordingly.

"I'll be right back, dear." Glen stands and heads toward the bathroom, which is near the exit. *Perfect.*

Lacie seems to pay Glen no mind and twirls her wineglass between her fingers. "My pig-headed son, Jesse, has signed up to fight in the Holiday Showdown. I think it would be good for publicity if you squared off with him. Knock some sense into his thick skull."

I blink. Several times. *Jesse? Lacie's son?* I feel as if the whole world has suddenly stopped, and my body is floating away into nothingness. *Was this really Jesse's dream all along or Lacie's?* Maybe Jesse doesn't know. He does come off as naïve and a little too ambitious. Should I break the news to him? "You're a sick woman to want me to beat up your son," I say.

Lacie scowls. "I have my reasons. A deal's a deal, Mr. Knox. See you in a week." She makes a small head gesture to Mason and his goon.

Mason shoves me in the back, away from the table. "Let's go."

I've half a mind to deck him here, but I need to keep my cool a little while longer. "I need to take a piss, first. Can I at least do that?"

Mason looks at me suspiciously and then nods. "Hurry up."

The two guys wait by the exit, and I head through the door to the lavishly decorated, gold-trimmed men's bathroom. Glen is at the sink, washing his hands. I look at the empty urinals and two stalls and make sure no one else is in here. He looks back at me, somewhat surprised, as he dries his hands on a paper towel.

"Mr. Richards," I murmur. "I need your help."

Glen glimpses the bathroom door as though anticipating someone to come through at any moment. I look over my shoulder as well, and my heart pounds. "I'll make it quick," I add.

"Look, this is all Lacie's business," Glen says. "Her empire. I swore not to get involved. Whatever she does, she does. I just love her for the admirable woman she is."

I raise my eyebrows. *Is he fucking serious?* "You call the way she treats your daughter and her own son admirable?"

He averts his eyes. "You don't understand what she's gone through. I . . . I love her."

I can't help but notice his hesitation in saying those three words. I shake my head. "I think you're trying to ignore what your heart is *really* trying to say. I think you know that woman is a criminal. Manipulator. That her type couldn't give two shits about your love so long as she gets her money."

His face gets another two shades paler. "I will admit I don't know all that she does. She assures me that she has the business under control, and I can trust her. At least, I think I can."

"You 'think'? Do you realize she's running an illegal gambling operation on the side?"

"I . . . think you're getting confused with Diamond-Sapphire's sponsors."

I study his face. I can see that he really has no idea. "No. You should listen to your daughter sometime. She knows a lot about what's going on."

He sighs. "Alexis has wanted nothing to do with me ever since I married Lacie. Those two never saw eye to eye."

"Well after meeting Lacie for only five minutes, I can see why."

"I didn't approve of the way she was talking to you—practically threatening you—which is why I got up and left. But it's her business, and what she does with it is hers. I can't and won't interfere."

"Did you ever sign any papers for Lacie?"

Glen furrows his brow. "I sign papers all the time. It's all part of the business, especially when you are married."

"You need to read the fine print, man. Especially the part about Extreme Blood and Bone Fighting, which has your name and signature on it."

Glen scrunches his face, creating small wrinkles around the corners of his eyes and the bridge of his nose. "What are you talking about?"

"Exactly. Think about what I said, man. Think about your daughter. She really does love you." I turn and walk out the bathroom, leaving him to his thoughts.

Glen seems to have a good heart, but he's as naïve as fuck. How the hell am I going to help him *and* Lexi?

I'm dropped off a few blocks from Ratty's Parlor. I wait for Mason's car to leave before I head there. It's a little after eight o'clock. The shop's closed, but I still see a few people inside cleaning the floors and wiping down equipment, Lexi among them. I rap on the door. Lexi stops mopping and comes over to answer it.

"You get lost or something?" Lexi asks with a chuckle in her voice.

I half smile. It's probably not the best time to tell her where I really was, so I reply, "Uh, no, my uncle and I stopped to get some dinner."

She nods and lets me in. "We closed about five minutes ago. We're just cleaning up, if you wanna wait around real quick."

"Sure." I park my ass on the couch in the waiting area.

Nash, who has been busily wiping down the countertop of his station, stops and looks in my direction. He grins and whistles. "It's Lex's booty call! How's it going, man?"

The two other employees make teasing whistles and cat-calls at me.

I clear my throat and nervously adjust my glasses, trying not to look too embarrassed. "Hey."

Lexi fights down a smile and then quickly resumes her cleaning. I spot a hint of pink around the exposed skin of her neck, and I smile.

My phone vibrates, and I whip it out. I pale when I notice Jesse's name. *Damn.* As if he could call at a more inconvenient time. The phone continues vibrating in my hand as I wrestle with the urge to answer it. I take a deep breath, close my eyes, and hit Answer. "What's up?"

"Hey, Knox, I have a few minutes to spare, so I thought I'd hit you up," Jesse replies.

I blink. "You're still at work?"

"Yeah, I managed to pick up some extra hours so I'll be able to afford the trip to Cali."

I chew my bottom lip. "So, you're still gonna do it, huh?"

"Fuck yeah! And guess what? I got an email saying that I'm going to be fighting in the main event! Can you believe that shit? My very first fight, and I'm gonna be facing off with the champ!"

The phone slips from my hand, but I manage to catch it and return it to my ear. I look around the shop to see if Lexi or the others noticed, but they're busy finishing up cleaning. "Are you serious?" I say, feigning my surprise.

"It's crazy, right? I was trying to find out who the champ was, but I couldn't find anything. All the ads just mention the main event but no names."

Thank God.

"But I'm ready," Jesse continues. "When're you coming to Seattle? I wanna show you some of my deadly new moves."

"I'm in Seattle now, but I'm staying with a friend."

"Oh, cool. Well, we need to hook up this weekend before I head to Cali next week."

I sigh. "You sure you wanna do this?"

"Yeah, totally sure. Nothing's gonna stop me, man. This is my big break, and I'm gonna take it no matter what."

I have to tell him . . . I have to—

"I gotta go now, Knox, but I wanted to tell you one last thing."

I freeze. The tone of Jesse's voice has gotten a little more edgy. "Yeah?"

"Thanks again for teaching me. You're awesome."

I swallow. "I didn't do anything."

"What're you talking about? If I hadn't met you, my fight would've been total shit. I've never felt so ready to do something before in my life. So thanks, man."

The words sting my gut in an odd way. Then I remember something Master Rho said back when I'd gotten my black belt: *"The value of a student's appreciation of a teacher is priceless.*" I chew my bottom lip and say to Jesse, "You're welcome."

Several voices speak in the background, and Jesse replies to them, but his voice is muffled. "Uh-oh, I'm being called back to work," he says clearly to me. "Talk to you later."

"Hey, wait, I need to tell you—" The call ends before I can finish my thought. *Damn.*

A blast of frigid air hits my face when Lexi opens the front door to her apartment. Carrying my duffel bag over my shoulder, I shuffle inside after her. "Geez, Lexi. I think it's colder in here than it is outside. What if your computers ice over or something?"

She grunts and flips on the lights. "That'll never happen."

I set my duffel bag by the futon and watch as she routinely goes to the kitchen, brews some coffee, then makes a beeline for her computer desk.

Placing a hand on her shoulder, I stop her before she can sit. "Lexi . . . "

She pauses, and I spin her around. I press my lips to hers before she can say anything. I kiss her deeply, eagerly. I've missed her taste. I've missed this moment.

No, I need to talk to her about what happened. I need . . .

She moans and returns the kiss, sliding her hands down my arms.

Fuck. That talk can wait.

I pull her body to mine so that I can feel the softness of her tits. I'm sure she can feel the hardness in my pants. Her tongue presses against my lips, and I eagerly welcome her with mine.

She finally pulls away.

"Holy shit . . . where did that come from?" she says breathily.

I smile and caress her cheek. "I've just missed you so damn much." I kiss her again more passionately. God, I want to take her right now, but with all the traveling and shit I did today, I could use a shower. It's my turn to pull away, though I'm reluctant. "Mind if I use your shower?"

"Really, do you need to ask?" There's a hint of mischief in her eyes as she says this. She draws her fingers across my lips then uses those same fingers to trace the visible cleavage of her scoop-neck shirt.

I'm fascinated by those fingers, which graze the area below the neckline where her nipples are faintly visible.

Damn, she's such a tease.

Grunting, I slowly pull away from her. She smirks, and her eyes move downward to the obvious bulge in my pants.

"Uh . . . yeah, so I'll be back in a few . . . " I hastily rummage through my bag for clean clothes, a bar of soap, and a towel.

Still smirking, she plops down in her desk chair and spins toward the monitors.

Alone in the bathroom, I turn the shower on. The warm water pelting my back relaxes and clears my head. So much has happened in four months—so much bad, and a little good—but I'm hoping with the new year will come a better start. And I think Lexi will find what she's looking for come Saturday.

Lexi. My dick, already stiff, throbs in my hand at the thought of her body on top of mine. She's everything I've always wanted in a woman—intelligent, funny, strong, unique, and drop-dead gorgeous. My past relationships are a blur now, while Lexi and I seem to have this genuine connection that I don't intend to let go of. I've never felt this way about a woman before. I've never felt so . . . certain.

I get out the shower, towel off, and put on my glasses. I'm checking my face to see how badly I need to shave when I hear the bathroom door creak open behind me. My heart pounds as I look through the mirror at Lexi, who pokes her head in and smiles. Neither of us speak, so she enters the bathroom . . . wearing absolutely nothing. She holds up a bright-green condom packet. I exhale and brace my hands on the counter top. My mouth waters as I admire her reflection—her beautiful, curvaceous reflection. She hugs me from behind and sets the packet on the sink. Pressing her tits against my back, she grinds her hips into my ass. Her hands clasp my lower abdomen, and I admire her manicured, black-painted nails.

"Lexi," I whisper amid my arousal.

"Shh," she says and begins to kiss my back.

My skin prickles with goose bumps at the touch of her soft lips and the cold metal lip ring. I grab the condom, tear it open awkwardly, and fumble with it as I try to slip it on. With it finally situated, I turn, facing her, and kiss her lips.

Not breaking the kiss, I heft her up and sit her on the sink's countertop. I play with her tongue with mine as I draw my hands down and grope her tits, massaging them and rubbing her nipples with my thumbs. Her back presses against the fogged-up mirror. She wraps her legs around my waist. I grunt as her thighs squeeze tight. I kiss across her jawline and down her neck. I draw my tongue down that forbidden line of her sternum until it gets lost in her cleavage. She runs her hands across my hair, breathing slowly. My tongue drifts down to her tits and across each nipple. Moaning, I suck on one greedily.

"Ah . . . Michael . . . "

More energy rushes to my dick when I hear my name uttered from her mouth. She's been the first girl to give new value to my name. *God,* she is incredible. I pull back and breathe hard, steady. She looks at me with dark eyes.

"I want you right now," I say between breaths.

"Then fuck me like you should."

Oh, hell yes.

I pull her to the edge of the countertop and slide into her without hesitation. I begin rocking a slow rhythm, and she braces herself on me, following my movements. I shove deeper until she clenches me tight, and then I thrust in and out of her, in and out. She cries and digs her nails in my back, gripping whatever she can. I feel pain in my back, but it's all eclipsed by the pure pleasure running though my dick. I groan, though it sounds almost like a growl in my ears. I lift one of her legs so that it's cinched around me and drive as far as I can go into her core.

"Oh fuck! Oh fuck!" she chants in time to our rhythmic movements.

Being so deep inside her like this makes me never want to let her go. She shivers in my arms, her core contracts, and I'm met with the hot rush of her orgasm. Seeing her in that trancelike state of bliss makes me work up my own until I'm seeing sparks. Panting, she rests her back against the mirror, and I collapse into her, my head resting on her soft, pillow-like tits.

I feel her hand run along my hair as I listen to the pounding of our attuned heartbeats.

"Michael," she mutters.

I lift my head slightly and admire her pink cheeks and kiss-swollen lips. "Hmm?"

"I love you."

I beam, her affirmation bringing new life to my dick. "I love you, too."

Yeah, the new year is going to start off great. I'll make sure of that.

Chapter 27

My scheduled fight with Jesse has remained under wraps, and I haven't had the guts to say anything to him. I did, however, finally tell Lexi about my encounter with Lacie, though I failed to mention anything regarding my fight with Jesse. She was already focused on dealing with her stepmother, and adding the shit about Jesse and me would have made her lose focus of her primary objective. I didn't want to fuck up any more than I already had. Lexi was pissed as hell about the news of her stepmother. She was also pissed at me for not telling her sooner and kept her pussy under lock and key for three days as "punishment"—well, *tried* to, anyway. Not even a full day had passed, and we were at it on her futon again.

I updated Dante, too, so he could call up his contacts and start putting things in motion.

"Dante, I don't want this place to be swarmed by cops," I told him. "I don't have enough information yet."

"Well, hurry the fuck up. This is the perfect opportunity."

It certainly is an opportunity tonight at the packed convention center. I linger around the lobby until the crowd starts ambling toward the main hall, where the fights will take place. A poster nearby showcases all twenty-four fighters and their opponents. But neither Jesse nor I is mentioned, and the Main Event listing only shows a picture of two silhouetted fighters with question marks in them.

I lean against the wall, my hands stuffed in the front pockets of my hoodie. Lexi's texting away on her phone. She's dressed in her gothic-punk style: a red-and-black-plaid button-down, left open to reveal a black T-shirt underneath with a vintage grunge-band logo on the front. On the bottom half, she's wearing a black pleated skirt over loose black pants with decorative buckles and chains. She sports a pair of calf-high boots with more buckles and chains as well as chrome spikes. The sleeves of her shirt are rolled up to show spiked wrist cuffs on her tattooed arms.

She's so much more alluring than the other people who walk by in their thousand-dollar suits and sparkling evening wear. They look our way and turn their noses up at Lexi and me. I wonder if they think we're hoodlums or something. But even in the sea of money, there are many others like me, dressed in street clothes. It's a public event, though the lavishly dressed people probably have the best seats.

"So, what have you and Nash been planning?" I mutter to Lexi.

She looks up from her phone. "Nash made a program for me that can pick up data through video images. I'm trying it out on some of the phones around here."

I lean over and peer at her phone screen, which currently shows a video image of people's legs. "Find anything useful?"

"Nope. Just testing it. I'm going to try it on Mason next."

"Mason's probably holed up somewhere with Lacie already."

She frowns. "Yeah, you're probably right. I need to find a way to get close to him. Or at least get to his phone."

I rub my chin as I continue staring out at the crowd. Security's posted everywhere. Lexi wouldn't get very far if she tries to look for him. I push off the wall. "I'll be back."

She says nothing and returns to her phone. I scour the lobby, getting a feel of the layout and the number of security guards. Many of the well-dressed spectators head for a set of stairs that's blocked off by a velvet rope with a hanging VIP sign. A guard standing there greets the spectators and allows them to pass. Other people head for the elevators, one of which is gold-colored and manned by a guard.

A janitor emerges from the crowd of lingering spectators, wheeling a large garbage can. *He might be able to tell me more about this place. It'll help me figure out how best to get to Mason.*

"'Scuse me, where's the bathroom?" I ask the janitor, even though I know full well where it is.

The older man tips his hat and then points. "Just down the hall there. Can't miss the sign."

"Thanks . . . uh . . . you usually work these types of events?"

His bushy grey eyebrows furrow, and he gives me an odd look as though he's not used to engaging in random conversations like this. "Sure. I'm employed by the convention center staff. I work all types of events."

"Are there usually a lot of fights here?"

"Nope. Diamond-Sapphire fights are the only ones I know about. This venue mainly hosts gardening and home shows. And the occasional comic convention—heh. But the annual Diamond-Sapphire fights definitely have the largest turnout."

"Security's pretty good here, then?"

"Yep, though Diamond-Sapphire only employs a few of the convention-center security people since they have so many of their own. See that guy over there with the blue-and-white armband?"

I follow the direction he is looking in and spot a suited man wearing a wireless earpiece in his left ear that blinks an intermittent blue light. He blends in well with the other suited spectators, but the difference is his armband, which has the Diamond-Sapphire logo printed on it. "He looks important enough," I say.

"Yep. Just don't be a knucklehead, eh?" The janitor chuckles.

I smile and give him a small salute. "Thanks, man."

"Anytime, son." He continues on, wheeling the garbage can along.

I walk toward the bathrooms—slowly—with no intention of going in. I spot several faint, blinking blue lights from farther down the hall. *They're swarming the place. That's how I can get in.* I casually make my way back to the main lobby. Lexi's still in her same spot and on her phone, but as I stand next to her, she looks up.

"I have an idea," I say.

She raises her eyebrows. "I'm listening."

"I'm gonna go talk to Lacie."

"Come again?"

"Mason took me to her before. I bet I can get him to take me to her again. They have tabs on me, and they know I have a pretty solid winning record. To them, I'm a bread winner. I'll bullshit with them for a bit while I scope out their hiding place for clues on how you can infiltrate it. Then I'll come back and let you know."

Her rigid expression changes, and she looks thoughtful. "That's it!"

I furrow my brow.

"I can use your phone to spy on them."

It takes me a moment, but then I nod. "Oh, I get it." I take out my phone and hand it to her.

She takes it, punches some buttons on the screen, and hands it back to me. "I've activated the camera and synched my phone to it. Just keep your phone hidden and make sure the camera isn't obscured. If there are any computers around, try to get close enough to them, or at least make sure the camera is pointing at the screen. Just don't be too obvious about it."

"Got it." I stick the phone in a side pocket of my pants and adjust it so that the camera lens is barely peeking out.

She looks at her phone screen and gives me a thumbs-up. "That's perfect. Okay, I'm going to go grab my seat in a bit. The event is starting in fifteen. I'll get in touch with Nash, so he can tap into the video feed and hopefully be able to crack something on his end." Her face softens. "Be careful, Michael."

I tug my lips into a smile, pull her close, and kiss her deeply. "I love you," I whisper.

"I love you, too," she whispers back.

I pull away from her and join a group of dressed-up people at the blocked-off VIP stairs. A few give me odd and condescending looks, but I ignore them. I step up to the suited guard as he lets the people ahead of me through. He looks at me and scowls, his eyes shielded by sunglasses. I note the Diamond-Sapphire emblem on his forearm band. A tiny device attached to his left ear blinks steadily with a blue light.

"General seating is that way." He points behind me to the main doors.

"I'm not a spectator," I say flatly, standing up against the guy even though he is about an inch taller than me. "The name's Knox, and I need to see Ms. Laughton. She knows who I am."

His jaw moves slightly, and he turns and mutters something in his earpiece. I cross my arms and wait. Another suited guard comes hurrying down the stairs and escorts me toward the elevators. I discreetly adjust the phone in my pocket, ensuring Lexi will be able to see exactly where I'm going.

The doors to the VIP elevator open, and we file inside. The ride up to the third floor is quiet and awkward. The guard stands rigid with his hands crossed in front of him.

The doors open to a lavish level with a marble floor and fancy hanging light fixtures. This definitely looks like a place where Lacie would stay. I follow the guard down the hall to the box-seating area, which is an enclosed room with plush seating and a full bar. The track lights cast a warm, inviting, multi-colored glow about the room. The far wall is open, and the sounds of the main hall below filter in. The steel cage looks like a dot from way up here. Why the hell do people spend so much money for seating like this?

Then I notice, on the opposite end of the room, a wall consisting of several big-screen TVs arranged together and synchronously displaying a single, close-up image of the empty steel cage.

The guard leads me over to Lacie, who's lounging on one of the couches. Mason is at the bar, a tablet and laptop on the counter in front of him. He's typing away on the laptop. I discreetly transfer my phone from the side pocket of my jeans to the back one as I approach Lacie, my back to the bar.

I hope I'm in a good position. It's then I suddenly realize my phone would be picking up audio, too. If I can get Lacie to admit to some crimes, it could be even more evidence to give to the police.

Lacie takes a sip at her glass of sparkling gold liquid and then acknowledges me with a scowl. "And what brings you here, Knox? Not thinking of backing out, are you?"

I lift my head slightly. "I never back out of a fight."

The clicking of computer keys stops abruptly. "Knox! What's he doing here?" Mason says.

I look over my shoulder and keep my back turned. "I came to make another business proposition."

Lacie sits a little straighter. "Oh? Now, this will be interesting." She lifts her thin, blond eyebrows. "Entertain me, Knox. What is your . . . *proposition*?"

"Since I'm fighting in the main event, I want ninety-five percent of my winnings."

She gawks at me, and for a moment, all goes completely silent. Then she suddenly bursts out laughing. "*Ninety-five*? A little too ambitious, don't you think?"

"I think my career record more than proves that I'm the best, and I want to be paid what I am owed."

"Diamond-Sapphire pays its fighters forty percent of all earnings. Non-negotiable." She takes another sip.

I shake my head. *Greedy bitch.* "Not enough, Ms. Laughton. Fine. Forty-percent and . . . a small share of your company."

She scoffs. "Diamond-Sapphire is not for sale to the likes of you."

"Oh no? Well, surely a large, established company such as Diamond-Sapphire has some affiliates, then? I want a piece of this, Lacie, since you're asking me to do this shit for your own entertainment. I'm talking about fighting your own *son*."

"I was never *asking* you. I was *telling* you."

"Whatever. So, do we have a deal?"

"You heard her," Mason said, not looking up from his laptop. "The company is not for sale."

"Hmm . . . perhaps I might consider EBBF . . . " Lacie taps her chin with her finger, her perfectly manicured nail glittering with a sparkly gold polish.

Mason snorts. "Why, Lacie? Glen is more than suitable bait."

This is great stuff. I arch an eyebrow, feigning ignorance. "Extreme Blood and Bone Fighting? That's *your* company?"

"Technically, it is. Though due to its . . . *nature*, I needed to keep the entities separate. I coerced my stupid husband to take it off my hands. He runs it now, for all intents and purposes."

"Your husband signed willingly?" I ask.

Her lips form a thin line. "You ask too many questions, Knox. I may be prepared to offer you a portion of EBBF. But you'll need to hold up your end of the deal, first."

"And what makes you think I would want your table scraps?"

"EBBF is quite profitable, actually. I'm talking internationally here. Glen is just the face of the company."

"So, I'll have to talk to Glen about getting a piece of it?"

"If you really want it, you let me know." She smirks. "The papers are all ready for you to sign." She makes a general gesture toward the bar.

I look at Mason again. He's focused on his laptop screen, seemingly oblivious to the conversation.

I hope Lexi is getting all of it.

The crowd noise grows louder, signaling the start of the event. The wall of screens pans to an announcer in a tuxedo and blue bowtie who walks into the cage and introduces the first fight of the evening.

I turn back to Lacie. "I'll consider signing . . . after my fight."

Lacie smiles sweetly. "Of course. Good luck, Knox. I'll be watching. Knock 'em dead." She chortles.

I cringe at her pathetic attempt at a joke and turn to leave. The security guard quietly escorts me back to the main lobby. Lexi is gone as expected, so I head toward the locker room, where the rest of the fighters are waiting. I check my phone along the way. She's already sent me a text:

Michael, I luv LUV LUV YOU SOOO MUCH!!!! <3

Grinning, I text back,

i take it u got what u needed???

Yup.

Do what u gotta do. I'm gonna get ready 2 fight...

I slip into the locker room and observe all the fighters warming up, practicing, talking shit, and getting pumped. Jesse's sitting alone in the corner, throwing practice swings at the air. I quietly head over to him, ignoring the stares and sneers I get from some of the other fighters. I sit on a bench, and leaning forward with my elbows on my knees and hands clasped, I watch my eager protégé. I see myself in that moment, eighteen years old, training for my first underground fight—the start of my career.

Jesse stops to rest and looks over to me with a start. "Knox! You made it!" He beams and comes over.

I smile weakly and hold out my hand. "Yeah. How's it going, man?"

He grabs and shakes it in a special way, kind of like the secret handshake my brothers and I used to have. "I'm good. Nervous as fuck about my fight, but good. Can you believe there's still no info about who my opponent is?"

I adjust my glasses nervously. "Yeah, uh . . . we need to talk about that, Jesse."

He arches an eyebrow.

I pat the empty seat next to me on the bench, and he dutifully sits, looking at me, his brow wrinkled. I heave a huge sigh and run over the thoughts in my mind. "Right, so . . . about this fight . . . " I bring my clasped hands to my lips and close my eyes. *Please, God, let him understand.* I open my eyes and look at him. "It's us."

He flinches, then his face scrunches. "What?"

I nod faintly. "Yeah, man . . . " I tell him the whole story. "No offense, man, but your mother is one sick woman," I finish.

Jesse stares blankly at the floor, silent a moment. "I already knew she was, but I never thought she would stoop this low. I had no idea she was promoting fights."

"You didn't know Diamond-Sapphire was her company?"

"Fuck no. I've stayed out of her way all this time. I wanted nothing to do with her. She once tried to persuade me to take some business classes in college. Probably wanted me to be-come a crooked mogul like her. Well, fuck that."

"Well, glad you didn't go that route," I say, trying to smile.

"Yeah." He glares at me. "So, all this was bullshit. My claim to fame, my dream. A fucking lie. And *you* knew!"

I hold my hands up in surrender. "Whoa, man. I'm sorry. I wanted to tell you, seriously. Some shit's about to go down tonight, I think. We need to do this fight—or at least act like it."

"Forget it. I'm not gonna do it. I won't give her the satis-faction."

"Look, I've got some connections, and if everything goes as planned, we'll get cops swarming this place in no time, ready to take Lacie away for this shit. We can't give her any reason to get suspicious."

He scowls. "I can't believe my own mother would want to see me fucked up in the ring."

"That's not all she's done—or said. I think all this mon-ey's corrupted her mind, man."

"Yeah, I know. That's why I left home as soon as I could. She totally disowned me afterward. It was crazy." He closes his eyes and slams his fist in his hand. "I wish she'd just be normal again, damn it. She wasn't always like that."

"Money makes you do stupid shit."

"Tell me about it." His frown lifts slightly. "All right. Fine. I'll go along with it. But I'm only doing this because I want to shut her down. I don't want this shit coming back to *me*."

"Don't worry. My girlfriend's got it." *I hope.*

CHAPTER 28

THE NIGHT GOES ON WITHOUT WORD FROM LEXI. I CAN only hope and trust that she managed to get what she needed because after a quick call to Dante to inform him of the situation, he immediately went ahead and called up his contacts and cop friends.

"You're going be surrounded by midnight, so be prepared to get your ass out of there well before then, kid," he said.

"What! Dante, I don't even know if Lexi got the info. And Jesse and I still have to fight."

"Lacie's there, doing what she does best and in plain sight. We will *not* get another opportunity like this again."

It's eleven o'clock, and there are five more fights left to go before the main event. The locker room thins out until there are only a few fighters left, including Jesse and me. Jesse slouches on a bench opposite to me and leans his back against the wall. He was pacing, practicing, and doing everything he could to stay active, but that was short-lived. He hasn't been paying attention to any of the fights that were broadcast on the TV mounted on the wall by the door. It's been the longest wait ever for the two of us.

I glance at the TV. It shows the current fight, which is well into the fourth round. Both fighters are winded, but the limber-looking one pummels his bulky opponent to the ground and gets him into an armlock submission. The referee bends and moves around, trying to get a good view of the situation. Suddenly, the bulky guy taps, and the referee calls the fight. He pulls the limber guy off his opponent and onto his feet and lifts his arm in victory. The crowd in the main hall goes wild, and the fighters in the locker room start chatting about the results.

"I don't like this, man," Jesse says, clenching and un-clenching his fists. "We're going to get caught, taken away, and probably never see the light of day again."

Not responding, I text Lexi again, hoping this one will go through, but it bounces back with a message-sending error just like the dozens of others I've sent tonight. She hasn't said anything since I left my meeting with Lacie earlier.

"Let's plan to leave five minutes to midnight," I say to Jesse.

"But what about our fight?"

I shake my head. "There's been a change in plans. We need to be out of this place by midnight."

"And we're gonna leave five minutes prior? Don't you think that's cutting it a little close?"

"Yeah, but—" My side vibrates from the phone in my pocket. I whip it out, and a text from an unknown number flashes on the screen.

It's done. Calling a taxi. meet me outside in ten. <3

I love the subtle way Lexi signs her texts. I look up from my phone to Jesse. "Scratch that. We leave now."

Jesse furrows his brow.

"My girlfriend took care of it. We need to get out of here—discreetly."

"Hmm." Jesse rubs his chin a moment then snaps his fingers. "The loading dock. It's just down the hall past this locker room."

I give a thumbs-up. "Perfect. Now, let's just hope that area is unoccupied by security guards."

He pales. "Oh shit, I forgot about those creepy bastards."

I get up from the bench. "No time to pussy out now. Come on." I flip up the hood of my sweatshirt and head for the exit. The few remaining fighters in here don't pay me any mind this time. I leave the locker room, not waiting to see if Jesse follows.

The hallway that leads to the loading dock is dimly lit by glowing Exit signs and advertisement marquees. I break out into a small jog down the corridor. Hopefully anyone who's down there won't pay me any mind. I'm just a fighter doing a little jog to stay warm and loose.

Footsteps behind me make me falter mid-step. I glance over my shoulder and see Jesse trailing not far away. I follow the signs to the loading dock, where, not to my surprise, a guard with an armband is standing outside the entrance.

"Hey, what are you doing here?" he says, holding out his hand, stopping me.

"Just going for a jog, man," I say, bouncing on my toes.

"Yeah, well jog that way." He points the way I came.

Jesse stops before us, and the guard stiffens. "Go, and take him with you," the guard says.

I partially pull out my phone from my pocket and glimpse the time. 11:38 p.m. I turn back to the guy. I listen for anyone else nearby, but all seems quiet. Time to use the last resort. I reach for the guard. He blocks my hand and follows up with a punch in the stomach, winding me a moment. I grunt and keel over. As I'm regaining my composure, the guard grabs for a gun at his belt.

"Requesting back—" he utters into his earpiece, but Jesse swoops in behind him and tears off the device. He grabs the guy's hand, which is now holding the gun. With a sharp twist, Jesse snaps the guy's wrist. He grabs a handful of the guard's collar and slugs him in the face repeatedly.

When Jesse starts to draw blood, I stop him. "Enough, Jesse." As much as I would love to see the kid finish off that guard, I can't let him lose control. Not if he's going to be *my* student.

Jesse cocks his hand back and stops short of the guy's face. He looks at me curiously then releases the guard. The man slumps to the ground in an unconscious heap. We head to the door and exit through the loading dock, where a few expensive-looking cars are parked, as well as Mason's white utility van from the other night. I'm betting one of the fancy cars belongs to Lacie.

A group of four well-dressed guys are gathered near a car, making a couple of discreet exchanges with plastic baggies containing white substances, and wads of cash. Lexi is amongst them, along with a guard, who has her held by the wrist.

I break out into a sprint. The guard pulls her toward the open back door of another car. She suddenly kicks him in the groin and follows up the attack with a palm strike—the same move she practiced on me that one night. The men halt what they're doing and tackle her to the ground.

I'm already on top of the guys, punching, kicking, breaking my way to Lexi. I get caught with stray fists and feet hitting my face and body. My arms are suddenly grabbed, and I'm pulled away. Pain shoots through my body. A man has my arms locked in submission.

Jesse rushes in to the group, growling like an animal. He tears one of the guys off Lexi and starts punching him repeatedly in the face.

I can't stop him this time, as I have my own problems. Lexi is scrambling away from the guys, who are distracted by Jesse's sudden entrance.

"Need backup in Dock Section C! I repeat, we need backup in Dock Section C!" one of the men says into his blue-lighted earpiece.

My captor lifts up, and I feel my shoulders about to pop out of their sockets. Gritting my teeth, I back kick him in the groin. He grunts. The pressure in my arms recedes, but he still has a grip on me. I kick him again. His grip loosens. I back sweep his legs, and he loses his grip. He falls backward against the front of a car. The fancy hood ornament impales the back of his head.

Another guard approaches me, holding a gun. He shoots just as I scramble around the car. The bullet ricochets off metal and concrete with a *pang*. I have no idea if I'm hit. I don't feel pain, but my adrenaline level is beyond maximum.

The gunman turns his attention to Jesse, who's squaring off with another guard. The pounding of many footsteps from inside the building starts to draw closer. I can also hear the echo of police sirens in the distance. *Damn, we need to get out of here fast.*

The gunman takes aim at the unaware Jesse. I pop out from behind the car and break his knee with a solid side kick. His bones crunch like paper, and he crumples to the ground. The gun slips out of his hand, and I swipe it up.

Jesse knees his final opponent in the solar plexus. He raises his elbow, about to finish the guy off, but I manage to stop him. "No," I say, grabbing his arm. "We need to go, now." I look behind me to see the exit door fling open and more guards emerge. A few already have their guns out.

"Let's go!" I say to Jesse.

We sprint toward the exit. I let Jesse run ahead of me while I hang back and fire toward the guards, making it harder for them to follow. Many of them duck and dodge, and some drop to the ground, though I have no idea if they were hit. The gun emptied, I toss it away and continue to sprint, not looking behind me. Shots fire back. I pray to God

I don't get showered with bullets. I escape the area and keep running. My legs are numb, and my chest is on fire.

As I cross the street, I can see scores of red-and-blue lights reflecting off the buildings several blocks away. There's a white light approaching in the sky and the sound of propellers. *Damn. Helicopters, too?*

A yellow cab is parked nearby, and two people are standing near it. Approaching, I realize they are Lexi and Jesse. They're looking at each other, surprised.

"Lex? What are you doing here?" Jesse asks.

"I should be asking *you* that," Lexi says. She notices me and rushes in with a hug. "Oh my God, Michael! You made it!"

I hug her back. "Yeah, so did you. Good move back there, by the way."

She grunts. "That guy was an idiot."

Jesse anxiously smacks his fist into his hand. "Hey, I think we need to get the hell out of here."

"Yeah," I say. "Dante said the place will be swarmed by midnight."

"It's 11:55. Dante doesn't fuck around, does he?" Lexi says.

I shake my head. "You don't know the half of it."

The three of us pile into the backseat of the cab, and we speed off to hell knows where.

We're crammed in the backseat of a taxi, me in the middle, Lexi and Jesse on either side of me. "Awkward" doesn't begin to describe this.

My adrenaline is just beginning to subside, and I can already start to feel the muscles and bones in my arms and legs aching. And I have a small cut on my left bicep. *How'd* that *happen?* Jesse has some bad bruises on his face, arms, and hands as well as a small cut over his right eyebrow. But he looks too excited to give a fuck. He's probably still riding that adrenaline high.

"Where the hell are we going?" Jesse asks, breaking the monotonous silence.

"Someplace far from here," I say and then look at Lexi, but she's busy typing something on her phone. Red-and-blue lights flash through the windows of the taxi as the cruisers drive by, toward the convention center. My phone buzzes, and I check it. Dante.

"Can't talk right now, man," I say quickly.

"They're on the way. Did you make it out?" Dante asks.

"Yeah, barely. Talk to you later." I end the call.

"This is fucking crazy!" Jesse says, peering out the window at the endless police lights zooming by. "It's like all of Cali's police force is out!"

"I wouldn't be surprised if they are," I mutter. I stare straight ahead and catch the cab driver's eyes on me from the rear-view mirror. He quickly looks away.

"Daddy, where are you?" Lexi suddenly says. I whip my head to her. Her phone's to her ear, and she looks distraught. "I'm coming home. Don't leave tonight. It's very important."

We stop at a red light, and Lexi leans toward the driver, showing him her phone. "Take us to this address."

The driver nods and punches the info in the GPS.

Jesse pales. "What? I'm not going home. What the hell, Lex?"

She shakes her head. "I got her, Jess. I finally got her! The info's already been sent to the police. Might even make it to the feds if we're lucky. Diamond-Sapphire is finished."

The taxi soon pulls up to a lavish mansion on the outskirts of the city. The sky is clear on this cold night, and the stars are out in full. Jesse sulks as Lexi pays the driver and gets out the car. She shuts the door and heads up the grand walkway, not stopping to wait for us.

"I can't believe I'm here right now," Jesse says, fingering the taxi's door handle.

"It's not like we're staying, right?" I say.

We get out, and I shut the door. The cab leaves.

"I hate being here. Too many bad memories," Jesse says.

I swallow. His words practically echo mine. "Yeah, I know how that is."

We walk together to the entrance, where the door opens before Lexi. Glen smiles and hugs her. "Oh, Alexis, you're back, baby girl." He kisses her on the cheek.

Lexi mumbles something to him, and he looks up from her to us. His gaze rests on Jesse, who slowly approaches and stops next to Lexi.

"Jesse," Glen says.

"Hey, old man," Jesse mutters, not looking up.

Glen lets us inside. The house looks even bigger than on the outside, and everything is bathed in money—marble floors, fancy paintings, next-gen electronics. I'm afraid to even breathe in here in case I damage something.

The TV is on, tuned in to the twenty-four-hour news channel showing a live shot of the convention center, which is surrounded by police cruisers and circling helicopters.

"You're a free man, Daddy," Lexi says.

Glen pales. "Yes, I . . . did a little investigation of my own while Lacie was out at the convention center. I can't . . . I can't even begin to . . . " He lumbers over to the pristine sofa and plops down. He rubs his hands over his face.

Lexi joins him and takes out her phone.

"I have all the evidence on here, and it's already been uploaded to the police networks. She admitted her extortion and a whole slew of other shit."

"I can't believe I loved her. Trusted her. All I wanted was for her to be happy. How could she do this?" Glen mutters.

Jesse and I stay put in the foyer, looking on at Lexi and Glen in silence. My eyes cut to the TV, which continues showing footage of the convention center. Diamond-Sapphire staff and security are handcuffed and being escorted into police vans. Scores of spectators are gathered outside the place and being questioned by authorities. This whole ordeal has made headline news with the caption reading: "Massive Illegal Gambling Ring Foiled."

"I'm sorry for not listening to you, dear," Glen says, and my attention returns to him and Lexi on the sofa.

Lexi shakes her head. "That shit's in the past now. All we can do now is move on."

"I found a copy of the contract on the computer in her home office." Glen pauses. "Well, that is until I was suddenly locked out."

"Mason's doing, I'm sure. But I'm glad you were able to learn the truth."

"Yeah, it was definitely the truth, because I'm hurting bad."

Lexi looks at her father with a look of genuine compassion in her eyes—something I've rarely seen in her. The two of them hug.

An anchorwoman's voice draws all of our attention back to the TV. She reports at the scene, and a camera pans to show Lacie and Mason being escorted in handcuffs into the back of a police cruiser. We watch the newscast in silence.

The story finishes, and the news cuts to a commercial. Glen covers his mouth and closes his eyes. "Oh, God. Lacie . . . "

Lexi purses her lips as she watches her father's grief. "Stop trying to replace Mom."

"I'm not. I just . . . your mother was very dear to me," he whispers, his face full of sadness and regret.

Lexi hugs him again. "Lacie was never worth your love. You deserve better."

Jesse watches them and walks to the door. "I'm outta here."

They break the hug, and Lexi springs up from the couch and rushes over to us. "Wait." She puts her hand on Jesse's shoulder.

Jesse shrugs her off and rests his hand on the doorknob. "Look, I'm glad you and your dad reunited, but I can't stay here. I don't want anything to do with this place anymore."

"Jesse?" Glen says, approaching us.

Jesse doesn't turn around. "See ya, old man." The door closes behind him.

I look to Glen and Lexi apologetically and follow. Jesse's already started down the driveway to the main street. *Does he intend to walk all the way home?*

"Hey," I call.

He slows his walk but doesn't stop. I catch up with him. "Where are you going?"

Jesse shoves his hands in his pockets. "I dunno. Might as well head back to Seattle, I guess. This was a fucking waste of money."

"Was it?"

"Yeah. I trained for the biggest fight of my life, and it ended up being bullshit."

"This isn't the only fight, you know." I pause, thinking about what I'll say. "I'll . . . I'll be your trainer, all right? I'll hook you up with some good, legit fights."

His face lights up. "Seriously? You'll do that?"

I nod.

"But you live all the way in New York. How's that going to work?"

"I'll find a way. Let's do things one step at a time. Do you want me to train you or not?"

"Hell yes."

I smile and pat him on the back. "You're a good kid. You'll go far with that attitude."

Oh my God. I've become Dante.

Chapter 29

"Turn here," I say to Lexi, pointing toward a street leading into Mama's neighborhood.

We top a steep hill, and I can see Mama's house at the bottom. There are Christmas lights strung about the house's trim and around the windows. Three cars are parked in the driveway.

We pull up behind Dominick's car, and Lexi shuts off the engine. She turns to me. "Are you ready?"

Not really. This will be the first time in eleven years we'll all be together. I managed to make amends with my brothers, but there's still a strange feeling in my gut—as if this gathering isn't supposed to happen. *Pops didn't want it to happen. That's why he did what he did.*

"Michael?"

Lexi's voice breaks me from my thoughts, and I feel her warm hand touch mine. I look down at her hand and then up at her face and smile. "Yeah, I'm ready." I lean in and plant a soft kiss on her lips.

She kisses me back and returns the smile. We get out of the car, gather our bags, and head up the walkway. When I reach the door, I take a deep breath and catch the faint whiff of onions and cooked meat. It's after seven; they're probably having dinner already. *Damn*, I don't want to interrupt, but . . .

"Well? Aren't you going to knock? Or should I?" Lexi gives me a curious look.

I swallow and shake my head. "No, I will." I take another deep breath and knock.

Uncle Adam answers, every bit of his tall, brawny frame filling the doorway. He beams at us. "Junior! You made it!" He scoops me up in an air-crushing bear hug.

"H-Hey, man," I say, catching my breath.

He finally lets me go, turns to Lexi, and inclines his head. "And hello, young lady. I'm Adam, Michael Jr.'s uncle."

She gives a cute little wave and smile. "Nice to meet you, Adam. I'm Lexi. Merry Christmas."

Uncle Adam lets us in, and we loosen the buttons and zippers of our coats. The house is comfortably warm, and the delicious smell of food cooking is overwhelming. I glimpse Mama in the kitchen along with the side of Denise's head and the back of Trinity's. The three women are hard at work chopping, garnishing, mixing, and stirring. A giant un-cooked turkey sits on a plate by the stove.

Lexi immediately leaves my side and runs to the kitchen to meet her friends. They all squeal happily the way high school girls do when they're around their best friends. They start talking up a storm—all at the same time. They talk so fast, so excited I have no idea what they're saying. How the hell can they understand each other when they do that? Must be a girl thing.

Mama smiles at them. Lexi points to me, and Mama's gaze travels my way. She immediately sets down her knife, wipes her hands on a dish towel, and hurries out of the kitchen to me. "Michael, baby!" She hugs and kisses me, and she cries freely now. But unlike before, I'm convinced that these are tears of joy because I feel my eyes water, too. As we hug, hot tears roll down my cheeks, and I quickly wipe them away. But Uncle Adam's watching us, and I think he saw what I did. He just smiles and gives one of those reassuring nods.

There's a blur of two figures in the corner of my eye, and I inch my gaze over to them. Kevin and Dominick stand at the edge of the hallway that leads to our rooms, Kevin's arms crossed and Dominick's hands shoved in his pockets. Still in Mama's arms, I swallow and force a weak smile at them. I slowly pull out of Mama's embrace, kiss the top of her head, and slide my feet forward toward my brothers. I stop about halfway and stare. They exchange glances a moment and then approach.

I nervously adjust my glasses. "H-Hey, guys."

Kevin tips his head. "Hey."

Dominick takes his hands out his pockets and offers a small smile. "'Sup?"

The small talk makes my heart pound with anxiety. My hands feel clammy, and I step closer. "I missed you both."

It's Kevin's turn to smile. He uncrosses his arms. "Missed you too, Mike."

I take another step closer. The three of us are mere inches apart. "Merry Christmas?" I extend my arms wide.

Dominick and Kevin hesitate a moment then step in, and we all do a group hug. It's just like old times, when one of us would do something awesome, like me winning a trophy, or Kevin winning a basketball game, or Dominick getting straight A's on his report card. Our hands and arms overlapping each other's, we hug tight as though we're trying to make up for lost time. I press my forehead against Dominick's and Kevin's and close my eyes. My tears fall, and unlike before, I don't bother wiping them away. I hear Dominick and Kevin let out small sniffles, too. This small, private circle we've created is our own.

"I love you guys," I whisper shakily through my tears.

Kevin sniffs again. "I love you, too."

"I love you," Dominick says.

I open my eyes and blink away the tears until I'm able to gaze clearly at my brothers. They lift their heads as well, and we break the group hug. Their faces are still wet, their eyes slightly bloodshot.

Mama and Uncle Adam watch us, looking relieved and excited—especially Mama, who can't stop smiling.

"This is the best Christmas ever. Praise the *Lord*!" Mama says, clasping her hands together.

Dominick, Kevin, and I go to Mama and give her a hug and kiss.

"And you're the best mother ever," I murmur in her ear.

Denise, Lexi, and Trinity join us from the kitchen. Denise and Trinity huddle themselves in Dominick's and Kevin's arms, and Lexi joins me. I wrap my arm around her waist and pull her close. She rests her head on my shoulder.

Uncle Adam beams. "I need to take a picture of the six of you." He retrieves his camera from a bag that's sitting next to the couch.

Mama claps her hands together. "Oh yes! Take it in front of the Christmas tree!" She ushers the three of us in front of the beautifully decorated seven-foot-tall tree. The girls laugh and chatter as we bump into each other trying to get assembled just the way Mama wants. I can't help but smile at the small bit of chaos and laughter.

As I stand with Lexi in my arms, I glance beside me at Dominick and Denise. Her left hand glitters with a sparkling diamond ring. I wonder what my life would be like if Lexi and I were to ever take that next step? Would she even *want* to marry me? Her friends seem happy, and my brothers, too. Could Lexi and I ever be happy like that?

I think I might be willing to take that chance, if she is. I've thought about it off and on while I saved up cash. Maybe she can come visit me in New York for the New Year's celebration. No place on earth does New Year's better than Times Square.

The sudden flashes and clicks from Uncle Adam's camera snap me out of my thoughts. He smiles and gives us a thumbs-up. We take another picture with just us brothers, and then one with us surrounding Mama. Everyone's laughing, smiling, and having a great time with one another. These were the moments with my family that I missed. Who would've thought I'd ever experience them again?

We have dinner in the breakfast nook. There're so many of us that Mama has to grab more chairs. It's a tight squeeze, but we somehow manage to eat comfortably. I eat so much food I feel like I'm going to explode. I've missed Mama's cooking. Hell, I've missed *Mama*. And I've missed my family. I'm glad that I was able to make it home this time and see everyone—especially my brothers. Mama finally got her wish. And I'm forgiven.

I may never be able to forget the past, but I can damn sure make a better future.

CHAPTER 30

Times Square, New York City, New Year's Eve

It feels as if all of New York is gathered in this one little section of the city. There's little room to walk. I hold Lexi's gloved hand tight as we're swept up by the sea of people flowing to nearby stages, where music artists are performing their latest hits. Lexi and I don't bother talking to each other. It's way too loud to hear ourselves. Lights flash in a dazzling display of colors, designs, and patterns that would rival Las Vegas. It's cold as fuck out here, and everyone's bundled like Eskimos. Some wear snow hats and funny eyewear with New Year's themes and logos of sports teams.

I still can't believe that I was able to get Lexi to come visit me for the New Year's holiday. After the awesome Christmas at Mama's, Lexi wanted to spend more time with me. Life is great. I have the job of my dreams working as a fitness and martial-arts instructor, and I have the girl of my dreams right here in my arms.

Lexi smiles at me, her lip ring glinting in the colorful lights. I kiss her, warming her cold lips. She kisses back, teasing me with that metal ring. I take her bait and deepen this kiss. But then I feel her body press against the small lump in my pocket, and I carefully push her back a few inches.

The crowd roars, the cheering becoming deafening.

"Here we go!" someone yells behind us.

We look toward the roof of the Times Square building and the giant ball that's lit up crazily with colorful blinking lights. Lexi squeezes my hand, and I squeeze back. My other hand slides into my coat pocket and fiddles with the small box I plan on presenting to her when the ball drops. After the Christmas holiday, I returned to New York and hit up the jewelry store. The thought has been nagging me for weeks. And now my heart won't shut up about it.

What the hell. Might as well try.

"Ten! Nine! Eight!" the crowd chants. Even Lexi gets caught up in the excitement. It's her first time experiencing New Year's in Time Square in person, so I understand.

I, on the other hand, have been here almost every year, so I know the deal. Still, it's always a sight to behold, whether you've been here once or a hundred times. While the chanting continues, I fish out the box and slowly let go of her hand.

"Three!" I get down on one knee. Lexi is too focused on the ball to take notice.

"Two!" I flip open the box.

"One!" I take her left hand and say a silent prayer.

"Happy New Year!" the crowd shouts, and confetti falls from the sky, engulfing everyone in colorful chaos. The majestic display over the Times Square building continues with fireworks shooting off, creating blinding, dazzling patterns streaking across the sky.

Lexi turns, but when she sees that I'm no longer right behind her, she inclines her head. Her eyes widen. I know she probably won't be able to hear me over all the noise, but I speak anyway, mouthing each word articulately so that she'll at least be able to read my lips.

"Lexi, I love you. From the first day we met, I knew there was something special about you. We've gone through a lot together—the good and bad—and I want to remain by your side no matter what. Will you marry me?"

Her jaw is dropped, and streaks of black mascara form lines down her cheeks in the wake of her tears. She covers her mouth with her free hand, and her eyes flutter closed. I stare at her face carefully, looking for the slightest of movements. I shakily bring her hand to my lips and kiss the back of it reassuringly. *I wish I knew what's going through her head right now.* She's probably all sorts of overwhelmed, and part of me thinks I might've gone a little too far.

But then her eyelids flutter open. She stares at me and gives me a single faint nod.

My smile suddenly grows. I slip the ring on her, stand, and kiss her madly. I pick her up, and she wraps her arms around my neck while we indulge in a deeper, more intimate kiss. Other couples around us are kissing, as well. TV-camera operators move throughout the crowd, getting close-up shots, but none of the couples seem to care, and neither do I. All that matters is the beautiful woman right here in my arms.

Renton, Washington

Leave that damn tie alone, boy. It looks fine," Dante says, scowling at me from the mirror.

I swallow and stare at my reflection, barely registering Dante's words as my hands idly fidget for the hundredth time with the silk-satin tie around my neck, undoing and redoing the knot. I wipe beads of sweat from my forehead. I haven't stopped sweating since my brothers and I, along with Uncle Adam, Dominick's friend Chris, and Dante, piled into Uncle Adam's SUV and zipped through town to Mama's church. The old wooden building with peeling white paint was a sight I hadn't seen in a very long time, sparking memories of coming here as a family and my brothers and I cutting up during service like I don't know what. We were asking for it when we got home, but most of the time, Mama would just embarrass us in front of everyone, with a hand to our asses.

Which is why I don't know why Kevin and Dominick thought having the big wedding here was a good idea. But the girls were all for it. They all love Mama, too.

"What did I just say?" Dante says, slapping my hand away from my tie. I snap out of my thoughts and look at him guiltily.

He raises his eyebrows at me. "Hey, don't even think about getting cold feet now."

"Yeah, man. I *guarantee* Lexi will fuck you up if you back out now," Dominick says from across the room. He slips on his white suit jacket, and Chris helps him straighten out the collar.

"Language, Dominick. Children present," Uncle Adam scolds as he fixes a button on his own light-blue satin shirt.

I glimpse the sharply dressed little boy standing next to Kevin. He's Trinity's nephew, Isaiah, and he doesn't appear to be older than five or six.

Kevin grabs a small brush from his pocket and goes over his slick fade. Isaiah watches and, when Kevin's done, takes the brush from him and mimics him.

"Look, I'm not getting cold feet," I blurt. "I've just never done this before. For *real*, I mean."

"Dude, not like we're experts at this either," Chris says, approaching me. He blows aside a wisp of feathered brown hair from his face.

Dante pats me on the back. "Just pretend it's another wedding rehearsal."

Easier said than done. I grab my silver handkerchief from the table beneath the mirror, fold it neatly, and slide it into my jacket pocket. Dante affixes a white rose corsage to my lapel.

Uncle Adam checks his watch. "All right, guys. It's almost two. Time to get out there."

I swallow a lump in my throat and follow everyone out of the waiting room and to the main lobby, where the rest of the participants are waiting—everyone except the brides, wherever they are. I peek through the double doors leading into the sanctuary, where the audience awaits our entrance. The organist continues playing a soft, mellow processional.

We—Chris, Uncle Adam, Dante, Isaiah, my brothers, and I—take our places behind Denise and Trinity's mothers, who will be at the head of the processional. They are dressed extravagantly in flowing silver dresses with red rose corsages pinned over their hearts. Seeing just the two of them makes me think about Lexi and the real mother she lost. The two older women smile back at us, Denise's mom looking a little teary eyed. Standing next to them is Mama in a matching dress and corsage. The dress slims her down so that she looks like a model, and the makeup and done-up hairdo make her look twenty years younger. She gives each of my brothers and me a hug and kiss.

"I'm so proud of you boys," she whispers. The anxiety fluttering around in my chest subsides a little.

"This is going to be some ceremony today," the pastor says from behind us. We all turn. He claps his hands together and beams. "This will be the first time in the church's history that we've had three simultaneous weddings."

"Yeah," Kevin said. "Whose bright idea was it for us to all get married on the same day, anyway?"

I clear my throat. "Yours, actually."

He rolls his eyes and huffs. "Yeah, well, I must've been drunk at the time."

We all laugh—Mama, too.

"Oh, I think it's great," Denise's mom says. "It's different. Unique. Memorable."

"Yes, yes, most definitely," the pastor says and then turns to Mama. "May the Lord bless you and your sons, Mother Anderson."

The organ music shifts and begins playing a little louder, more articulately, signaling the start of the ceremony. The doors before us open, and Denise and Trinity's mothers enter and walk slowly down the aisle. The audience fixes on the two women as they descend and sit in the front pew on the brides' side of the church.

Afterward Chris, Uncle Adam, and Dante proceed, as we all rehearsed a hundred times before. But this time it's real. I swallow a lump in my throat once our three best men stand at the altar.

Mama turns and smiles at us. "Here we go."

I take deep breaths to calm my nerves. Dominick stands on Mama's left and Kevin on her right. They interlock their arms with hers. I stand behind her. Isaiah, who holds our rings on a satin pillow, stands beside Kevin. We walk together in a small group. As we go through the double doors and into the main sanctuary, I look out at the audience and notice a few members of our family—mainly distant relatives I've not seen since I was a baby, much less remembered—some of Kevin's friends, his sports agent, his basketball coach, and a few of his teammates, and Dominick's friends—most notably a group of biker guys sitting together, wearing their coordinating leather vests—and the rest of the pews are occupied by Denise, Trinity, and Lexi's families and friends. Jesse is sitting in the last row in the back. He smiles proudly at me and waves.

I hear Mama sniffling when we're halfway down the aisle. I lower my head and place my hand at the small of her back, guiding her until we reach the altar. We take our places on the right side, and Mama stands between us. Isaiah remains at Kevin's side, still balancing the rings on the pillow.

The pastor enters then and takes his place at the center of the altar, an open Bible in his hand. He adjusts his glasses, lifts his head, and smiles. My mind starts to wander, again, to Lexi and how beautiful she'll look in her wedding dress. But my thoughts are suddenly interrupted when the bridesmaids, Bianca and Cherie—Denise, Trinity, and Lexi's best friends—and Faith and Charity—Trinity's sisters—descend the aisle, carrying bouquets of white roses. They're all dressed like fanciful princesses in long, flowing, strapless gowns of light blue and silver. Their hair is adorned with floral headpieces. Charity, Trinity's youngest sister, brings up the rear, scattering white petals down the aisle as she walks.

The organist abruptly stops playing the mellow processional and starts the Bridal Chorus. I swallow, the nervousness quickly returning. Everyone in the church stands and looks toward the double doors at the rear. I clench and unclench my hands as I stare, unwavering, at those doors. Denise is the first to appear, escorted by her father. She is every bit gorgeous in a shimmering white gown with a long train dragging behind her. Through the sheer white veil covering her face, I see her smile. I glance over to Dominick, who's grinning widely. I couldn't be happier for him right now. Denise reaches the end of the altar, and her father offers her hand to Dominick. Inclining his head, Dominick gently takes her slender hand, and the two of them stand before the pastor.

Trinity descends the aisle next, escorted by her father. The dress she wears accentuates every curve of her full body. A train falls from the back of her headpiece, but it's not nearly as long as Denise's. Despite Trinity's size, she walks with elegant grace. Around her neck is a crystalline necklace that twinkles in the light as she moves. She has a lovely face, and her smile is contagious. Kevin definitely lucked out on this girl. Trinity reaches the end of the aisle, and Kevin takes her offered hand.

Mama sniffles and wipes her face. I rub her back with assurance.

I stare at the double doors, but no one else appears. I feel my mouth go dry, and I swallow repeatedly. *Did she back out?* I look toward my brothers. They stare back at me, Kevin raising his eyebrows slightly. I look toward the audience and to Jesse in the back, who's craning his neck, trying to look beyond the entrance doors. He looks back at me and shakes his head solemnly.

Mama holds my hand, and I lower my head. Maybe it wasn't meant to be. Maybe I rushed the marriage thing when I proposed to her on New Year's Day. At least Kevin and Dominick will be happy.

But then I feel Mama squeeze my hand, and I look up at her. She's smiling now, and her face has brightened. I follow her gaze to the double doors, through which Glen escorts my purple-haired bride. She's walking in a form-fitting, lacy white dress that spills over her feet and cascades in a small train behind her. The strapless top presses against her chest, creating a healthy dose of cleavage. All of the tattoos on her arms and chest are fully exposed, bringing out her exotic beauty. Her ears have diamond studs in them, but she still wears that sexy lip ring that I love. I watch, unblinking, as she descends the aisle, and Glen offers her hand to me. I stare at her face, which is made up like a model's, with the little blemishes carefully powdered away. She smiles at me. Smiling back, I take her hand, and we face the pastor.

"Dearly beloved, we are gathered here today in the presence of the Lord, and before you, as witnesses, to join Dominick Anderson and Denise Ramsey, Kevin Anderson and Trinity Brown, and Michael Anderson Jr. and Alexis Richards in holy matrimony."

The ceremony continues, but at this point, I'm paying little attention to it. However, my hands move when they need to do the ring exchange, and I manage to recite my vow when it's my turn. As I stand here, I can't stop staring at the beautiful woman beside me, this woman who will become my wife. I never thought it would be possible with my life having been what it was. But Lexi showed me that even I can turn around from my mistakes. I can't believe that after all this, the six of us will be one big family. It's everything Mama has wanted and more. Finally, I think she's found the peace she needed.

"And now by the power vested in me by the State of Washington, I pronounce you husband and wife." The pastor grins. "Gentlemen, you may now kiss your brides."

And do we ever, in beautiful unison. The past is never going to take hold of me again. Because I'm committed to the future—my beautiful bride and my family—and I'm never going to give up.

About the Author

Marie Long is a novelist who enjoys the snowy weather, the mountains, and a cup of hot white chocolate. She's an avid supporter of literacy movements like We Need Diverse Books (WNDB) and National Novel Writing Month (NaNoWriMo). To learn more about her, visit her website: www.marielongauthor.com.